PRAISE FOR

HOW LONG A SHADOW

You can smell the stone dust in this richly imagined and deeply researched book. Cheryl Ossola's *How Long a Shadow* evokes a long-ago but still deeply resonant world rife with discrimination, bitter labor disputes, and hotly contested questions about a woman's place in society. *Brava*!

—**MICHAEL DAVID LUKAS**
author of *The Oracle of Stamboul*
and *The Last Watchman of Old Cairo*

Intimate and sweeping, *How Long a Shadow* is a powerful historical novel of immigrant life, family loyalty, and hard-won female awakening.

—**JUDITH TURNER-YAMAMOTO**
author of *Loving the Dead and Gone*

Ossola is a writer of extraordinary empathy and precision. . . . *How Long a Shadow* swept me into a world I didn't want to leave.

—**DANIELA PETROVA**
author of *Her Daughter's Mother*

I loved these people so much; I was truly sorry when I turned the last page . . . unforgettable.

—**STEPHANIE COWELL**
author of *The Man in the Stone Cottage*
and *Claude & Camille*, American Book Award winner

Ossola masterfully makes the reader feel the anguish of love and death, choke on the dust of cut granite, smell the sweat of men fighting on the picket line . . .

—STEVEN MAYFIELD

author of *The Penny Mansions* and *Treasure of the Blue Whale*

How Long a Shadow is a love letter to all the ways we make art, seen and unseen.

—MARCO RAFALÀ

author of *How Fires End*

Ossola's compelling novel follows an arc of gestation—labor, transition, and howling life.

—CAROL LaHINES

author of *Miracle Grow of the Mind*, *The Vixen Amber Halloway*, and *Someday Everything Will All Make Sense*

How Long a Shadow is an achievement of wisdom.

—KAREN BJORNEBY

author of *Hurricane Season*

A little-known sliver of the Italian American story.

—DOMENICA MARCHETTI

author of *Italian Cookies*

and numerous other books on Italian home cooking

A fiercely beautiful novel, warm in its humanity . . . a gripping narrative of family history and political upheaval.

—ROSANNA STAFFA

author of *The War Ends at Four*

Best father–daughter novel I've ever read.
—**MARK WISH**
founding editor of Coolest American Stories
and author of *Necessary Deeds*

An evocative and exciting tale of early
twentieth-century New England.
—**RUSSELL BELDING**
Barre, Vermont, historian

HOW
LONG
A
SHADOW

ALSO BY CHERYL A. OSSOLA

The Wild Impossibility

HOW LONG A SHADOW

CHERYL A. OSSOLA

CHESTER CO.,
PENN.

PUBLISHED BY CENNAN BOOKS
an imprint of Cynren Press
Chester County, Pennsylvania
http://www.cynren.com/

An excerpt from an earlier version of this book was published by Bordighera Press in *VIA: Voices in Italian Americana* 35, no. 2 (2024).

First published 2026

Printed in the United States of America by TPS

ISBN-13: 978-1-970676-08-2 (pbk)
ISBN-13: 978-1-970676-09-9 (ebk)

Library of Congress Control Number: 2026935978

Content Warning: This book contains themes of Industrial disease; Suicide; Pregnancy loss and infant death; Difficult childbirth; Labor strike violence and deaths; Abortion; Sexual assault attempts; References to domestic violence; References to animal cruelty; Workplace exploitation and unsafe conditions; Family estrangement and conflict.

Cover art is from Cyprien Eugene Boulet, *Woman with Green Shawl*, 1927
Cover design by Roderick Brydon

For my father

The history of progress is written in the blood of men and women who have dared to espouse an unpopular cause, as, for instance, the black man's right to his body, or woman's right to her soul.

—EMMA GOLDMAN

For in the last analysis, the grand adventure—which is liberty, the true inspiration of all idealists, poets and artists—is the only human adventure worth striving and living for.

—EMMA GOLDMAN

Stand up and see how long a shadow you cast in the sunlight!

—EUGENE V. DEBS

CONTENTS

PART I

LABOR

April 1903

BY DAWN ON A DELICATE SPRING DAY in Barre, Vermont, when the stone dust flew thick, frosting the railroad tracks and striping the river, Aldo Nappi was dead. Another stonecutter, another statistic. Not that anyone was surprised. They found his body on the railroad tracks, out of town a fair piece on the Williamstown line, split like a chicken under a butcher's knife, said the men who retrieved the body. To spare his widow, they fetched the coroner and a pallet and took what was left of Aldo Nappi to Socialist Labor Party Hall. Cause of death: clear to anyone who had eyes. Reason for death: suicide, like too many stonecutters before him. Aldo Nappi had *mal d'america*.

ONE

AT QUARTER TO EIGHT IN THE MORNING on the day Aldo Nappi died, Rosina Bottinelli hurried across Burnham Meadow to the stone sheds crouched between railroad spurs along the river. The cool air tasted of stone dust, earthy and metallic, lethal for the lungs but pretty on this sunny morning, swirling in the breeze. This was the industrial heart of Barre, alive with sound and energy. She paused to watch a derrick crane swing a block of granite the size of a wagon from train car to shed, a marvelous feat. And a dangerous one. She quickened her pace. Fifteen minutes, that was all the time she had to drop off her father's lunch pail and get to work before her boss would swear at her for being late.

Her father claimed that the Meadow was too dangerous a place for girls or women, but she liked it there. She thought it magical, this colony where stonecutters, artists and alchemists to a man, turned rough granite into polished beauty. The rough-cutters hewed and shaped the quarried blocks while the sculptors, her father and brothers and uncle among them, translated lines on paper into shapes they coaxed out of the stone—columns and cornices, markers and monuments, gates and gravestones and balustrades. It was man against stone and the men always won, though in the industry's early years they hadn't known the price of victory. The stone bled dust.

Inside Ugo Lombardi's shed, Rosina covered her ears against the deafening clatter of pneumatic chisels and the insistent whine of polishers. A tool boy hurried past, weighted down with buckets of blunted chisels. Rosina stepped over air hoses and wound past granite blocks twice her height. Already dust was everywhere, drifting and settling like snow. Shafts of light from high windows pierced the white fog, isolating dark beards, the glint of steel, muscled forearms. They looked like ghosts, these men who carved markers for the dead.

At her father's station, she set down the lunch bucket and waved at her twin brothers, Paolo and Nico, conferring over a half-carved jagged tree trunk, a symbol of a life cut short. Barre's cemeteries had too many monuments like that, decorated with trees cut in half, broken columns and pillars, unopened flower buds.

"Papà, you forgot your lunch," she said when Carlo silenced his chisel. "Mamma says you worry too much and that's why you're forgetful."

"Your mother is always right." Carlo smiled, whisking dust off a lily.

Rosina traced the edge of a petal, rough against her fingertips. "*Che bello*." It always surprised her that something so delicate could be made of stone. If only she could make something that would last nearly forever like the *scalpellini* did, leave a beautiful mark on the world. They could walk past buildings and statues and cemetery monuments and think, *I carved that. And it will stay on this earth for centuries.* Art had power, Zio Gabriele always said.

"I have to run, Papà. Zucchelli throws a fit if I'm late." It was a five-minute walk to her dreary job at the Labor Hall's basement store, where there was no art, only coiled-up ropes of sausage, stacks of cheese and salumi, impatient customers, and Luigi Zucchelli's grabby hands.

An hour later she waited impatiently while two women contemplated cheeses as if the wrong choice would end their marriages. A jangle of the bell as the door opened brought news delivered by a busybody eager to tell it. "No! Not Aldo Nappi!" Rosina said, fighting the urge to slap the insensitive woman. She liked Mr. Nappi, a kind, sweet man about her father's age. Her throat clenched. *Had* liked him. How dreadfully he must have suffered. Men who got *mal d'america* had two choices—endure a long, agonizing decline or end it all quickly. The result was always the same. No cure, no hope.

The news spread quick as spring runoff, and the morning passed in a blur of hushed voices sharing bittersweet memories. Mr. Nappi had been the first to greet the Bottinellis when they arrived in Barre, showing up on their doorstep in the Italian North End with wine and sweets and an offer to acquaint them with the town. In those first disorienting months, when Rosina spoke no English and everything about America confused her, he would stop her in the street to ask how she was settling in, whether she liked school or had found any friends yet. His eldest girl spoke English well and Rosina was welcome to stop by to practice if she liked. His eyes reminded her of her uncle Gabriele's, deep-set and kind, vibrant with warmth.

And now he was gone.

At lunchtime Rosina gathered the cheeses and meats Zucchelli had agreed, grudgingly, to give to the new widow. Walking across town, dodging sprawling puddles and islands of blackened snow, she passed a man whose rattling cough promised blood. Making the sign of the cross, she said a quick prayer for her father and brothers and uncle, then hurried on, steeling herself for what she'd find—the bereaved's sorrowful eyes and clinging hands, the army of weeping women, the darkened house that smelled like grief. She would leave the widow's house heavier than when she'd arrived, carrying part of the woman's burden and a darkness of spirit that would linger for days.

Her mother, Clementina, opened the widow's door. "Rosi, *cara*, I hoped you would come. Please help with the children, in the kitchen."

"Of course." Rosina kissed her mother, hiding her irritation. Was it intentional, this habit her mother had, of putting her daughter in the company of children? Did she think the proximity would convince Rosina to marry that tiresome Giorgio Marelli?

An hour later, with the children fed, she sat at the table listening to the lilting flow of women's voices conveying sadness or grief, some in Italian, some in dialect. Two boys playing marbles sprawled at her feet, their hands nimble, faces intent. Good subjects for a sketch, she thought. She was better at drawing gardens and houses than people, but she had to keep trying if she wanted to improve. So said Zio Gabriele. After six years in America, though, Rosina had begun to ask herself why she bothered when her choices here were the same ones she'd had in Viggiù—to marry and have children, or to teach and not marry, or to waste her life and her mind and her talent doing a menial job like the one she had. She could barely remember the excitement she'd felt on the ship from Le Havre to New York. What she did remember was the incessant swell of the ocean, the heave of her innards, the stench of vomit and unwashed bodies. For six long days she'd envied her brothers' cast-iron stomachs, the ease with which they'd buried boredom in games of *scopa* and *tresette*. She had lived for the moments on deck, gasping in the salted air that froze her lungs, her eyes focused on the unchanging horizon. Until there it was—New York Harbor, embraced by the Statue of Liberty, gated by Ellis Island. A new land, a new life. True and untrue. If America was the land of opportunity, it was for men, not women. Rosina was proof of that—two years at the store, two years wasted. And all the while her mother and Giorgio, poor patient, deluded man, waited for her to admit defeat.

She would not. She would marry for love or not at all, find meaningful work, make a life for herself that justified leaving Italy. Children weren't the gold ring on the carousel if the carousel wasn't to her liking. Far better to be a shriveled-up spinster with ink-stained hands, living in a small, sad room papered with drawings, than to marry Giorgio or any dullard like him.

Playing at their game, the boys laughed and crowed, shoving each other in warlike competition, hints of the belligerent men they might become flashing across their faces. Taking a small notebook and a pencil from her cloak pocket, Rosina captured the hunched curves of their skinny backs, the energy in their flung arms. But their hands, oh, at those she failed miserably! She erased them, tried again. It was no use, they looked wooden, inhuman. Dead, even, like poor Aldo Nappi.

She tossed the pencil aside, pressure building in her chest. She'd seen him only yesterday, pale and bent, handing out peppermints in the street as he always did, looking older than his years but still alive. Did he know then what he would do this morning, or had he risen before dawn planning to live another day, then changed his mind? She stilled her breath. She mustn't cry in front of the children.

One by one, the mothers came to fetch their young. When only the Nappi children remained, Rosina joined her mother in the parlor. "We'll stop by tomorrow," Clementina was saying, her voice soft.

"My deepest condolences, Signora Nappi," Rosina said. "Your husband was always kind to me. I'll miss him."

The women there that day had promised comfort and they would be true to their word. By now they knew what to do. Two or three of them would come daily for as long as the widow required, bringing food and flowers, jars of their red sauce and bottles of homemade wine or their husbands' prized grappa, conversation or sympathetic silence. It was what they did, this North End family of theirs. Though they came from various towns in Italy and spoke different dialects that created barriers there, here they were simply Italians, united by displacement. Whether *lombardi*, *piemontesi*, or *toscani*, they needed one another, needed the common ground that most of them, most days, were glad to have beneath their feet. Even so, on days like this one, Rosina wished her family had never left Viggiù.

TWO

A FEW DAYS LATER ROSINA WAS RUNNING ERRANDS on Main Street when she saw her aunt Donata halfway down the block. "Zia, it's been ages!" she called, hurrying over to chat.

"Rosina, how lovely to see you! Forgive me for not stopping, I'm in a terrible hurry. Mrs. Puricelli's baby is coming sooner than expected. Regards to your family." Donata paused at the door to Halliday's Pharmacy. "Come to think of it, do you have time to do me a favor?" She fished a list from her bag and handed it over. "Have Mr. Halliday pack up these things for me and bring them to number 8 Pearl Street. As quickly as you can. Thank you, dear." She hurried off.

Angus Halliday's caterpillar eyebrows scrunched as he perused the list. "I'll have it ready in two shakes," he said, already turning away.

Ten minutes later Rosina was in Pearl Street, where the door to number 8 stood open. "*Scusate*! *Buongiorno*!" she said, stepping into the corridor. "I'm looking for my aunt. The midwife?"

A frantic-looking man rushed out of a ground-floor flat and ushered her in. "In there!" he said, pointing at a door that promptly banged open. A teenage girl dashed out.

"Zia, I'm here!" Rosina called through the open door. The girl rushed back into the room, this time laden with clean linens, and Rosina followed her. A sweating mountain of a woman lay on the bed atop sheets soiled with blood and feces and between her splayed knees sat Donata, leaning forward and murmuring encouragements. Rosina had barely taken in the scene—the word *battlefield* entered her mind, then *che schifo*, how disgusting—when her aunt held up a wet, squalling baby and announced it was a boy. Then, to her surprise, she was following Donata's commands, opening a bottle of phenol, dousing a washcloth in warm water, wiping the mother's face and neck, with no time to stop or think until the baby was bundled and in the arms of his tearful mother. She felt oddly exhilarated.

"My dear, I can't thank you enough," Donata said, swooping in to kiss her. "This is the first time in years I've been caught unprepared."

"Zia, do you need a helper?" The words were out before she had a chance to think twice. That her aunt was a midwife Rosina had known as long as she could remember, but she'd never considered that path for herself. Babies had no place in her life, not now and maybe not ever. Babies were for women like her mother, happy on their narrow paths of tending to husband and family. But this—two women working together to bring a child into the world, her aunt joyfully in charge—this was different. "Working at Zucchelli's is terribly boring. This seems"—Rosina regarded the disarray—"interesting, at least."

"A helper, no, but I'd be happy to train you. Barre could use another midwife. How much are you paid now?"

"Four dollars and fifty cents a week."

"I'm afraid I can't match that. Three dollars, regardless of the hours." Donata smiled. "We are at the mercy of babies, my dear, day and night."

Rosina hesitated. Her family counted on her earnings. Her father sent money to his mother in Italy every month, was generous with the sick stonecutters and the widows. Still, it was a good opportunity, and a midwife was more respected than a lowly store clerk. Her parents, or her mother at least, would surely approve.

"I'll talk to Mamma and Papà tonight."

"No," said Carlo at dinner. "*Assolutamente no*. The wages are too low and you don't know how much you'll work. In terms of money, midwifery is a crapshoot."

"You can't tell me what to do, Papà. I'm not a child."

"I can and I will as long as you live under my roof." Carlo pointed his fork at her. "Use your head. The money isn't the only problem. My sister lives in Vittorio's house and eats his food. She's beholden to him, which means you would be too. I won't have it."

"But she's the best midwife in Barre. I'm sure she pays her share of the household expenses."

Carlo snorted. "Marietta would never take her money. If Vittorio thinks she does, he's a fool."

Rosina fixed Clementina in a pleading gaze. "Mamma, you'd like me to be a midwife, wouldn't you? It's good work." She searched for a more convincing word. "Honorable work."

"Honorable?" Paolo laughed. "Hardly."

"*Zitto*!" Rosina glared at him, a finger to her lips. "Please, Mamma, I'm so bored at Zucchelli's."

Clementina hesitated only a fraction of a second, but long enough to give Rosina hope. "What I'd like is for you to marry a good man. Once you're a wife and mother you'll dream of being bored. You heard your father. Either stay at Zucchelli's or find something else that pays as much." She softened her words with an apologetic smile, then stood, signaling the end of the conversation. "Now who wants cake?"

"Poor old Giorgio," Nico said to Rosina. "He'll be ninety and toothless before he gives up on you."

"His choice." Rosina rose to clear the plates while the men sat there, elbows on the table, taking no notice of the clutter around them, expecting it to miraculously disappear and cake to arrive in front of their noses. As it would.

"Papà, is it true what I heard today?" Paolo leaned forward, his voice charged. "Is Big Bill Haywood coming here to speak?"

"More likely Eugene Debs, but nothing is definite yet. Keep it to yourselves for now. *Acqua in bocca.*" Carlo zipped finger and thumb across his lips.

The three of them huddled together like conspirators, Carlo and the twins, talking among themselves as if the women were invisible. Zio Gabriele, always the quiet one, sat back and listened. Rosina sighed. Politics as usual, excluding her as usual. She'd given up trying to join their conversations. The only one who understood her was Nico. He was always kind and sweet to her. To everyone. He was so nice he'd probably scooted aside in the womb to let Paolo be born first. When it was only the two of them, Nico asked her about life, and work, her drawings, her thoughts about events in the news. And he listened! After all, she read the *Barre Daily Times*. She knew what the socialists had against the anarchists and what both of them had against capitalism. She'd heard the stories about Haymarket a hundred times, and she'd rather hear them another hundred times than chat about recipes and dress patterns. She had opinions about things outside the front door, things that mattered. She knew the value and power of a union, and its limits too. And women's suffrage—imagine if women could vote and be heard! Maybe midwifery wasn't the best way into the big world she read about every day, but it would be better than dying a slow death at Zucchelli's. Or as Giorgio Marelli's wife.

As Clementina handed out slices of walnut cake, Rosina leaned against Gabriele's shoulder. "Would you look at my new drawings tonight? I'm afraid I've made a mess of someone's hands."

He kissed the top of her head. "With pleasure, my dear."

Her uncle had taught her to draw, taught her everything she knew about art. Back in Viggiù they would visit the churches together to study the paintings and frescoes. He would explain how the artists worked, the symbolism they used, why they chose certain colors or brushstrokes. Rosina loved seeing how emotion emerged through technique, how artists used composition and color to capture a feeling, how they made gestures and expressions say more than words could. At home she would watch her uncle draw whatever was at hand, always amazed that in those two-dimensional sketches she could see something of Gabriele himself. Everything was a choice, he explained—color, medium, angle of perspective, realism or abstraction. Everything. Art was his voice, he always said, and it could be Rosina's too if she worked hard. Clementina considered it a waste of time, saying if Rosina liked pretty things she could take up something useful like embroidery. Rosina ignored her, though she'd drawn in secret at first to avoid her mother's sharp words. Bits of her world, captured however poorly, tucked away in a notebook yet somehow always a part of her. Though a few years ago, at Gabriele's urging, she had stopped hiding her drawings. Now she tacked her best work on her bedroom wall where she could study what was good and note what was lacking. Her mother had never said a word, and Rosina wouldn't care if she did. She was done pretending her art didn't matter, sick of being told what she could and couldn't do.

The men scraped back their chairs, collected their things, and left the house. Waiting for the kettle to boil, Rosina cleared the plates, scrubbed the table, tossed bits of pork out the window for foraging cats to find. How lucky they were, free to do what they wanted, like her father and brothers. Still, she was determined not to be a sheep, stupid and easily diverted. And though her parents might never understand her, Zio Gabriele did, and Nico too. That counted for something.

The kettle whistled. Pouring water over the plates and utensils, Rosina watched them disappear into steam and suds. She smiled, her spirits lifting. That was another beautiful thing about art—it never disappeared. Once you'd seen a painting or sculpture, it was there inside you, always visible in your mind's eye, a repository of joy. No one could take it away.

THREE

FOUR DAYS AFTER ALDO NAPPI DIED, Angelo Lucci was hauling buckets of tools in Ugo Lombardi's stone shed, sweat running off him like the Winooski River at flood stage. Hurrying past Carlo Bottinelli, he caught a glimpse of the garland he was carving, with lilies so fine you'd have to touch them to know they weren't real.

The mood in the shed had been grim since Aldo's suicide. Carlo blamed the shed owners for Aldo's death and that of every other man cut down by *mal d'america*, and he didn't care if Lombardi heard him say so. In fact, Carlo said things like that all the time—the dust in the air was killing the men, the shed owners didn't give a damn, the stonecutters should strike. It made sense that he was a union leader, president of the Barre Local. One of these days, Angelo would be a union member himself. Not soon enough.

"Lucci, move your ass!" Lombardi was coming at him, yelling so hard his molars showed. Lombardi spoke terrible English—except for swear words and insults, he was fluent in those—which was probably why he hired mostly Italians. The men in the shed spoke Italian, sometimes peppered with English, but not Angelo. He spoke English every chance he got. How else would he get ahead in this town? And he was good at it, if he did say so himself.

"You think Gallo over there is standing around scratching his balls?" Lombardi yelled. "You don't work hard, he can't work hard, *capito*?"

"Got it!" A fellow couldn't even stop to spit as far as Lombardi was concerned. Angelo beelined to the blacksmith and dumped his load, exchanging dull chisels for sharpened ones. He worked plenty hard, got there early most days, shoveled slag during lulls even though it wasn't his job. Lombardi probably didn't notice.

Angelo had never thought to be a tool boy, but it was steady work and a foot in the door. The money wasn't what he'd make as a stonecutter, especially one like Gabriele, who could make any design look a thousand times better in stone than it did on paper. Some men could only do the shaping, some the lettering or simple designs, but Gabriele, he was a true artist. The best *scalpellino* in Viggiù, everyone said, and Angelo knew for a fact he was the best in Barre. Carlo was good too, but he fell short of his brother, maybe because he was a divided man, a socialist first and an artist second. Angelo tried to stay on Carlo's good side, partly because he hoped to become a stonecutter and Carlo could help him, and partly because Carlo was Rosina's father.

Make that mostly because he was Rosina's father. Damn if she wasn't the prettiest girl in Barre, and smart too, third in her graduating class at Spaulding High even though she didn't speak English when she got there. They hadn't been in the same class, him being a year ahead, but he'd noticed her right away, and if he'd stayed in school he might have had a chance with her. He'd lost that chance when he dropped out, not that he'd had a choice. Still, he could never let go of the idea that she was the one for him. There was something about her that he couldn't name. She had this . . . he wasn't sure how to describe it, a kind of presence, he supposed. Like a rare spark wrapped up in familiar cloth. It wasn't a physical spark, though there was that too—he swore if she ever touched him he'd light up like fireworks. No, the spark was more than that. What he felt for her was nothing like what he'd felt with other girls, even the ones he'd been with. Something connected them, him and Rosina. Or it would if she'd ever notice him.

His buckets loaded, Angelo hightailed it to Gallo. Out of the corner of his eye he saw what Gabriele was carving, a pretty little weeping angel leaning on a headstone with her chin propped on her folded arms and her wings rising behind her, as tall as she was. Those wings were trembling, swear to God, as if love and sadness and joy were pouring out of the angel all at once. He'd kill to be that good someday.

Back to the blacksmith's room, hustling now. His neck and shoulders were killing him, but if he slowed down he might get fired, and he couldn't risk that. A quick stretch and he was off, buckets loaded with tools still warm from the anvil.

Passing Gabriele's angel again, he thought of his mother's plain, flat stone, all his father could afford. When he got his chance to carve, when he was as good as Gabriele, Angelo swore he'd make an angel for his mother, with a face as sweet as hers. He blinked hard. *Porca miseria.* He never could think of her without tearing up. Couldn't let Lombardi see him like that. He kept going, making the rounds, doling out sharp tools, collecting the dead ones. He missed his mother a lot these days, even more than in the months after she'd died. She'd taken sick on the boat over and then never gotten well. He was fifteen then, horrified by her wasted body and trying not to show it. Whatever had grown inside her had taken everything, a greedy son of a bitch. When she died, her skin looked like sunburned daffodils. He tried not to think of her like that, tried to remember how she was before that terrible time, when he was young and they were still in Carrara, before they'd ever thought to come to America. When she taught him to draw. They'd spend hours together, filling pages with Madonnas and saints, gladiators and monsters. She told him he was good at it, bought him paper and pencils with coins from the household money jar. When his father objected, saying the money was for necessities, not idle pleasures, she'd stood up to him. Their son had talent that must be allowed to grow, she'd insisted, and besides, what point was there to life if it held no pleasure? She used to say, so often that he knew her words by heart, "Angelino, *tesoro*, listen to me. *Ascoltami bene*. Don't let anyone keep you from something you love, *capito*? *Mai*. Not ever. And don't you do that to anyone else. We all deserve the life of our dreams."

He stopped to wipe his face. He was trying, he was, but he'd had to put his dreams on hold after his mother died. Except for Rosina. He would never stop dreaming of her, even though he hadn't gotten up the nerve to act on his feelings. Not yet. The day would come, though. He could wait. As his mother used to say, *la gatta frettolosa fa i gattini ciechi*. He said it in English: "The cat in a hurry gives birth to blind kittens." It sounded strange, with no hint of his mother's voice.

Dio santo, he missed his mother. She would have liked Rosina, no question.

He'd barely gotten moving again when the whine of the polishers deepened and chisels chattered to a halt. Voices rose as the stonecutters formed a ragged circle around two men apparently fixed on killing each other. Angelo scrambled onto a granite block to get a better view. Enrico Baggio, built like a steam engine, had stringy-looking Franco Contini in a headlock and was beating him in the face with a gloved fist. Contini swung in the big man's grip, flailing and kicking as the onlookers shouted, voices overlapping: "Destroy him, Baggio! *Distruggerlo*!" "You call yourself a union man, Baggio? You're a fucking two-faced traitor!" "Let him go, you *figlio di puttana*!"

A man thrust a crowbar toward Baggio. "Bust his teeth out!" As Baggio grabbed it, Lombardi flew across the shed waving a pistol.

"*Basta*! Break it up! I said break it up, you fucking morons! Do I have to use this thing?" The fighters froze and the watchers backed off. "Drop it, Baggio." Dust mushroomed where the heavy bar landed. "Now let him go."

Baggio released his prey and Contini limped away, wiping blood off his face.

"Nobody fights on company time, you *stronzi* got that?" Lombardi shouted. "What the hell's this about?"

Baggio pointed at Contini. "Son of a bitch wants to strike."

"Yeah?" Lombardi spat into the dust. "You want to fight about political shit, you go ahead. Far as I'm concerned you can cut each other's balls off. But not here and not on my time. You're both fired. Get out of my shop." He jerked a thumb toward the door. The men slunk off amid jeers and protests and Lombardi swung around, the pistol at arm's length. "That's what strike talk and fighting will get you in this shop, hear me?" His aim jumped from one man to another, fast and unpredictable. "You union assholes want trouble? I'll give you trouble and plenty of it if I hear one more word about your goddamn strike. Now get your lazy asses back to work, and don't think I'm not watching you. I'll fire anyone who doesn't work his balls off today."

As Lombardi stalked toward the office, Angelo jumped off his perch, charged with newfound energy. With two men gone, Lombardi would be hiring. No point in approaching him now, when he was pissed off, but he'd have to do it soon, before someone beat him to it. He glanced at the wall clock. An hour until the lunch break and four more hours after that. Enough time for Lombardi to cool off. Then he'd talk to him, and if the answer was yes he'd go to Zucchelli's to splurge on some sausages for dinner, and if Rosina was there he could say hello, tell her his good news. With luck, she'd do more than give him the time of day.

When the closing bell rang five hours later, Angelo punched out, then stood before Lombardi's closed door, fist raised to knock, heart dancing in his throat.

"The bear's left the cave." It was Nico, his jacket slung over his shoulder. "Whatever business you've got with him, I'd leave it for a while. Unless you like getting your head bit off."

"But he might hire someone else."

Nico looked surprised. "You want to cut stone? Ever done it?"

"No, but I know I can. I'm a good artist and a fast learner."

"Maybe so, but he'll want someone who knows his stuff."

Angelo sagged. So much for his good mood.

"Listen, I'll teach you the basics. Lunchtime tomorrow, all right? You can try your hand. I'm warning you, it's not easy."

"Yeah, okay. Thanks."

"Don't worry. You get good enough, Lombardi will hire you like that." Nico snapped his fingers. "Let's go have a beer, what do you say?"

"Sure." He didn't want to see Rosina now anyway, not when he felt so blue. But the way her face lit up when she smiled, that sure would have cheered him up. Her eyes, her lips . . . Shaking off the thought, he followed Nico outside. He could torment himself later, like he did every night, lying in bed gazing at the portrait he'd drawn of her, hoping she'd come to him in his dreams. He kicked at a pebble, sent it flying. For now, dreaming would have to do.

FOUR

ON THE FRIDAY AFTER ALDO NAPPI'S BODY WAS FOUND, Vittorio Bottinelli was at his desk at the Hotel Milano, poring over a partnership contract with Ugo Lombardi that would, without a doubt, raise his brother Carlo's ire. A pity, but nothing new; they'd been at each other's throats for years. A pity too, about Aldo Nappi. No man deserved such a death. But life went on, and for Vittorio, this week had been good indeed. He locked the contract in his desk drawer, then collected his coat and hat. On Monday morning, pretending to have cold feet, he would ask Lombardi to show him around. As if Vittorio didn't know how a shed operated! Lombardi knew his history, should realize that Vittorio understood the industry as well as anyone who'd grown up cutting stone. But the man was an imbecile, incapable of connecting the dots. Vittorio would enjoy watching him sweat.

Outside, he fired up his Oldsmobile Curved Dash and trundled down Main Street, noting the admiring gazes of the men and boys he passed. Up ahead, good progress was being made on the Wortham Block expansion. He nodded approvingly. That was Barre for you—thriving and forward thinking. It was hard to believe it had been nothing but a mill town until someone discovered what the surrounding hills had hidden for millions of years—a granite core said to be four miles long, two miles wide, and ten miles deep. Once the trains came, connecting quarry to shed and shed to builder, the granite industry took off, and thousands upon thousands of stonecutters and quarrymen arrived, mostly from Italy and Scotland, all hoping to make a good living and send money back to the old country, all eager to make a good home, a good life. Not all would live to see it.

America held promise, though. When Vittorio had arrived in 1896, eager to escape the poverty strangling Viggiù since the local quarries shut down, Barre was booming, exciting, alive with noise: hammers and saws, wheels and hooves, the sweet songs of trains and the clash of metal on stone. Now, seven years later, streetcars rumbled for miles, the occasional Stanley Steamer or Ford puttered across town, park benches were more common than hitching posts, and new houses dotted the hills. And all of it thanks to Barre Gray, a granite in high demand and of endless supply. A fine-grained mix of quartz and feldspars whose dust sliced lungs to ribbons.

Vittorio had been smart, worked hard and saved, then traded pneumatic chisels and stone dust for the calm elegance of the Hotel Milano. Too bad his brothers had refused to do the same. No, they chose to labor in the sheds, to carry home mica-laced dust in their pores and their lungs, praying every day, like every stonecutter did, that they wouldn't develop a cough, the first terrifying sign of *mal d'america*. The blood came later, and after that the pain of inhaling a hundred razor blades with every breath. And all the while, loved ones watched, helpless. Knowing what would come had driven more than a few men to suicide. Aldo Nappi was the latest, but he wouldn't be the last.

Vittorio turned onto Washington Street, heading home. Life had a strange habit of going in circles, because when he'd bought the Milano two and a half years ago, on the cusp of a century that promised opportunity with a capital *O*, he couldn't have imagined returning to the granite industry. Yet here he was, about to do exactly that—only this time without getting his hands dirty. Or his lungs.

On Monday morning Vittorio left the Milano and strode down North Main, the brass head of his walking stick firmly in hand. A walk to Burnham Meadow on such a fine day would be good for his spirit and his waistline. The day promised a new beginning, though not without a few wrinkles along the way. Not with Lombardi. It was Carlo he'd have to face, and Gabriele, the twins. Vittorio had hesitated when Lombardi proposed a deal, because he knew Carlo would take the partnership as a personal insult. But the man was right—it was an opportunity Vittorio wasn't likely to get again. "You left the granite business," Lombardi had said, aiming his stubby cigar at Vittorio, "and the shed owners won't forget it. They're not as open-minded as me."

Near the Labor Hall the air grew hazy with dust. Deadly stuff, Vittorio thought. Carlo and Gabriele hadn't known about the dust before they'd followed him here, and he should have told them. But if he'd warned them that Barre had an underbelly that could kill them, they might have changed their minds, stayed in Viggiù or gone to Switzerland to find work there instead. And he'd wanted them here, the three brothers together. Bottinellis in America.

He had planned all along to ask them to buy into the Milano, convinced they'd want to leave the sheds once they understood the danger. He'd been blinded by his own hopes, unable to see how stubborn they were. They were artists, they said, not businessmen. He and Carlo had drunk too much that night, said things they shouldn't have. Despite the drink, he remembered all too well. "What you are"—Vittorio had slurred his words—"is goddamn socialists. You care more about your precious brotherhood than your family." Carlo had accused him of being a capitalist sell-out, throwing the workingmen to the wolves or some such rot; Vittorio had called him soft, a man with no ambition. Gabriele had stayed out of it, nursing a beer and letting them say words they'd regret. In the end, as Vittorio had known he would, Gabriele sided with Carlo.

Past the Labor Hall now, crossing Burnham Meadow, almost there. Vittorio's pulse quickened. First a hotel owner, now soon to be co-owner of a stone shed. Not bad, not bad at all. In fact, he'd have no complaints if he hadn't been forced to do both without his brothers. Their snub cut him like glass even now. Thank God his sons were cut from his cloth, at his side without fail. It comforted him daily to see them so competent, Daniele handling the budget and Cosimo the hands-on management. If the Bottinelli name was going to be a big one in Barre—and Vittorio would aim for that until his dying day—it was up to him to make it happen.

Crossing the last few yards now, his breath coming short. Was it his thickening waist, the tick of time? Or the step he was about to take, the pain he knew he'd cause his brothers? All of it. But there was Marietta to think about, and their sons. His family's future, soon to include a grandchild. Today he would play cat and mouse with Lombardi, and then he would sign that contract. A done deal.

Carlo had been hunched over a run of scrollwork for a solid hour when he paused to stretch. Paolo waved to get his attention, then jerked his head toward the opposite end of the shed. Vittorio and Lombardi were there, Vittorio lit up like he held all the aces and Lombardi, that *maledetto coglione*, showing off his pride and joy like proud men do.

"*Cazzo*," Carlo muttered. Whatever game the two of them were playing, it couldn't be good. He looked over at the twins, caught their eye and put a finger to his lips. Then he flagged down Angelo. It took the boy all of twenty seconds to get to him, a pace that would kill him within the year if he kept it up.

"Whoa there, slow down. Lombardi's distracted now, you don't need to impress him." Carlo tossed two chisels into the boy's bucket.

"Right." Angelo puffed a few times, then drew in a deep breath and coughed. "*Porca miseria*, I need to remember not to breathe."

"Only if you want to live to see fifty. Listen, did you hear what they're talking about?" Carlo jerked a thumb toward the two men, now strolling from station to station.

"Nah. I tried, but . . ." Angelo waved his hands head high, indicating the noise. "Uh-oh, I'd better go." He scurried off as the men approached.

"Good morning." Vittorio planted himself at Carlo's station and checked his pocket watch as if deciding whether he had time for his brother. Lombardi sidled up next to him like the fawning *pezzo di merda* he was.

Carlo nodded a greeting and pretended to study a sketch, keeping his chisel running and Vittorio waiting. He noted with satisfaction the film of dull gray on Vittorio's shoes, no doubt freshly shined that morning. What a piece of work his brother was, coming here in his tailored suit and silk pocket square, carrying that pompous walking stick. He might impress Lombardi, but the stonecutters wouldn't care if he dressed up like goddamn King Emmanuel the Third. Vittorio wasn't one of them anymore.

Carlo eyed Vittorio, then returned his attention to the sketch long enough to make his point. Finally, his tone loaded with disinterest, he asked, "What brings you here?"

"I'm getting the grand tour." Vittorio beamed. "Ugo and I have been discussing a partnership." When Carlo didn't react, he raised his voice. "For a new shed. We'll sign the contract today."

Carlo shrugged and pushed his bit into the stone, sending dust onto his brother's pant legs. Vittorio raised an eyebrow, then moved on. The twins kept their heads down, and Gabriele, next on Vittorio and Lombardi's circuit, suddenly had reason to talk to someone on the opposite side of the shed. Well played, brother, Carlo thought. Then he frowned, noting Gabriele's hand at his mouth. He was coughing a lot lately.

As soon as the two men were out of sight, Paolo rushed over. "Did he say a partnership? This can't be happening! Did you know about it?"

"No. We'll talk about it later. Go on, get back to work. Don't give him the pleasure of seeing you mad."

"*Testa di cazzo*!" Paolo kicked at the dust.

"Calm down," Carlo said. But his own pulse pounded in his temples. If he'd had any hope for the Bottinelli brothers to act like a family again, it was as long gone as the ships they'd taken to America.

FIVE

ROSINA LEANED ON THE COUNTER AT ZUCCHELLI'S, wondering if she dared put her head down and close her eyes, if only for a minute. She'd stayed up late sketching, inspired anew after a short lesson from Gabriele, and then slept poorly, dreading telling Zia Donata that her parents wouldn't allow the apprenticeship. She'd found her aunt at home early this morning, fortunately. Better to give bad news quickly than to encourage false hope.

"What a shame, I was looking forward to it," Donata had said. "And I confess that I'd hoped our working together would be good for the family. I love my brothers, but this feud they're having—well, they're acting like children. Self-important little brats." She'd laughed then, though tears shone in her eyes. "I fear they will never be close again. Unfortunately the rest of us must suffer the loss too. Ah well, I'm sure you'll find another post that your parents will approve of. I wish you the best, my dear."

Rosina had no desire to find another job like the one she had, which would almost certainly be as bad or even worse. Zucchelli might be disgusting, but he never did more than touch her bottom. Her friend Giulia hadn't been so lucky. Her former boss had made a habit of jumping her like a water snake, touching her breasts one day and kissing her the next. She'd asked him to stop, and when he wouldn't she'd slapped him and gotten fired. Fortunately she'd found work at the tailor's shop, where the owner's wife kept her husband on a short leash. Where could Rosina go? She couldn't picture herself on Main Street, selling fine jewelry or stationery or silk scarves to the wives of wealthy businessmen, not that a single one of those shop owners would hire an Italian. No, she was stuck at Zucchelli's, slowly turning into a shell of herself, a woman incapable of intelligent thought.

Zucchelli was headed her way. Rosina dashed out from behind the counter to a towering display of tinned foods near the door. "*Sta per crollare*," she said. "I swear I saw the whole thing sway. What a mess it'd make if it toppled." Zucchelli watched her rearrange the perfectly stable tower, no doubt plotting his next move. It wouldn't be so bad if he were young and handsome. Like Marcello Battaglia, for example, who managed to look not only *bello* but elegant in a bloody butcher's apron. She wouldn't mind flirting with someone like him, who surely had the decency to keep his hands to himself. Not that a handsome, elegant man would be enough of a prize to convince her to marry. She hadn't thrown up all the way across the Atlantic only to scrub some man's kitchen and iron his undergarments for the rest of her life.

Her mother said Rosina was stubborn, which was true, and unreasonable, which wasn't. As far as stubbornness went, it was *il bue che dà del cornuto dall'asino*, the bull calling the donkey horned, because Clementina refused to give up on her pet project, marrying her daughter off at the first opportunity. Her most recent "eligible" find was the hopelessly boring Giorgio Marelli, pale and potbellied, with a receding hairline (already!) and hairy knuckles that made Rosina shudder.

His idea of a fun day was taking her to watch his father shoe horses while explaining how well he'd be able to provide for her once he took over the family business. One day not long ago, over ice cream, he'd explained in numbing detail the many physical problems his father had after years of crouching over hooves and pounding hot metal, not to mention the several times he'd been kicked by ungrateful horses. His father planned to retire in a few years, Giorgio said, which meant he and Rosina had time to enjoy a long courtship. He blushed when he said this, as if imagining what such a courtship might include, though he'd done nothing so far except launch a few sloppy surprise-attack kisses. He was so enthusiastic about his plans that he didn't notice she had little to say. Smiling faintly and nibbling on her ice cream were apparently sufficient.

She could endure Giorgio, considering his cowardice would keep him from proposing for some time. If he ever did produce a ring, she would refuse it. So what if her mother was determined? Rosina was earning her keep. No one could force her to marry. Let the twins give their mother the grandchildren she wanted.

The bell on the shop door rang, announcing the arrival of the two snottiest women in the North End. Rosina greeted them with a smile that surely looked as fake as it was. For a fleeting moment, compared to these intolerable days at Zucchelli's, Giorgio seemed like a better option.

After work, Rosina headed to the Battaglias' butcher shop to pick up a lamb shank her mother wanted. Maybe she should flirt with Marcello after all. He'd been a top athlete on the baseball team at Spaulding High, and Rosina was far from alone in having a crush on him. They'd met when she'd slipped on some wet leaves on the entrance stairs and fallen, slicing open her knee. When he came to her rescue, all it had taken to make her lightheaded was one glimpse of his warm brown eyes, fringed with lashes longer than hers. After that, he said hello whenever they met in the halls, often making silly jokes about her inability to stand or walk down a flight of stairs. Ever hopeful, she'd taken his friendliness as a sign of romantic interest, only to find out he was seeing a girl in his class, a blonde from Turin who thought herself sophisticated. By then they'd been an item for several years already and, according to Giulia, had spoken of marriage. But there had been no wedding, not even after Marcello graduated—Rosina had checked the posted marriage banns each Sunday and scoured the "Talk of the Town" column in the *Daily Times*—which gave her hope but not courage. By the time she'd graduated two years later and her mother started shoving men at her, she'd realized she didn't want Marcello or anyone else.

An ill-fated romance, though—that would be perfect. He would be a much more pleasant suitor than Giorgio.

She was trying to remember if her mother liked Marcello when she arrived at the shop to find him in the clutches of Mrs. Colombo. The old woman asked one question after another about the cost and freshness of the pork loin and—Rosina couldn't help laughing at this—whose farm had produced the pigs. Finally she left, having bought only a lone chop of unknown origin.

Rosina waltzed over to the counter. "*Scusami giovanotto*," she said in a quavery, old-lady voice. "Do you know precisely which pig produced those ribs over there? And what was its name, pray tell?" She peered at him through a mimed pince-nez.

Marcello laughed, wiping his hands on his apron. "The spareribs are very good, though I'm afraid I don't know the pig's name."

"Oh, then I can't possibly buy them." They both laughed, and Marcello reached for the spareribs. "Wait, I haven't decided yet," Rosina said. She cast around for something else to say. "How is your aunt, by the way? I seem to remember my mother saying she was ill for quite some time."

"She's well now, thank you."

"Wonderful, I'm glad. *Allora* . . ." Perusing the meats, Rosina bit her lower lip and shifted her weight to one hip. "Now I'm thinking maybe a lamb shank—"

"Marcello!"

Isabella Bianchi stood in the doorway, face aglow, chest heaving as if she'd run ten blocks. Sweeping past Rosina, she claimed Marcello with a hand on his arm and a lingering kiss on his cheek. It figured, Rosina thought. Isabella, with satiny, true-black hair, porcelain skin, and a bustline envied by every girl in the North End, was a known heartbreaker. Of course Marcello would court someone like her.

Rosina raised her voice. "A shank, Marcello. Lamb, please. On credit if you'd be so kind."

"Oh, excuse me," Isabella said. "I didn't see you."

"Four pounds, please." Smiling sweetly, Rosina turned to Isabella. "How nice to see you. Say, I heard you were engaged to Andrea Ferrario. What a shame it didn't work out." Another sweet smile, then the wrapped shank was in her hand and she was out the door.

Walking home, she chided herself. She shouldn't have been rude to Isabella, whose face had gone blotchy with embarrassment. On the other hand, was it so terrible to want to shake things up, to spark her boring existence with—what? For a mad minute she imagined tossing the shank in the shrubbery and running off in search of adventure. She could take a train to the end of the line, wherever that was. Simply disappear. Or live a nomadic life selling her drawings in town after town. Or run off with a man who had plenty of hair on his head and none on his hands, and no expectations. Someone as handsome as Marcello, preferably.

But she would do none of that because her family depended on her. Apparently she was not destined for an adventurous, scandalous life.

She walked on, the wrapped shank like a shackle on her arm. At the corner of Berlin and Vine, two women in black stood chatting, their shopping bags huddled at their feet while their hands flew. They were exchanging little stories about their errands, their families, enjoying a moment of connection that was probably the best part of their day. Was this what they lived for, this recognition they saw in another woman's eyes, along with whatever pleasure they took in caring for home and family? Was it enough? Rosina wanted to ask them, though she knew their answer would be yes. They had their pride, these women.

Whatever long-held desires they still harbored, whether muted or halved or nearly forsaken, would remain cloistered under those black dresses. And the widows among them, the Mrs. Aldo Nappis, what hope did they have, what pleasure? Did they wake each morning wondering how long the day would be?

"Well, you've put yourself in a fine mood," Rosina said under her breath.

That evening after dinner, when Clementina had dozed off over her mending, Rosina sketched her mother's face, beautiful in repose. What did she dream of? Surely more than the next day's dinner or what was on sale at Camolli's grocery. Perhaps she dreamed of her husband, or some long-ago suitor before him. In her dreams, would she be young again like her daughter was, twenty years old and ready to take on the world? With her life ahead of her, the known and the unknown, would she dream of possibility?

SIX

PRIMO MAGGIO, THE FIRST OF MAY, dawned clear and warm with a lightness in the air. It wasn't always so, because a Vermont morning in early spring might arrive warm and sunny, with crocuses popping up by lunchtime, or cold and crisp, with a blustery wind scattering early petals and smothering them in snow. Spring brought water too, and with a fast melt or days of downpours, the river would jump its banks, roaring like a prisoner set free. A Vermont spring was a changeling with the crazed energy of a hopeful gambler, the threat of unpredictability.

The weather today was a stroke of good fortune, thought Vittorio as he and Daniele arrived at the Labor Hall, because there would be nothing else good about the day. Primo Maggio, the workers' holiday, was a socialist celebration if ever there was one.

Socialist Labor Party Hall, a simple brick building with granite trim, sat on Granite Street a little more than halfway from Main Street to the river. Vittorio had helped to build it. Still proud to be a stonecutter back then, still buying into the socialist ideals, he'd put his back and his sweat into this building alongside Carlo and Gabriele and a hundred other men. Now it pained him to be here.

Trudging up the granite steps, he glared at the carved stone medallion above the entry, an upraised hand wielding a hammer, nested in two oak branches. Beneath the branches were the letters "SLP," for Socialist Labor Party, whose Barre members, for the most part, were stonecutters with callused palms and scarred fingers. Vittorio couldn't fault the socialists' ideals of community and concern for their fellow man, but that was all they were, ideals. To get somewhere in this world, a man had to be practical, and wise to the nature of man and his society. Some ideals were little more than pipe dreams.

"Hello?" Vittorio's voice echoed in the empty room. He checked the time. Whoever had written the note shoved under his front door last night had promised information about Ugo Lombardi, and given how new their partnership was, and how incomplete Vittorio's knowledge of the man, ignoring the summons had been out of the question.

"The note said ten o'clock, damn it."

"It's barely two minutes past," Daniele said.

As they waited, faint voices filtered in, people marching to the picnic grounds on the outskirts of town. Vittorio could make out the words because he knew them so well: "Workers of the world unite: You have nothing to lose but your chains!" In Barre, no Primo Maggio could pass without those words being said. How many times had he chanted them himself, marching arm in arm with his brothers and compatriots? It wasn't that he didn't still believe in some of the socialist ideals. He cared about family and community; he didn't want children to starve or men to die in pain. Societies should take care of their people. But he had a right to own a business, to make money without feeling shamed into giving it away at every turn. Families in need were a fact of life.

Daniele wandered over to the stage, readied for the evening's performance. "I'll bet you can't wait to see *Il Primo Maggio* again, right?" He laughed.

"That piece of drivel." The thought set Vittorio's teeth on edge. Lombardi had said one of them should be there, making it clear that Vittorio was the designated one. A show of diplomacy, Lombardi had called it, and Vittorio wondered why a man who didn't give a damn about his workers would bother with diplomacy, such as it was. Vittorio would be the pariah in the room that night and Lombardi damn well knew it.

"No one's coming," Daniele said. "It must be a prank, a stupid one if you ask me."

The voices again, farther away now, singing "Inno del Primo Maggio." Vittorio swore he could hear Carlo's scratchy baritone. How loudly he and his brothers used to sing, marching arm in arm. "*Vieni o maggio, t'aspettan le genti, ti salutano i liberi cuori, dolce Pasqua dei lavoratori, vieni e splendi alla gloria del sol.*" He caught himself humming along. Christ. Fortunately, Daniele, now pondering the portrait of Karl Marx on the wall, gave no sign he'd heard. Such a fine young man, smart and strong and confident, worthy of his father's pride. He would be a father himself soon, a responsibility he would no doubt take on as willingly and easily as he had the Milano's books. A serious young man, that one, with an admirable devotion to his wife. How different he was from Cosimo, who loved nothing better than a night accompanied by drink and women. Yet the two boys had always been close. They shared an easy companionship, rarely marred by harsh words, that couldn't be more different from the bond between Vittorio and Carlo, who from boyhood had shared a combative kind of love. Carlo used to torment Vittorio by flirting with the girls he liked, though he never followed through—and he could have, easily, because girls went weak in the knees at Carlo's sweet-talk, not to mention his body, like a goddamn Adonis. Then there was the story Carlo loved to tell, about the time when Vittorio came home drunk and he'd doused him with water from an upstairs window. Vittorio's hollering woke their mother, and she'd slapped him as if he were a child. It still made Carlo laugh and Vittorio bristle. Carlo hadn't spared young Gabriele either, thrilling him with lewd talk of girls, then teasing him for not knowing that the woman who smiled at him in the piazza, the woman he'd had a crush on since the day his voice changed, was the town's most infamous *puttana*.

Those were good times, the best times. But enough of the past. He was moving forward.

"It's been twenty minutes," Daniele said, abandoning the portrait and striding toward the door. "Let's go, Carmela is waiting. She wants to go for a drive if you don't need the car."

Vittorio peered out the window. The street was maddeningly empty. No one was coming, and he was a damn fool.

Rosina sat fuming on the Bottinellis' picnic blanket while Giorgio Marelli droned on and on about . . . she didn't know what, because the mere sound of his voice put her to sleep. She had always loved Primo Maggio, but not this time. She'd give Giorgio five more minutes, and after that her mother could listen to him because Rosina had better things to do, like go home and scrub the floors or lance someone's festering boil. Tuning him out, she let her gaze wander over chatting couples, blankets laden with food baskets and wine jugs, children playing tag, half a dozen men setting up a bocce court. Near the ticket sales table, three old-timers sat smoking, accordions at their feet. And there in line for tickets were Marcello and Isabella, ridiculously perfect together, laughing as if their lives were as perfect as they were. Rosina was about to indulge in self-pity when a young man stepped up to their blanket and said hello. He was fairly tall, a little too lean, with brown hair tipped red in the sun and a patchy beard that did him no favors. She remembered his name right before he said it.

"I'm Angelo, Angelo Lucci. Nico invited me." He shifted his weight, kept his gaze on Clementina so that Rosina wouldn't leave him tongue-tied. Clementina was wearing an enormous hat loaded with yellow flowers, very much like one his mother had owned. For a second he saw her eyes gazing out from below the wide brim.

"*Benvenuto*, Angelo," said Clementina. "Nico told me you were coming. Please, sit down. I'm sure you know Rosina, and this is Giorgio Marelli."

Rosina said hello, relieved that Angelo was here at Nico's invitation and not her mother's. One undesirable suitor was enough for one picnic. Still, now she'd be expected to make conversation. And when was her mother ever going to learn English? She snapped open her handheld fan and beat the air. Everything bothered her today.

Angelo wavered between sitting next to Rosina and across from her to see her face better, then chose a spot halfway between the two. He hadn't expected to see Giorgio here. Bad luck, since he must be courting her, judging by the way he looked at her. Judging by the way she looked at Giorgio, though, he was having a tough time of it. Good. He took a beer from Clementina, grateful to have something to hold on to. It was hard not to stare at Rosina, pretty in a pale green dress dotted with flowers. Her hair was only half pinned up so that a cloud of curls fell onto her shoulders. Tearing his gaze away, he searched for something to say.

Rosina snapped her fan closed, interrupting the awkward silence. "How do you know Nico?" she said without disguising her lack of interest.

"From the shed. We work together." Angelo dared to look her full in the face and feared his bones would crumble.

"That's hard work you do," Giorgio said. "Good work. It builds character, my father always says."

"I suppose. I'm a tool boy now, but it's temporary. I plan to cut stone someday—the sculpting like your father and brothers do, Rosina. Not the rough stuff. See, I'm an artist." He gulped his beer, hoping he didn't sound like a braggart. "A fellow has to start somewhere."

"Haven't I seen you at the park now and then, selling your sketches?"

She remembered him! "That's right. It was a while ago, though. I see you at Zucchelli's sometimes."

"Yes, of course." There was another awkward pause, which Rosina used as an opportunity to escape. "Excuse me for a moment, please. I need to talk to my friend."

Angelo scrambled up. "I'll walk with you." For a second he thought Giorgio would say he'd come too, but then the poor fellow's shoulders slumped and he turned to Clementina.

"Very well, but I'm not going far. Over there." Rosina pointed toward a family seated a few yards away. "Giulia!" she called, waving.

"That's all right. I should go find Nico anyway. Say, are you going to the play tonight?"

"Of course, doesn't everyone?"

His hopes faded. She sounded distracted, like she didn't care that he was there now or would be at the Hall later. Well, no one had ever accused him of being a ladies' man.

"I'll see you later, then." He trudged off. For a second he imagined taking her hand, the two of them running off together, laughing and . . . He was an idiot. She probably had plenty of suitors besides Giorgio.

"Angelo! *Eccoci*!" Nico waved from the edge of the clearing where the Bottinelli men stood, a bucket of beer at their feet. "We've got something to tell you!" He elbowed Paolo, who snorted with laughter.

"What's so funny?" Angelo accepted a beer, chugged half of it. He wasn't in the habit of getting drunk, but now seemed like a good time to start.

"I was about to ask the same thing," Carlo said.

"It was Nico's idea." Paolo nudged his brother. "You tell them."

"We sent a note to Vittorio that said—" Nico laughed, hands on his knees. "*Oddio*, I can't breathe!"

"It said to go to the Labor Hall at ten o'clock," Paolo said, "to meet someone who had, and I quote, 'information about Ugo Lombardi that will interest you.' What I would have given to see his face when he figured out he'd been played!"

"You boys don't think things through," Gabriele said. "He has a right to go into business with Lombardi or anyone else, whether you like it or not. Making him mad doesn't do any good."

"It does if I get a laugh out of it," Paolo said. "There's more too. I bribed the director of the play to change one of the anarchists' names to 'Vittorio.' I can't wait to see his face tonight!" He steepled his hands, eyes closed. "*Dio, vi prego,* make him show up."

Gabriele and Carlo exchanged irritated looks. "He'll show if he's smart," Carlo said. "I'd think any shed owner would want to hear what Eugene Debs has to say about union developments."

"He's coming, then? It's definite?" Nico said.

"Last I heard. Come on, let's go eat."

Carlo and Gabriele headed off, Angelo trailing behind them. The twins probably expected him to side with them, but truth was he agreed with Gabriele. Besides, he had nothing against Vittorio.

When everyone had gathered, Clementina served up plates of rabbit stew and polenta. Rosina showed up a few minutes later, her face stony as she doled out utensils and bread. Paolo and Nico kept side-eying each other and laughing like schoolboys until Carlo's glowering face shut them up. After that, everyone ate in silence.

Finally Rosina put down her plate and fork in disgust. "Excuse me, but what is going on? Are we at a picnic or a funeral?"

Paolo shrugged. "You don't seem too chipper yourself."

"Nothing's going on," said Carlo, "except that your brothers played a juvenile prank on Vittorio that only they find entertaining. Naturally he'll think I was involved."

"Sorry," Nico muttered. "We wanted to get back at him, that's all."

"For what?" asked Clementina. When the boys said nothing, she glared at her husband. "Carlo," she said, the single word a drawn-out warning.

Carlo sighed, brushing crumbs from his mustache. "I wasn't going to tell you until the deal was done, which it may be by now. Vittorio is going into business with Lombardi."

"What!" Clementina said. "I don't believe it."

"It's not so bad," Gabriele said. "He's helping Lombardi finance a new shed. He won't be our boss." He sipped his beer, then coughed. "Went down the wrong pipe," he said when Clementina looked at him in alarm.

"I hope that's all it is," she said.

"He left the industry, so why is he coming back?" asked Paolo. "It's like he's trying to prove he's better than us."

"Doesn't matter, he already acts like he is. It's a shame." Carlo stabbed at a piece of meat. "He gets rich from the Milano and what does he do? Help us fight for what we need? No, he sides with the shed owners. Meanwhile, more men get sick and die. Now it's the Panetta boy. It's criminal."

"I saw his mother yesterday," Clementina said. "The poor woman is beside herself. Carlo, couldn't this be an opportunity? Couldn't Vittorio help you get the equipment you want? Ask him if you haven't already. After all, we are still family."

"Wishful thinking, I'm afraid. The shed owners make improvements for one reason only." Carlo rubbed fingers and thumb together. "Why did they go to pneumatic chisels? Because they increase productivity. They make our hands and wrists numb, but they don't care. We get *mal d'america*, they don't care. One man dies of the dust and another takes his place, it's all the same to them. There's no profit in clean air. They won't buy the vacuum system unless they're forced to."

Clementina paled. "You don't mean a strike? People still talk about the last one. They say it went on for months and families were starving."

"They exaggerate." Carlo waved a dismissive hand. "We'd have to scrimp, but we wouldn't starve. It's only talk for now. But you know I'll do what I have to, when the time comes."

"We could change sheds," Nico said. "A friend of mine at the Smith shed says they're decent folks."

Carlo shook his head. "No, son. We need to show my brother we don't give a damn what he does. You two boys see him nosing around the shop, ignore him. If he talks to you, be civil, but take your concerns to Lombardi and only Lombardi. Understood?"

"Understood," the twins said, their faces glum.

Angelo wiped his mouth to hide his delight. A new shed! This was the best news he'd heard in ages. He felt bad for the Bottinellis, but a new shed meant more jobs. This could be his lucky break. What a day this was turning out to be! And tonight there would be music and dancing, and he'd bet his bottom dollar Rosina loved to dance. Most girls did. He could see them now, spinning around the dance floor while Giorgio watched them, sidelined. Could he get two lucky breaks in one day? He damn well could.

By six o'clock the picnic grounds were emptying out, everyone headed home to rest and prepare for the evening's festivities. Angelo walked back to town with the Bottinelli men. No point in walking with Rosina, who still looked like a storm brewing. Women were a mystery. You might think you were on safe ground with them, and then bam! you blinked twice and you weren't.

When he got home, his father wasn't too far into a bottle, so Angelo cooked up some pasta and beans and convinced him to eat. After a quick wash and a clean shirt, he set off for the Labor Hall, an hour before the doors would open. He liked to arrive early, wherever he was going, liked seeing a place when it was still quiet, waiting for whatever might unfold, the yet-to-be-known. It was like the places were alive, paused between slices of life, and he was bearing witness to the before and after of something bigger than he was. He could have explained this idea to his mother, and she would have understood. They were alike, him and her. *Due gocce d'acqua*, she used to say. Two drops of water. She said people like them didn't have both feet on the ground, not all the time. Sometimes they floated, half in, half out of the real world. He wondered if Rosina floated, or if she would think such talk was nonsense.

Tonight, though, his mind kept veering toward other things, like whether Rosina's dress would move with her body, what her waist would feel like beneath his hand, how crazed he'd feel with her warm fingers in his. He pictured the two of them spinning together in the half-light, the music carrying them to a place where no one else existed. He ached at the thought.

It was dusk when he arrived at the Hall. The lights were on. Probably the actors were rehearsing, or the women were setting out cookies and cakes while young men hauled chairs up from the basement. From across the street, he watched daredevil bats swoop past ambered windows and cruise the roofline. Maybe tonight he would be that daring. Though the bats didn't think they were daring, did they? They were hunting, bent on survival. For them, daring was normal, a part of daily life. Fine, then. Tonight he would dare.

An hour later the Hall was standing room only, filled with laughter and bright faces, women in silk dresses and socialists with red handkerchiefs tucked into their breast pockets. The Bottinelli men stood near the windows, their faces flushed with drink. Clementina was at the dessert tables, Rosina nowhere in sight. Angelo was about to look for her when a man called for everyone's attention and announced that the play was about to begin.

It was the same play every year, based on the Haymarket riots in Chicago, and Angelo knew the story by heart, spoke the lines along with the actors under his breath until a woman shushed him. Finally, near the end, came Paolo's prank. An actor moved center stage, right fist raised, and shouted, "My name is Vittorio and I fight for the common man!" The crowd went quiet, then roared with laughter. Everyone knew the character's real name was Gianluca and that of all the men in Barre named Vittorio, it was Bottinelli who was being mocked. Angelo searched the crowd, found Vittorio standing rock still near the windows, eyes glued on the stage. Poor fellow had to be steamed as hell, though he didn't show it. Then the actor mimed throwing a bomb and the stage lights flashed. The play ended a few minutes later and the same announcer, now shiny with sweat, said there'd be a fifteen-minute break before the speeches.

Angelo snagged a handful of cookies, then wandered until he found Rosina talking to her friend Giulia at a dessert table by the window,

Giorgio slouching nearby like a discarded puppy. He was about to head over there when Clementina interrupted the girls, and within seconds they were refilling trays of cookies as fast as they could. He drifted into the crowd. Trying to talk to Rosina now wouldn't be daring, it would be stupid. Better to wait for the music.

Moments later the announcer came back onstage. "Attention, everyone. Attention! It's time for our first speaker tonight. Please welcome Gavin Donachie, who would like to say a few words on behalf of the Scottish stonecutters."

Donachie, a short man with a porcupine beard, didn't take long to start yelling about Barre's shameful lack of proper revolutionary spirit. Primo Maggio was a call to action, he said, a renewal of the socialists' goal to challenge capitalist oppression. By the time he worked himself up to calling wealthy businessmen selfish parasites that fed on laborers, a cluster of men at the back of the Hall, most of them young and none of them sober, were shouting at him to get off the stage. Raising their fists, they began to chant in a mix of Italian and English. "*Né Dio né padrone*! *Né Dio né padrone*! Neither God nor master! Neither God nor master!"

Anarchists, Angelo thought, and up to no good. He'd bet they were here to heckle Debs. A flask was going around, the drunk getting drunker. Not good. Any mob was dangerous, but a drunk one was worse. The women should leave now. He craned his neck, searching. Rosina was still at the dessert table, but now she was talking to a tall fellow, broad shouldered and attentive. Too attentive. Angelo shoved through the crowd, got close enough to see who it was. *Merda*, it was Marcello Battaglia, and he was touching her arm! She was all lit up about it too, a goddamn lighthouse. So much for his lucky break.

Another speaker took the podium, a leather-faced quarryman named Brasi. The chanting had died down and in its place came shouts of "Where's Debs?" and "Quiet, let Brasi talk!" Mouth open, Brasi tried to see past the stage lights. He hadn't said ten words when a scuffle broke out at the back of the crowd. Amid cries of "Hands off!" and "*Basta*!" and "Simmer down!" and "*Calma, calma*!" a body hit the floor and women screamed. Then everyone was up, turning, shoving, trying to see what was happening.

The announcer rushed back onstage. "Any of you folks can't act civilized, I've got to ask you to leave. We're here in solidarity tonight as workers and brothers." He mopped his neck with his handkerchief.

"Says who?"

"Where's Debs?"

"Goddamn socialists!"

The front door opened and a dozen men surged in, pushing through the crowd like rats down a snake's gullet.

"Where's Debs?" "*Dov'è* Debs?" More voices this time. "He talking tonight or not?" A skinny man with eyeglasses stepped onto a bench and turned slowly, chanting, "We want Debs!" and pounding fist to palm with each word. "We! Want! Debs!" A few people took up the chant, then more and more. Fists jabbed the air, faces went red, voices bellowed. "We! Want! Debs!"

"He's not here!" someone yelled. "Goddamn socialist liars!"

"Debs! Debs! Debs! Debs!" Then waves of shouts and obscenities drowned out the chanting and the mob spun into a free-for-all, chairs wielded as weapons, flesh smashing into flesh, bodies slamming onto the floor. Women screamed and dragged their children toward the exit, calling for their men. The man on the bench pumped his arms and chanted, his shadow flapping on the wall.

Angelo dodged chanters and brawlers and panicked women, trying to reach Rosina and Giulia, huddled next to the windows with Clementina. Marcello hovered over them, talking urgently, then herded them toward the door. Giorgio had disappeared.

"Papà!" Rosina's eyes were panicked. "Marcello, let go of me!" She stumbled back toward the mob. "Nico! Paolo!"

Marcello reached for her but Angelo cut him off and grabbed her hand. "Take those two and go! *Vattene*!" Marcello swept Clementina and Giulia away.

"Let me go!" Rosina shoved Angelo. "Papà! Paolo! Nico!"

"They'll be all right! They can't hear you, let's go!"

They were almost to the door when the air splintered. Rosina whirled around, her face ghost white, as the man on the bench spun off his perch, a bloody hole in his chest. Angelo grabbed her again, forcing her forward. They were only feet from the exit when six men barreled toward them, five of them hustling the sixth toward the door. Rosina escaped with seconds to spare. Angelo fell back out of the men's path, then hurtled down the stairs after them in time to see them pile into a waiting car. It chugged off, headlights cutting through a swarm of scurrying figures.

Debs, Angelo thought. That had to be Debs. Then a hand clamped onto his shoulder and Carlo's voice was in his ear. "Let's get the hell out of here."

SEVEN

ON HER WAY TO WORK THE NEXT MORNING Rosina kept picturing the man on the bench falling, falling, again and again, his shirt drenched with blood. She'd dreamed that he landed on top of her when he fell, suffocating her while Marcello watched, frozen and helpless. When she finally managed to struggle free, the man rolled over and she saw his face, vacant eyes to heaven. It was Aldo Nappi. She woke sweating and horrified, her heart wild in her chest, and now she couldn't stop thinking about how a life could be undone in a moment.

She was crossing Granite Street, lost in thought, when Angelo hurried toward her, calling her name. She was in no mood to chat, but it was a choice between ignoring him or stopping, and her mother hadn't raised a callous girl.

"I lost you last night," he said, catching up to her. "What a shock, huh? How are you holding up?"

"I'm all right, considering." The warmth of his tone and the concern in his eyes were unexpected, and surprisingly welcome. "I can't stop thinking about that poor man who got shot. I dreamed about him last night, only he was Aldo Nappi. I keep seeing his face." She shivered. "It's so stupid," she added with sudden fury, "all this violence. I'm sick of it."

Stupid, and a way of life, at least for the men of Barre. Maybe for men everywhere. They didn't know how to listen, especially when they were butting heads. Oh, they were quick enough to put up their fists or draw their guns, but talking things over came second or not at all. She would never understand it. No matter how nasty women could be—no matter how much they gossiped about their neighbors or let personal feuds go on for years—the hurt they inflicted, insults and cold shoulders and curses and the *malocchio*, drew no blood. Well, not most of the time. When it came to jealousies and love affairs gone wrong, some women took their battles to the ground. Still, men were far worse.

"You men, it's always the same, you talk with your fists," Rosina went on. "I hate it. And nothing will change unless women get to have their say, and that won't happen until we get the vote. We have a lot to say, I'll have you know. Men should listen. Why are you smiling? I suppose you think I'm being hysterical."

"No! You speak your mind, is all. I like that." Angelo was surprised to find it was true. In fact, she had more pluck than some men he knew.

"Well, good, I suppose. Not that it matters. No one listens to me except Nico. Papà goes on and on about the union and politics, but does he ever let me say a word? No. Honestly, I've given up trying."

This was an open door if he'd ever seen one. "Listen, seeing as you're interested in politics, how about going to a union meeting with me? There's one Monday night."

She sniffed, tossing her head. "Oh, but women aren't allowed. Don't you know we need to stay home and knit?"

If eyes could cut a man down, hers would, and with no hint of mercy. He was tickled by her fierceness, had to stifle an urge to laugh. She might think he was ridiculing her.

"Sorry, I should have said listen to a meeting, not go to one."

Her stance softened. "How?"

"Leave that to me. I'll wait for you outside your house, say, eight thirty?"

"Yes! We're in Scampini Square, number 5," she said, her face alight.

"I know!" Angelo took off at a run. He'd never been so happy to be late to work. Lombardi could dock him double for all he cared.

He had almost reached the shed door when a scowling Vittorio charged toward him. "Out of my way, boy!" Angelo followed him inside and dashed to punch his time card. Then he picked up some buckets from the blacksmith's room and hightailed it after Vittorio. If there was going to be a fight, no way in hell was he going to miss it.

Vittorio wound through the shed as quickly as his throbbing head allowed, under siege as it was from last night's drink. With each step his head pounded harder, exactly what he wanted to do to his goddamn brother. By the time he reached Carlo, he was trembling with rage.

"It was you, wasn't it?"

Carlo silenced his chisel. "*Cosa*?"

Vittorio ignored the Italian, continued in English. "That note summoning me to the Hall, that was your idea of a joke? And my name in the play? Well done, brother, well done. Though I'm curious to know what gives you the right to shame me when I have done nothing wrong, absolutely nothing!" Christ, he was screeching like a fishwife. He lowered his voice. "My partnership with Lombardi is my business and mine alone, it has nothing to do with you. If you don't like it, it's your problem."

"Nice speech, but it wasn't me." Carlo checked a drawing, then shifted his gaze to the slab of rock before him.

He wasn't lying, damn him. Deflated, Vittorio watched him contemplate the granite block. He was picturing where to drill the reference holes needed to lay out the design, Vittorio realized. He rubbed his temples, fighting an unexpected urge to see the design, ask him how he planned to translate two dimensions into three, toss out a few ideas the way they used to, one stonecutter to another, with some arguments and laughs, an affectionate slap on the back. How he missed that. In that moment he wanted nothing more than to forget the pranks, ignore this chasm between brothers. And he might have done that if he hadn't noticed his nephews' smug faces. He marched over to Paolo and Nico, his fury reignited.

"I trust you enjoyed your bit of fun at my expense?"

"Fun? That's what you call a riot and a murder?" Paolo nudged his stonecutter's hat back, a gesture so insolent that Vittorio wanted to backhand him.

"I know the note was your doing."

"Note?" Paolo frowned, scratching his head. "Nico, dear brother, do you know anything about a note?"

Nico pretended to think. "I don't think so, Paolo, dear brother. What kind of note?"

Vittorio propped his fists on his hips. "You know damn well. And planting my name in the play was juvenile and idiotic."

"That's what you're thinking about the day after a man was murdered?" Paolo said. "Sounds like you've got your priorities in a twist."

Vittorio wanted to fire him, both of them, all three of them, on the spot, but he was powerless without Lombardi's buy-in, which he'd never get. This wasn't his shed, and the Bottinellis were too damn good. He should have known better than to waste his time. Well, as long as he was here he might as well have a sit-down with Lombardi, blow off some steam. It was early yet, but Lombardi's whiskey bottle paid the hour no mind and he sure as hell could use a drink.

As he turned to go, Angelo jumped out of his way. "What are you looking at, boy?" Vittorio bellowed. Good God, it was like being a clown in the center ring of a circus.

Lombardi wasn't in the little cubbyhole that served as his shed office. Swearing, Vittorio hurried to the Main Street offices, arriving out of breath, each inhalation tainted with the stairwell scent of stale cigars and old sweat. The door was ajar. Stay calm, he told himself. Lombardi was the hothead in this partnership; it was up to Vittorio to play counterpoint.

"*Buongiorno*, Ugo." He swore he'd coax some halfway decent English into the dullard's head eventually; it was the language of business, after all. "Do you mind some fresh air?" He heaved open a window, then collapsed into a chair. "I'll take a whiskey if you have it."

"I bet you will. Heard about the play last night." Lombardi grinned, rolling back in his chair to collect a bottle and two glasses. "That your brother's doing?"

Vittorio grimaced. "My nephews'. Make it a double, will you? Is that all you heard about? The play?"

"And this." Lombardi held up the *Daily Times*. "SOCIALISTS, ANARCHISTS CLASH," the headline blared. Below it: "One Man Dead After Uprising at Labor Hall."

"A tragedy. Idiots, all of them, and drunk as sailors on leave. Did you know the man who was killed?" Vittorio sipped the whiskey, grateful for the glow chasing the bite.

"Nah." Lombardi lit a fresh cigar. "An out-of-towner, is what I heard. Part of that mob wanting to cause trouble for Debs. Apparently they don't like all this talk about one big union, all trades and nationalities. Me neither. Crazy idea. It'd kill us."

Vittorio nodded. "The IWW, yes. Unfortunately, it's the kind of thing Carlo will jump at. It worries me." He downed his drink, needed another. In fact, what he needed was a leisurely meal in a private booth with a good bottle of wine and some business talk that would raise his spirits and restore his pride. "Listen, how about lunch at the Milano, say, one o'clock? We can talk about the business over the best food in Barre. On me, of course."

"Today? Can't do it. Tuesday's good though."

He always had to have the upper hand, Lombardi did, making it abundantly clear that while he was happy to take Vittorio's money, he wasn't about to concede a whit of power. Vittorio mustered patience from a reserve he didn't know he had. "Very good, Tuesday at one."

"Make it one thirty." Lombardi snapped open the newspaper.

Vittorio wanted to snatch the paper from him, tear it to pieces. Lombardi's infuriating need to have the upper hand was bad enough, but that goddamn word "CLASH," big and dramatic, was worse, shouting in his face. He'd had enough clashing what with Carlo, the union, the socialists and anarchists, hell, even Marietta this morning, nagging him about God only knew what. He'd tuned her out. He'd had enough for a lifetime.

On Monday night Rosina lied to her mother about where she was going and escaped the house. Angelo was waiting outside as promised, and ten minutes later they were on Granite Street, hidden in the shadow of a cluster of pines.

"We have to wait until everyone's arrived," he whispered. "It won't be long, the meeting's about to start."

"But what are we doing?"

"You'll see."

A few minutes later he announced an all-clear. They ran across the street and squeezed through a bank of forsythia, emerging into a small clearing beneath the north windows.

"I used to eavesdrop on the meetings before I started working at the shed," Angelo said, his voice low. "I miss it, sort of. It's fun listening when no one knows you're there."

"You're in the union now?"

"Not yet, but your father lets me go to the meetings anyway, seeing as I work with him."

Side by side under the windows, backs to the cool bricks, they listened to the buzz of conversation. Rosina's arm was only inches from his and he could feel her warmth. To kiss her, all he'd have to do was turn his head.

"Welcome, men," Carlo said. "As president of the Barre Local of Granite Cutters International, I now call this meeting to order."

"This is exciting!" Rosina whispered. Her eyes were huge, her face lit up. Angelo was already eager for the next meeting so they could do this again. Until tonight, he'd never missed a meeting. He smiled in the darkness. Still hadn't, actually.

The first point of discussion, Primo Maggio and the shooting, had everyone yelling in less than five minutes. "Calm down, calm down," Carlo said, raising his voice to be heard. "I don't want to start an argument here." When the men quieted, he went on. "The point is, what happened could happen again, or worse. I know this tragedy will taint all of our memories for some time to come. But take it as a warning, I beg you, to keep your tempers in check."

"Papà's English is so good now," Rosina whispered. "I'm proud of him."

"What about Debs?" someone said. "Is he coming back here to talk or not?" Voices rose again, loud, impatient, urgent.

"Damn it, Carlo," said a gravelly voice, "we need that big union he's talking about or we'll all die before we meet our grandkids."

"I hear you, Marco," Carlo said. "We're working on getting him to return. You all know about the union he's talking about? If you haven't been coming to meetings, you need to keep up. Debs is organizing it with Big Bill Haywood and a bunch of others. They call it the Industrial Workers of the World, the IWW." A murmur of recognition. "The thing is, Marco, I want to live to see my grandchildren too, but nothing's going to happen overnight. The important thing is, the IWW is gathering steam. If they can unite workers in all industries, small locals like us will have a bigger voice and more power. That would make a strike threat a much more powerful weapon."

"Isn't this fun?" Angelo whispered, and Rosina shushed him. "Seems like you like it," he said, and she shushed him again, this time with a frown. Good. Like a mouse to cheese, she'd want to come back and he'd be right here with her in the near darkness, in this private place where the two of them were as good as alone. And once she got to know him better, maybe she'd start looking at him the way he looked at her.

"A national union is our only option," said a tenor-voiced man. "You old-timers who were on the line with me in the '92 strike, you know I'm right."

"That strike nearly killed me and my family," said a man with a Spanish accent. "I won't do it again, not for five months. Not without a national union backing me."

"You've got a point, both of you," said Carlo. "Like I said, though, the IWW won't happen overnight. Are you willing to wait years for the vacuum equipment in order to have them behind us? I'm not. How many more men are we going to let die before we take action?"

"We got no proof the dust is making us sick," said a nasally voice. "The docs say it's tuberculosis." The man stopped to cough.

"It is *not*!" Rosina said into the sudden quiet that followed. Angelo put a hand over her mouth and she grabbed his wrist, her eyes huge with fright.

"What was that?" someone said. "I didn't hear nothing," someone else replied. Then the coughing stopped and the debate continued.

Angelo removed his hand. "Sorry, I shouldn't have done that."

"It's all right. You surprised me, that's all." Rosina was about to pat his arm to reassure him, then stopped. It was the strangest thing. His palm had felt good against her lips, warm and dry, with a faint scent of soap, and that wouldn't do at all. It was best not to touch him, even his arm.

"Not to argue," a raspy voice was saying, "but Doc Carson don't say that. He says the lung disease comes from the granite dust. It don't spread like TB. Think about it, Enzo—if it did, the dead men's wives and kids would be dead too. What people are saying about us being dirty and spreading it around because of that, and bringing it on ourselves, that's bullshit. I'm with Doc Carson, it's a job hazard, plain and simple. We get the dust out of the air and we don't get sick. Ask him if you don't believe me."

"Well said, Enrico," said Carlo. "And now I'm going to say this again, as plainly as I can—we can't wait around for Debs and Haywood. I know it's a hard truth, but we'll breathe deadly air until we strike, likely more than once. Until then, it's time all the citizens of Barre knew the truth, not only us stonecutters, and to that end I've written a piece explaining our position. It'll be in the *Daily Times* early next week."

A scattered chorus of "Hear, hear!" Then an argument broke out, a loud jumble of words impossible to follow.

"I wish they wouldn't all talk at once," Rosina whispered.

"All right, all right, everyone simmer down!" Carlo said. "Keep it civil or we're done for tonight."

After more discussion about air filters and suction equipment and a good half hour arguing about whether to strike, Carlo said it was time to move on. Before it got too late, he wanted to say a few words about Aldo Nappi.

Voices rose in collective dismay. "Damn shame." "A tragedy." "Hell, I'd do the same thing."

Carlo interrupted them. "Aldo was a good man and a damn fine stonecutter, not to mention a devoted father. He left five children behind. All of you know as well as I do that he shouldn't have died. He was healthy two years ago, for God's sake. Some people will say he sinned to step in front of that train—"

"You said it, Carlo," said a voice as deep as the bottom of a well. "It's not right for a man to take his own life."

"Walk in Aldo's shoes and then say that," Carlo replied. "You all know he spared his family from a living hell. I call that courage. Now it's our turn. We must find the courage to strike. All right, I've said my piece. The point is, we're not here to pass judgment on a good man. If anyone else wants to say a few words about Aldo, now's the time. My hat will be on the table by the door if you can spare a few coins for his widow on your way out."

Four or five men shared stories about how steady Aldo had been, a hard worker who loved to tell bad jokes and sang like Caruso, who was quick to share his lunch if another man's came up short. Then someone shouted, "God bless our brother Aldo!" and the men echoed him, their voices spiraling out the window. "God bless Aldo, may he rest in peace!"

"We should go, they'll be leaving any minute," Angelo whispered.

Quickly, quietly, they slipped away. "Thank you," Rosina said as they walked toward Scampini Square. "I learned something tonight."

"You can see how hard it is to get things done, can't you? Too many opinions, and the Local's not strong enough even when they do agree."

"No, no, no!" She erased his words with her hands. "I know all that, Papà talks about it all the time. I meant they didn't say anything a woman shouldn't hear. I wish I could tell my father that."

"Don't let on you know about anything you heard here or he'll ask how you know."

"I'll try not to, but if I do, I'll say you told me. We're friends now, aren't we?"

Friends. An ugly word, cruel, like a knife through the heart. "Sure we are."

"When is the next meeting? I'm sure I'll hear about it at the dinner table, but it's easier to get out of the house if I know ahead of time."

"Should be in two weeks. It's hard to get away?"

"Of course. Mamma doesn't like it when I go out at night, even to see my friends. Barre isn't the safest place for a woman alone, especially near the Meadow. She'd have a fit if she knew where I was tonight. Papà too."

The exasperation in her voice took him by surprise. "I suppose. I never thought about it."

"Pfft, spoken like a man. You can go anywhere and do anything whenever you want to, and no one thinks a thing of it. Or questions your virtue."

They were back at Scampini Square, the street empty except for a few rough-looking men passing time near a lamppost. The town was theirs, their body language said, and the neighborhood, the world. Rosina's skin prickled with alarm. "I'd better get inside. Thanks, Angelo. I'll see you around."

He moved in for the traditional double kiss, nothing romantic, but she spun around as if she hadn't noticed. She had, he was sure of it, which meant she was ducking him. *Porca miseria*. Well, he'd have other chances. He watched her go inside, imagined her entering the apartment, warm with light and family. Nothing waited for him at home except a lonely cot and a father who might as well be a stranger.

Rosina crept upstairs, praying that Mrs. Calcagni, that old *pettegola*, wouldn't poke her head out to ask where she'd been. Luck was with her because the gossip's door stayed closed, as did the doors on the second floor. She slipped quietly into the apartment, hoping to ease unnoticed into her room.

Her mother's voice stopped her. "*È tardi*, Rosi," Clementina called from the kitchen. "Why are you late? Be aware of the hour next time."

"I will."

"Who was there tonight?"

So much for avoiding the usual prying questions, bad enough when she wasn't lying. She was terrible at it, transparent as glass. "Oh, the usual girls." Rosina went as far as the kitchen door. Her mother was at the table, where two sealed envelopes lay on the table next to a box of stationery, her weekly letters to the family back home. "Who are you writing to?" Rosina said, hoping to distract her.

Clementina laughed and put down her pen. "Who do I always write to? Now tell me, how many booties did you girls make?"

"I guess a dozen pairs? I'm not sure, Mamma."

"You chatterboxes must have done more talking than knitting."

"We always do, don't we?" Rosina faked a yawn. "I'm off to bed now, unless you need me to do anything."

"Go along. *Sogni d'oro*."

Rosina sat on her bed, her body charged. A door had been opened tonight, and though she wasn't allowed to step through it she'd seen what was on the other side. Nothing had changed, not yet. Still, she felt more hopeful than she had since she'd left school. America was young, a country without the centuries and centuries of traditions and beliefs Italy clung to. America was still figuring out its path. Maybe she was wrong in thinking her choices here would always be the same as they'd been back home.

She rose to close the curtains. The men by the lamppost were gone, but Angelo stood where she'd left him. Whatever was he doing? She raised a hand in case he'd seen her. A rare fellow, he was, talking to her as if she had a brain, as if he didn't know women were supposed to want nothing more than a life that revolved around the kitchen and nursery. Talking meant nothing, though. In time he'd want what every man did, a woman who knew her place. He might listen to her ideas, but he'd still expect his shirts to be washed and ironed, his dinner on the table when he got home from work, his children waiting to greet him with scrubbed faces and combed hair.

Yet there was something different about him. She'd felt safe, even in the dark with no one else around. Even with his hand pressed to her mouth.

As soon as Rosina's window went dark, Angelo took off at a clip. *Dio santo,* he was so charged up he could have run to City Hall and back, twice, and still had plenty of breath. What a night! He liked knowing which room was hers, where she slept. He turned around, gazing into the darkness, imagining her in her bed. He'd see her again, he knew it. They had a secret now, something that bound them. Who knew what might come next?

Up ahead, a maple leaned over the street. He took a running start, leaped for a low branch, swung high and let go. For a few seconds he was flying.

EIGHT

ON WEDNESDAY MORNING Vittorio woke up to news that made his teeth grate. There in the *Daily Times*—not in the *Cronaca Sovversiva* paper, that piece of socialist propaganda, but in Barre's main mouthpiece, supposedly the home of serious journalism—was a long-winded screed written by his brother, laying out the stonecutters' demands for new equipment that would, he claimed, save lives. What would happen if they didn't get the equipment wasn't implied, oh no. Carlo point-blank threatened they'd strike. Which meant it was only a matter of time. Which very possibly threw a wrench the size of the Statue of Liberty into his plans to build a shed with Lombardi.

He sipped his coffee and grimaced. "Good God, Marietta, did you boil this all night? It's undrinkable." He tossed aside the paper, which she had placed, as always neatly folded, next to his breakfast plate.

Marietta sighed and turned to Daniele and Cosimo, her furrowed brow suggesting they do something about their father's foul mood. When Daniele said nothing, his wife, Carmela, nudged his arm.

"Oh well, I uh . . . I wouldn't worry too much, Papà," Daniele said. "It's an opinion piece, no one will take it seriously."

"He's right," Cosimo said, gesturing at his brother with a half-eaten brioche. "By tomorrow people will be lining their birdcages with it."

"Save your breath." Vittorio pushed back his chair. "Damage done is damage done. I'll have my coffee at the Milano in peace and quiet. And I am *not* being temperamental." He stomped to the entry hall for his hat and coat.

"Marietta, the coffee is delicious as always," Carmela said.

"Thank you, dear. How are you feeling this morning? You seem to have more of an appetite."

"I'm famished!" Carmela patted her belly. "I think this little one got twice as big overnight."

Daniele kissed Carmela and his mother goodbye. "I'll go see if I can calm the monster."

"Better you than me," Cosimo said. "I'll be hiding behind the bar today."

Vittorio spent the morning holed up in his office and snarling at his secretary. He was tempted to write a rebuttal to Carlo's diatribe, but he could imagine what Lombardi would say: "You're not a shed owner yet. Best keep your opinions to yourself."

At quarter past one he went to the dining room to wait for Lombardi. He hadn't known the man for long, but he knew one thing—he'd be intentionally late. Vittorio took a bottle of whiskey from behind the bar and settled into a corner booth.

The Milano was gratifyingly busy, packed with businessmen plotting deals, travelers taking respite on their way to Montpelier or Boston, shopkeepers and clerical types chatting over beers at the bar. Proof, in Vittorio's eyes, that the hotel's food and drink, not to mention its atmosphere, were the best in Barre. Normally he'd enjoy observing this world he had created—the polished wooden tables and velvet-soft banquettes, leaded glass windows and graceful chandeliers—but today all he could appreciate was the glass of Hiram Walker smooth against his palm. He slugged the liquor, poured another.

He and Carlo used to drink together, back in the day, before they'd gone in opposite directions. It happened sometimes—brothers once close becoming strangers. But the distance now between him and Carlo was a step beyond estrangement. Christ, they were practically enemies, divided by the very thing they'd once shared.

The door opened with more new arrivals, and Vittorio caught each one's eye, welcoming them with a nod. People here knew him, knew what he'd accomplished. He laughed now whenever he thought about the business ventures he'd admired in Viggiù. No comparison. In Barre, fine new buildings went up with speed and frequency, each one filled with offices and shops, proof of a healthy economy. In Viggiù the finest buildings were churches, eight of them for only five thousand people, good only for the eyes and spirit. No town needed eight churches; they were a waste of buildable land. Still, Viggiù had one advantage over Barre—no lethal granite dust poisoned the open courtyards where the stonecutters worked with hammer and chisel and the air carried only the pungent smells of horse stalls and smoldering iron.

It was a large advantage, Vittorio had to admit. Even so, he'd been smart, very smart, to come to Barre. He'd known it was his way out of stonecutting, though he hadn't told anyone but Marietta. He'd written to his brothers every week, describing the plentiful work, the sheds that kept multiplying. A sales pitch so enticing that they'd been eager to join him. But they hadn't understood how different life would be in Barre, and neither had he. Adjusting to the new place, the language, the strange American ways, Vittorio had focused on the wages he was earning, the bright future he envisioned. Not once did he think seriously about the closed sheds and pneumatic tools that forced dust into the stonecutters' lungs. But then, no man believed *mal d'america* would come for him.

"*Buongiorno*. Nice place you got here," Lombardi said, startling Vittorio. "I see you're drinking the good stuff." He seemed to be in a surprisingly cheerful mood.

"I am indeed, and now so are you." Vittorio gave him a magnanimous smile and poured.

With food and wine ordered and small talk dispensed with, Vittorio jettisoned his plan to discuss the details of the new shed he'd be paying for. He'd put up half of a six-thousand-dollar shed, no small change, and would reap half the profits, a deal he'd been happy to sign. But first the damn thing had to be built, and a strike could dash their plans.

"You saw Carlo's piece in this morning's *Times*, I assume?"

Lombardi leaned back. Taking his time, he lit a cigar, puffed it to life, anchored it in a cut glass ashtray, sipped his drink. "Sure I did."

His tone was chilling. This lunch, which Vittorio had envisioned as a chummy meeting of like-minded partners, might well become a test of his loyalty.

"Yes, well," Vittorio said, "this vacuum equipment the men want—I've heard something about it. An air filtration system of some kind, I believe."

"That's right."

"They claim it would prevent *mal d'america*, or at least lower the risk."

Bowls of olives and pickled vegetables arrived, giving him a few seconds to choose his words. Lombardi's piercing gaze never wavered.

"Is there any truth to it? If so, is it worth considering? I suppose," Vittorio added hastily, "it's quite expensive."

"You suppose right."

Vittorio nodded. "Of course, of course. At least initially. But with the savings in time lost to illness—"

"Wrong. No time lost, you understand? Man goes out, man comes in. No shortage of stonecutters in town and plenty more willing to come here."

"Yes, yes, of course." Vittorio forced a laugh. "What was I thinking? I guess I've been out of the business long enough to forget that."

The conversation ebbed as red wine and two plates of ossobuco arrived and the men busied themselves with the food. Vittorio cast about for a reasonable change of subject, but too late.

"So tell me," Lombardi said through a mouthful of veal, "you been out of the business long enough to forget anything else? I seem to recall you going on and on about your experience in the sheds, all that knowledge you got, how you'd bring more to the table than the money I need." He aimed a loaded fork at Vittorio. "Were you lying then, or are you lying now?"

"Neither, I assure you! I am a man of my word, you can count on that. To be frank, Carlo's little public tantrum threw me off. I'm not myself today."

"Make it the last time. Or is this going to be a problem, you having family in the sheds?"

"No, no, not at all. You have my word."

"I'd better." Lombardi polished his plate, sopping up meat juices with bread. "Cheesecake sounds good if you got any."

Vittorio flagged the waiter and ordered dessert and grappa, wondering how fatal this meeting would be to his future. He was rattled, should keep his mouth shut for now. Yet faced with Lombardi's displeasure, he felt compelled to explain away his error.

"Regarding the equipment, I, ah, I was thinking generally, simply in terms of business investments, that's all. An eye on the future."

"Investments. That's what you're thinking about. Not your brothers' lungs." Lombardi leaned forward, directing smoke at Vittorio's face. "I'm going to say this once and only once—keep business and family separate. In my shed, we make purchasing decisions based on cost and gain, not because you want to protect your family. That's if—and it's a big if—*mal d'america* has anything to do with the sheds, which according to me it doesn't. Now, are you in or are you out? Because we can go to my office right now and tear up that piece of paper you signed and you can find somewhere else to shove your money."

"I'm in, Ugo, I'm in, of course." A long pause filled with smoke and wine and regret. Vittorio felt like a chastened schoolboy, and he'd be damned if he'd let Lombardi do that to him again. The day ground broke on the new shed was the day Lombardi had better begin treating him with respect.

He cleared his throat. "Can I ask what you think about this strike business, in terms of the shed going up? I'm sure we'd both like to avoid any delays."

"Strike?" Lombardi snorted. "This"—he crushed out his cigar—"is what I think of the strike. They're fools if they walk. So what if working conditions were better where they came from, that doesn't matter when a man can't feed his family. You know that as well as me. Here they can put food on the table, send money home, and still get drunk after work. If they decide to give all that up, fuck them. The scabs will be ready. We break ground as planned."

If the coffee and grappa hadn't arrived then, Vittorio would have bitten the man's head off. He downed his grappa. "Very good, I'm glad we're on track," he said in as measured a tone as he could manage. "Out of curiosity—that's all, I assure you—regarding the cost of the vacuum equipment, what kind of numbers are you talking about?"

"Big ones. A central system with one hose per man would run us thousands of dollars. You want to invest in that or the shed I want? Can't do both."

"Of course expanding is the smart move."

"Lombardi-Bottinelli Granite Works—sounds good, no? And I'm thinking about one of those new bridge cranes. Rossi has one, go take a look." Lombardi reached for his hat. "Thanks for the meal. Regards to Marietta."

Vittorio poured another grappa, his hands unsteady. He'd been an idiot to rock the boat this early in the game. He had to approach the granite business the same way he had the Milano, with clarity and a profits-first attitude. Get the new shed built, then think about new equipment. Because in that respect, he disagreed with Lombardi, whose vision was clearly limited. Vittorio had his eye on the future, and it would stay there. He had more than the shed to look forward to. Come November he'd be a proud grandfather, and it was up to him, and Daniele of course, to give that child—may it be a boy!—a future brighter than their own. Cosimo should settle down too. More Bottinellis, that was what Barre needed. Bottinellis who would do more with their lives than cut stone.

Vittorio donned his hat, palmed his walking stick. Outside, the afternoon sunlight was soft and warm with a floating breeze. He inhaled deeply, the sweet air filling his lungs, and then suddenly he was coughing, his throat seizing up like it wanted to kill him. Like he was breathing the air in the stone sheds, thick with dust and anything but sweet.

NINE

ON SUNDAY ROSINA WOKE UP with an idea so obvious she couldn't believe she hadn't thought of it sooner. If Angelo sold his drawings, why couldn't she? She could set up an easel in the park, show her sketches to anyone who stopped by. She tossed back the covers, invigorated.

"*Buongiorno a tutti*!" Rosina sang as she entered the kitchen. "Mamma, let me do that." She took the coffeepot from Clementina and hummed as she filled the men's cups.

"Aren't you in a good mood," Clementina said.

"I am. I've decided to sell my drawings in the park like Angelo Lucci used to do."

"Good for you," Nico said. "I'll be your first customer."

"No you won't," Carlo said. "No daughter of mine is going to stand on a street corner and sell art or anything else."

"Who said anything about street corners?"

Clementina looked at her in dismay. "No, Rosi, I agree with your father. It would be . . ."

"Tacky?" said Paolo. "Is that the word you're looking for?"

Clementina eyed him with exasperation and put a gentle hand on Rosina's arm. "It's not a good idea, *figliola*. What would people say?"

"Hopefully that they like my drawings!" Rosina slammed down the coffeepot. "Zio, what do you think? You keep saying I should do more with my art. Well, I'm trying!"

"I admire your spirit, but I agree with your parents," Gabriele said. "For a different reason. Selling your work doesn't make you an artist. Yes, do more. Make art, grow, learn. Perhaps one day you will find an audience"—his voice softened—"but not today."

"Because I'm not good enough." Rosina crossed her arms, hating the childish petulance that turned her voice into a whine.

Gabriele held up his hands in protest. "I didn't say that! You have talent, *cara*, I would never lie to you about that. You are young still, you need time. Art takes more than an instrument in the hand."

"Sorry to interrupt this touching moment," Paolo said, "but the game is about to start."

"*Testa di cazzo*." Nico swatted Paolo's head. "This is important to our sister."

"Language," Clementina said to Nico.

"*Va' a cagare*, Nico," Paolo said with exaggerated sweetness. "I'm going. See you at the courts."

"Language!" Clementina kissed Rosina's head. "Patience, *cara*. Everything comes to those who wait."

What a tired old saying. Rosina wanted to bean Paolo in the head with his precious bocce balls. He and Nico could go off and have fun while women and children filled the pews at St. Monica's on Sundays. The only men who went to church anymore were the ones too old and decrepit to walk to the courts. She felt sorry for them, deprived of a lifelong pleasure, but at least no one told them they weren't allowed to play. At least they didn't have to rush home after Mass to prepare a meal. At least—her selfish thoughts faded—at least they weren't dead before their time.

After Mass she took a walk to settle her mind. She wouldn't fight her parents about selling her drawings, but only because Zio didn't think she was ready. Maybe she would never be ready. Maybe her work was destined to stay on her bedroom wall forever. What a distressing thought.

Wandering down Main Street, she passed shuttered shops and passersby going home or to a relative's house for Sunday dinner. Before Zio Vittorio and his family moved to the mansion on Washington Street, when all the Bottinellis lived in the North End, in the same tenement, they always had Sunday dinner together. She missed them. Her aunt Marietta had always been delighted to see her latest drawings and listen to her stories about school, and no matter what her father said about Zio Vittorio, he was a good man. Back in Viggiù, when Rosina was small, he took her to the store for candy or ice cream on Saturdays, her riding on his back. He made a good horse, she used to tell him, steady and strong. When she was eight, he'd convinced her mother to let her keep a stray kitten, then helped her feed it for weeks. She was his unofficial daughter, Zio used to say, since he didn't have one of his own. And now they were strangers. It was so sad.

She missed that cat, left behind in Viggiù. Her darling Topolino, gray like a little mouse. She missed her grandmother too, and her endless complaining about everything, including her dead husband. She missed her best friend, Elisabetta, and the piazza where they played after school, and the donkeys that pulled carts up and down the hill, and visiting her cousins in Besano and swimming in the lake at the edge of Switzerland. She missed the wild asparagus she used to gather and the roasted chestnuts hot on her tongue in winter and the garlic pesto she could never get enough of. She ate those foods here too, but they weren't the same.

A gentle breeze toyed with her hair, reminding her that the day was fine. Crocuses and hyacinths brightened the winter-drab city, lightening her mood. Where Main Street veered south at City Hall, people wearing their Sunday best milled about, chatting on the sidewalks and park benches at the Common. A group standing in front of the Universalist church broke up, and there was Marcello! Oh, and Isabella. Rosina wrinkled her nose. Their mothers were with them, the four of them chattering like magpies.

Choosing a bench on the opposite side of the park, she sat to watch them, tipping her head back now and then, eyes closed, so that if Marcello happened to see her he'd think she was taking the sun. *Mamma mia*, he was a sight in a perfectly cut suit and a bowler hat. How dashing he was!

Mrs. Battaglia finished whatever tale she'd been telling and everyone laughed. Then Marcello looked Rosina straight in the eye and walked over as if he'd known all along she was there. She hid her delight with a look of mild surprise because Isabella was watching them, her displeasure obvious. She said something to her mother, who shook her head and stilled her with a hand on her arm.

"Good morning!" Marcello stood three feet away, hands tucked in his pockets. "It's a nice day, isn't it? Say, that's a very pretty dress."

"Thank you. I didn't expect to see you here."

"We were at church." He gestured over his shoulder. "Over there."

He wasn't Catholic, then. She'd been inside the Universalist church, recalled it as plain, its only glory slivers of stained glass windows. When her family had first arrived in Barre she'd gone into all the churches, looking for one that reminded her of home. None of them did, not even the Catholic church, Saint Monica's, which didn't look Catholic at all. Where were all the chapels devoted to the Madonna? She missed her favorite church in Viggiù, the Madonna of the Cross, with its beautiful altarpiece fresco of a sweet-faced Virgin with long, delicate fingers and a chubby baby Jesus.

"Do you know my mother?" Marcello said. "Come and say hello to her and the Bianchis. They're leaving tomorrow, back to Italy for the summer. Too bad for me."

Was it? He didn't seem terribly sad. Then Rosina was standing next to Mrs. Battaglia and introductions were being made, three pairs of eyes giving her a once-over.

"Isabella and I know each other from school," Rosina said, at which point Isabella's face went blank. "Oh, don't you remember the spelling bees? I beat you three years in a row." She smiled, then turned to Mrs. Bianchi. "Marcello says you're going to Italy for the summer. That's lovely."

"Yes, we go every year, Isabella and I. My husband's work responsibilities keep him here. He's a bank manager," she added with obvious pride.

"I see," Rosina said. "What a shame he can't go too." Did the woman expect congratulations for nabbing a husband with enough money to ignore her? Condolences seemed more appropriate.

"I'd rather stay too," Isabella said, slipping her arm through Marcello's. "I'm going to miss this fellow so much." She kissed his cheek. "Now, you be good while I'm gone. You know all the girls will flirt with you." Her eyes bored into Rosina, cool and cutting.

"It's only a couple of months, Bella," Marcello said. "You'll be back in no time."

Rosina announced she was late getting home and bade them goodbye. Isabella might be right to worry about Marcello, she thought as she hurried off. Why introduce her when he could have simply waved hello or pretended not to see her? Maybe she would have a shot at him after all. If so, and if she convinced her mother she was serious about him, then it would be goodbye, Giorgio, at last. How good an actress could she be, pretending to be in love?

Except Marcello wasn't Catholic. Her mother wouldn't be happy about that. Still, in her own view that was good, another very good reason a courtship with him wouldn't last.

A storefront window box caught her eye, nasturtiums in vivid shades of red and orange, flaming in the sun. She'd have to remember to come back to sketch them. Better yet, she'd buy some paints and capture those colors. Watercolors, she thought. Something new.

She walked on, pleased with the turn the day had taken. Another tired old saying, her grandmother's favorite, popped into her head:

"*Il buon giorno si vede dal mattino.*" It wasn't always true—a good start to the day didn't always bode well, and a bad start didn't mean the day couldn't turn out well. Like today, for example, a very good day, and hidden until now.

Almost home, she passed the Battaglias' shop, shades drawn, waiting for morning. The next time she stopped by, she would find out exactly how much Marcello was pining for Isabella. If her instincts were right, it wouldn't be much.

Two days later—waiting required patience, and she had very little of it these days—Rosina went to the butcher shop to prove herself right or wrong. Six people were waiting. As she took a number, Marcello saw her and winked. He was talking to Mrs. de Bella, who apparently had asked why he'd decided to be a volunteer fireman.

"*Ecco com'è andata,*" he said. "Our neighbor had a kitchen fire, you see—"

"*O Madonna santa*!" The woman's hand flew to her mouth.

"Exactly what I said. It could happen to anyone, couldn't it?" Marcello was oozing charm that Rosina swore was aimed at her. He went on and on, finally ending with, "And when I saw those men leap off the fire engine and knock those flames out in no time, I said to myself, 'Now that's important work.'"

"Indeed it is! I thank you for your bravery."

Santo Cielo, the woman was practically swooning. Rosina watched in amazement as Marcello leaned toward her, his face melting with gratitude. He probably would have taken her hands if his own hadn't been slick with raw meat.

"*Grazie a Lei*, Signora de Bella, for respecting the men who keep you safe."

Rosina spun around, hand over her mouth to keep from laughing. What a performance! If the poor woman had known he was trying to impress a girl instead of her, she probably would have slapped him.

"More work, less talk," Mr. Battaglia said, emerging from the back of the store. "We can't keep these people waiting, son." He stepped up to the counter. "Next in line!"

Marcello dispatched his next few customers with great speed, his timing perfect so that when Rosina's turn came his father was already occupied. "*Buongiorno*, Signorina Bottinelli, how can I help you?"

She tossed off her sunniest smile. "I'd like a pork loin for six people with leftovers, please." Marcello moved at a snail's pace, poking and prodding and weighing, until his father had finished with the last customer.

"Call me if there's another rush," Mr. Battaglia said, wiping his hands on his apron. "Afternoon, Miss Bottinelli."

Marcello plopped the wrapped meat on the counter. "One pork loin, the best we've got. Anything else?" An undeniably flirtatious tone.

"Is that story true? Are you a fireman?"

"I am! Although I haven't gone to a fire yet. To be honest, I'm less worried about fires than about the engine boiler blowing up." He laughed, then noticed Rosina's shocked face. "Sorry, I shouldn't joke about that. Actually, I think I'm more likely to get bitten by one of our horses. They're ornery as can be, every last one of them."

"I don't blame them, they must be terribly afraid all the time. Well, I suppose I should get this roast home."

"I suppose you should," Marcello said, his tone suggesting the opposite.

As far as Rosina could tell, nothing in his voice, face, or demeanor suggested loneliness or heartbreak. She might as well test the waters. "Oh, by the way, I meant to ask if you've heard from Isabella."

"Not yet. She should have arrived in New York today. Their ship leaves tomorrow."

"Of course, how silly of me."

"Say, I've got a long, lonely summer ahead of me," Marcello said without an ounce of dismay. "Would you like to walk with me sometime? We can talk about pigs' names and ornery horses."

There it was, proof that he was as faithful as a snake. "Thank you, but I'm seeing Giorgio Marelli these days. And I'm sure Isabella—"

"Isabella won't mind. A walk, that's all. No harm in that, is there? I promise not to steal you away from Giorgio." Marcello snorted a laugh, then leaned in, his arms folded on the counter, his tone irresistibly inviting. "What do you say, tomorrow at lunchtime? One o'clock at Currier Park?"

She couldn't believe his nerve, lying to her when he knew she'd heard Isabella warn him about other girls. A thrill of excitement brought goosebumps. This was fun—dangerous fun. "All right, a walk. As friends! Until tomorrow, then."

Outside, she watched him through the window, reaching into the display case, apron snug around his slim waist, sleeves rolled taut against his forearms. He was no Giorgio, that was for certain.

The next morning Rosina put on her favorite dress, the green one she'd worn on Primo Maggio and never wore to work, hoping her mother wouldn't notice and ask her why. That hope lasted all of five minutes.

"*Dove vai oggi*?" Clementina said when Rosina walked into the kitchen.

"Nowhere. To work," she said, hurrying to set the table.

"Who is the young man, Rosina?"

"I swear you're a witch!" Avoiding her mother's eyes, she fussed with a napkin. "Oh all right, if you must know, it's Marcello Battaglia. We're going for a walk, that's all."

"While Isabella Bianchi and her mother are in Italy for the summer? Don't be foolish, he can't be trusted. *Quando il gatto non c'è, i topi ballano*."

Her mother was right—when the cat is missing, the mice dance. What her mother didn't know was that Rosina wanted Marcello to dance.

"And people will talk," Clementina added.

"Talk about what?" Nico said as the men trooped in.

"Nothing," Rosina muttered.

"Your sister seeing Marcello Battaglia while Isabella Bianchi is away," Clementina said, casting yet another disapproving look at her daughter.

"I don't like his family's politics," Carlo said as Rosina poured the coffee. "You can do better."

"You mean like Giorgio?" Paolo laughed. "I'm with my sister on this one."

"Thank you, Paolo."

Clementina sniffed. "If he isn't a two-timer, I'll put my hand in the fire."

"It's a walk, Mamma, that's all."

"So you said. A pretty face isn't everything, remember that."

Rosina arrived promptly at one. Marcello was waiting for her on a bench, one arm stretched along the backrest and one long leg crossed over the other, ankle to knee. From fifty yards away he looked sculpted, as beautiful as a Roman statue. He jumped up and gave a little bow as she approached, and they began making slow circuits around the park, he with his jacket slung over his shoulder and she with her hands behind her back so that people wouldn't think they were courting. They probably would think that anyway, what with Marcello watching her the way he did, as if she were a morsel to consume or a prize to be won. She suspected he was the kind of man who liked the chase. Fine, then let the chase begin. She would make sure it was a long one.

Their conversation stumbled along in fits and starts, finding the most secure ground on the topic of his training with the fire brigade. By the time they'd made their third round, propriety dictated that Rosina ask about Isabella.

"Surely you miss Isabella by now. Will you write to her?"

Marcello shrugged. "I suppose so. If my mother had her way, we'd marry in the fall."

"I see." She hadn't planned on their engagement, a most disappointing twist. If her mother knew about it, she'd keep shoving Giorgio into Rosina's path.

Marcello insisted on walking her back to work, which Rosina took as a gentlemanly gesture until they'd crossed the train tracks at Granite Street and he pulled her behind a standing boxcar. With his arms an iron clasp around her waist, he kissed her.

She pulled away. "Marcello!" Despite her doubts about his character, she hadn't expected this. Or at least not so soon. "What about Isabella?"

"What about her? We're having a little fun, that's all. You want me to stop?" He kissed her again, and this time she let him. Waves of heat flew from her lips to her core. His kiss was needy, animal-like, raw, not the least bit romantic. The few kisses doled out by her other suitors seemed brotherly in comparison, dry and timid or overly polite.

He nuzzled her neck. "You're very pretty. And different from Isabella. You like this, don't you?"

He was a two-timer, as her mother had said. And dangerously appealing because of it. Rosina wanted to throw herself at him, but that would be a mistake. This was only the beginning of the chase; she couldn't let him think he'd won her over so easily. Not to mention that being seen as a homewrecker wasn't part of her plan. Even though he and Isabella didn't have a home to wreck, if they were engaged, Rosina had to be careful. People were quick to make accusations. She could already hear the gossipy women she waited on at the store: Marcello *l'infedele*, Isabella *la tradita*, Rosina *senza cuore*. The unfaithful, the wronged, the heartless.

"I don't let engaged men court me," she said as primly as she could.

"But you let me kiss you. And who said I'm engaged?"

"You said your mother—"

"I said if she had her way I would be. I haven't proposed."

"Well then," Rosina said, straightening her hat, which had been knocked askew in their embrace, "if you'd like to court me, I'll consider it after you've ended your relationship with Isabella. And any other women you're seeing. Although I should tell you my mother is awfully fond of Giorgio."

"And who are you fond of?"

"No one. Certainly not you. I'm not at all fond of two-timers."

He laughed, the insult rolling off him like rain. "Ah, but wait until you get to know me." He reached for her hand and she whirled around, skipping out of his reach.

"Give my regards to Isabella," she said over her shoulder.

"I don't give up easily!" he shouted after her.

"Neither do I!" she shouted back. She swung her skirts, pleased by her success. A fake courtship with Marcello would be fun. He'd be a delightful diversion and, even better, a handsome deterrent to other suitors. And since he was obviously a rogue, she was quite certain he wouldn't mind playing her game. Not that he knew it was one. He had better get to work on his letter setting Isabella free—no, a telegram, because a letter would take forever. If he was a decent man at all, he would word it kindly.

Oddly, she didn't feel guilty about her plan, even though she did, occasionally, feel bad about poor Giorgio. About Marcello, not a whit.

That afternoon Rosina smiled whenever she thought about his kiss. She couldn't wait to tell Giulia, who disliked Giorgio too, though she didn't think it was fair for Rosina to string him along when she had no plans to marry. "It's my mother's fault," Rosina always said whenever the subject came up, to which Giulia always replied, "Even so. You're going to break his sad little heart." If that was what she worried about, then she would think Marcello a better choice. No chance of heartbreak there.

TEN

IT TURNED OUT THE SCUFFLE AT LOMBARDI'S, the one before Primo Maggio that had sent Lombardi running out of his office brandishing a gun, was nothing compared to what happened the third Friday in May. For Carlo, it meant push had come to shove.

It happened where the Stevens Branch of the Winooski River sliced through Burnham Meadow, where nearly fifteen hundred men worked in stone sheds fed by train cars and long-armed cranes. They were hard-working men, men who'd seen plenty of hardship, who spoke different languages and knew different cultures. You couldn't throw Scots and Swedes and Greeks and Italians into a volatile boomtown like Barre and not expect conflicts. Not when plenty of those men spoke only a smattering of English, making misunderstandings common, and not when those crippled conversations were about wages and hours and politics and strikes.

What happened was that a few dozen shed workers went to the river after work to drink beer and blow off steam. The usual harmless stuff—playing cards, joking around, complaining about the boss. By ten o'clock any sober men had gone home, and the others had moved on from cards and jokes to that most dangerous of topics, politics. What had begun as a somewhat friendly debate between the socialists, which most of the men were, and a handful of anarchists—about using violence as a means to a good end—accelerated within minutes. And from there the argument got specific. Up for dispute was whether the men were dying due to the dust in the air—it was hard to admit that doing the thing you loved was likely to kill you—and whether the new vacuum equipment Carlo touted would be the miracle solution he claimed it was. Aldo Nappi, being the most recent man to die, was brought up, again, as either a tragic figure or a pathetic coward who had abandoned his family. That got the men heated. Then the strike advocates, the doubters, and the old-timers who'd seen the ugly reality of a prolonged strike heated things up even more, and the argument shifted from opinions to threats to fists, then to knives, rocks, and broken beer bottles. Someone with a cooler head than the rest of them took off and called the police, and it took the three officers who came at a run, armed with clubs, twenty minutes to shut the fight down. There were several injuries, one that warranted a trip to the hospital.

That wasn't the worst of it, not in Carlo's book or anyone else's.

The worst of it was that two ten-year-olds, Roberto Rossi and Leonardo Casagrande, had sneaked down to the river hoping for some excitement. Imitating their hotheaded fathers, they stood on the banks of the swollen river calling each other names and threatening beatings until Roberto lobbed a rock and Leonardo took it on the forehead and fell into the water. No one had known the boys were there until Roberto came running. The search party numbered in the hundreds, but the current was strong and swift after a week of rain and the fallen boy's body wasn't found for hours.

It was only going to get worse, that much Carlo knew. There would be no reconciling the two sides with rational discussion, and in the meantime, every cough or fevered night made fear flare up like bottle rockets. It was time to move on, to end the debate. Time for the vote they all knew was coming. Not that it would end the violence. There was no such thing as a peaceful strike, not when men's pride and livelihoods and families were on the line. But at least the violence born of a strike could end in good, in the triumph of the workingman, a tangible and moral victory, whereas the kind of violence that led to the death of a child was nothing but senseless tragedy.

The next day dawned as gray and grim as Carlo felt. The night before, he'd told Clementina he planned to call a vote, and now she was giving him the cold shoulder, which he expected would continue for some time. Gabriele said Carlo was doing the right thing given the boy's death, and his quiet support gave Carlo strength.

He called an emergency meeting, laid out the argument in favor of a strike, and announced the date for the vote one week hence, on Saturday the twenty-third of May. If the vote was *yes*, they'd walk out the following Monday morning. He asked the men to help spread the word to those who weren't at the meeting. He wanted more than a quorum, he wanted a *yes* vote down to the last man. Then he went home without hearing a thing Gabriele and the twins chatted about as they walked, because all that was left to do was to wait and worry and ask himself, over and over again, if he'd made the right decision.

The vote was *yes*. Cast, tallied, and kept secret until Monday morning when the stonecutters converged on Burnham Meadow with picket signs and a statement of their demands, one copy tacked to each shed door before dawn. Fourteen hundred men chanting "*Sciopero*! *Sciopero*! Strike! Strike!" hoisted signs shouting "On Strike" and "Air Not Dust" and "Save Our Lungs!" in two languages. Carlo stood among them, exhausted and relieved and determined, reconciled to the hardship ahead. It could be a long road. It would be a hard one. Today the men marched in solidarity, but if the strike lasted for months, if people got desperate, friendships would fail and families would grow silent. Despite the reassurances he'd given Clementina, he knew the stories were true about the nightmarish toll a prolonged strike would take. On everyone, not only the stonecutters and their families but the city too. God willing, it wouldn't come to that. Carlo's stomach knotted at the thought. But what else could he do? Too many men had died, and too many more would die if nothing was done.

A cutter from the MacClery shed pumped his sign, shouting "Follow me!" and a river of men set off for Main Street. The plan was to loop south on Main to City Hall, then back to the Labor Hall, keeping the line going around the clock in six-hour shifts. The shed owners watched the mob, some with disgust, some with anger, all of them with a chilling lack of worry. Lombardi crumpled the notice tacked to his door, then leaned against the frame with his arms crossed. It wasn't hard to read his mind: *Have it your way, you sorry bastards.*

"Carlo!" Angelo emerged from the throng. "I'm here, can I get a sign?"

Carlo's eyes were on Lombardi, now talking to Vittorio, who seemed nervous as hell. "This isn't your battle."

"But I'm with you, a hundred percent! I breathe that air all day too." But his stomach clenched at the thought of food cupboards too empty even for mice. For years he'd scrambled for work, delivering goods, mucking out stables, whitewashing fences, baling hay, living with constant uncertainty until the tool boy job fell into his lap. He dreaded having to scramble again, and it might come to that. But he'd be a union member someday, and he was a stonecutter at heart, and a body was a body when it came to holding a picket sign.

"Good." Carlo squeezed his shoulder. "Now do me a favor and find out what Lombardi and my brother are saying. Don't let them see you."

Angelo spotted a tool boy he knew standing a few feet from the two men. He sidled over to him and exchanged a few words, keeping his eyes on the picket line.

"They think they're mighty today," Lombardi was saying, "but they'll change their tune when the first scabs get here. With any luck, and if they're smart, they'll change it fast and we can get back to business as usual. In the meantime, we've got to get the new men working as soon as we can. It'll be a busy couple of days."

"When will they arrive?" Vittorio asked.

"Some are here already. As soon as word gets out, every train will be packed with hungry men." Lombardi jingled the keys to his padlocked shed.

"You must not have seen the *Times* today, then," Vittorio said grimly. "I spit out my coffee when I saw the headline. One word, all capital letters. You can guess what it was. The news is out."

Angelo circled back to Carlo to report what he'd heard. "Nothing I didn't expect," Carlo said. "Come on, let's walk."

By late afternoon, scabs were pouring into Burnham Meadow from Depot Square. Some of the shed owners waited on the platform, launching job offers as soon as the men stepped off the trains. Vittorio wanted to do the same, but Lombardi said there was no need. There would be plenty of scabs to go around, he said. Vittorio should relax, the men would come to them.

By evening Carlo's feet were like stone, his arms on fire, his throat raw. Eight times the men in line had linked arms to keep the scabs out, and five times the blockades had produced cracked heads and bloodied faces. Nothing would stop the scabs, though. They'd swim across the river—hell, they'd tunnel underneath the damn thing in the middle of the night if they had to. There wasn't much anyone could do to stop a man from doing whatever he could to feed his family. The strikers knew what they were up against, and so did the scabs. They knew what the workers were fighting for, understood that their own lives were at risk too. But you couldn't tell a man whose stomach was empty today that a job might kill him tomorrow. The most Carlo could hope for was that the scabs weren't skilled and productivity would suffer. A hit to their profits was the only thing that would bring the shed owners to the bargaining table. The question was whether the union men could hold out long enough.

When the line circled back to the Labor Hall, Carlo stepped out, dropping onto the stone steps to rest. The day had been relatively calm, but the next would be worse, as would every day after that. The men would face fatigue, hunger, sunburn, blistered feet and palms from walking the line, and their wives' short tempers and sharp words when money ran short. If the strike ran to months, some of the men might cross the line. Time and hunger and desperation would reveal how deep their resolve ran.

Carlo pushed to his feet, rejoined the endless line of chanting men. Before he could sleep tonight, he needed to talk to the shift leaders he and Gabriele had enlisted to keep the line going day and night. Four men would keep things organized, the lines of communication effective. They'd pass out coffee and bread, settle arguments, assign shifts. As time went on, they'd make new signs, stoke the men's spirits, replace the coffee with something stronger. It would be a long haul, and boredom and despair were the enemies of bravado.

Rubbing one aching shoulder, then the other, Carlo thought of Aldo and the rest of the men who'd died from the dust. The strike had come too late for them, though it might not make a difference anyway. It was going to be hard, this walkout, no matter its length. How much easier it would be to get through it with both his brothers at his side. Together, each would have eased the burden on the others. But ease was the most his brothers could have offered Carlo. The *yes* vote was his doing, and his alone. Once again, he hoped like hell that he'd done the right thing.

PART II

TRANSITION

ELEVEN

THE STRIKE DIDN'T SHUT DOWN THE GRANITE INDUSTRY; the scabs saw to that. Productivity continued at an acceptable pace, yet uncertainty strangled the city. No one knew how long the strike would last; no one knew when, or if, negotiations might give them hope. Fearing the worst, housewives tightened their purse strings, and soon shop owners did too, reducing their stock or shaving their hours. Others, like Luigi Zucchelli, panicked and cut their staff, which was why, on a Thursday morning in early June, Rosina was out of work. Zucchelli was sorry, but times being what they were, his hands were tied. She should come back after the strike ended, he'd be glad to take her on again.

She walked home that evening plagued by worry. Here she was, at last free of her hated job yet unable to rejoice. Her family needed every penny of her earnings. Her mother was taking in sewing now, but so were other housewives. Rosina had to find work, anything, no matter how poor the wages.

Up ahead, a woman pushing a baby carriage crossed the street, and there the idea was, right in front of her. The strike might hurt businesses, but nothing stopped babies from being born. And in times like these, wouldn't men seeking escape or comfort turn to their wives in bed more often than not? All those babies arriving nine months from now would be perfect timing for a new midwife building her reputation.

But none of that mattered unless Zia Donata was still willing to train her.

Rosina reversed direction, feet flying. Her father wouldn't like it, but he'd simply have to swallow his pride where Vittorio was concerned. Work was work.

At Vittorio's house, a turreted white Victorian halfway up the Washington Street hill, a housekeeper answered the door. As instructed, Rosina waited in the foyer, a warm space with a stained glass window that threw jewel tones onto the gleaming hardwood floor. All was quiet until a distant clock chimed the hour. Rosina took two cautious steps into the corridor, which opened onto a parlor on the left, where amber drapes framed a half circle of windows and a brocade settee dug its carved feet into a rug patterned in burgundy and gold. To the right was the dining room, where crystal candlesticks and a cutwork cloth topped a table big enough for twelve. Imagine living in such a palace!

"My dear, what a lovely surprise!" Donata hurried toward the foyer, silk skirts swishing. "Please come in."

"Thank you, Zia, but I can't stay. I came to ask if you would train me after all."

"Your father has agreed?"

"No, he doesn't know I'm here, but I don't care what he says. I lost my position at Zucchelli's and I need work."

"In that case, I can't imagine he would object. Though neither he nor Vittorio will like it. However, that's their problem, isn't it? It's settled—a midwife you shall be. Does your tenement have a telephone?"

"Yes, on the first floor, next to Mrs. Calcagni's door. She likes to answer it."

"Good. Tell her you will be expecting important calls and that someone must answer, day or night. If you're not at home when I call, I'll send a boy to find you."

"And my wages, will they be what you said before?"

Donata smiled. "You'll make a good businesswoman someday, my dear. Yes, three dollars a week for whatever is needed—lying-ins, home visits, errands. I won't always have work for you, but I'll commit to paying you every week for as long as the strike lasts. That's fair, isn't it?"

"More than fair, thank you."

"It's hard work, and it can be exhausting, but when all goes well it's joyful too. You'll see. Now then, Mrs. Ambrosini is due for a home visit tomorrow, and I need to pick up a few things first. I'll meet you at Halliday's Pharmacy at nine o'clock."

On her way home, Rosina prepared herself for her father's anger. Even more worrisome, though, were her aunt's words: *when all goes well.* She hadn't thought about the possibility that a birth wouldn't end well. She hadn't thought about births much at all, and certainly not about babies dying, which she should have because of her baby brother Carletto. Still, there would be a lot to learn, and it would be exciting to be out at all hours, to never know when the telephone might ring or a boy would stop her in the street and say she was needed, perhaps urgently. She must always be ready. She was ready now—for the unknown, for new experiences to spice up her predictable life. She couldn't count on Marcello for spice, having heard nothing from him since their kiss. Maybe she'd misjudged him and he truly cared for Isabella.

Rosina arrived home to the tang of garlic and the woody smell of oregano, familiar and welcoming. The house was quiet. The men would be on the picket line as usual. It might be hours or days before she could speak to her father, and there was no time to waste.

She found her mother in the kitchen, rolling out long twists of pasta while tomato sauce bubbled on the stove. Her mother looked older these days, her face strained with worry, her hair streaked with new strands of gray. Her face crumpled when Rosina told her Zucchelli had let her go, then brightened at the prospect of other work.

"*Brava, hai fatto bene*," Clementina said, patting Rosina's cheek. Surprised by the praise, Rosina flushed with relief when her mother brushed off the lower wages, saying that anything was better than nothing, and besides, she would be proud to have another midwife in the family. And Rosina wasn't to worry, she would deal with Carlo herself. "You will do well, *cara*. Now then, go dig some potatoes for me."

Rosina took a trowel and basket from the landing and went downstairs to the building's shared garden. Digging into the damp earth, inhaling the rich scents of growth and decay, she wondered what Marcello would think if he saw her now, kneeling in the dirt. That she was where she should be? That she was a hard worker, a suitable choice to give him children? Isabella had probably never dug potatoes in her life—would that make her more desirable to him?

Rosina paused to push back some strands of hair. What did it say about her that she wanted to lure Marcello into a courtship that would lead nowhere and would cause Isabella pain? It meant she was selfish. Cruel. Shallow. And what if Marcello fell in love with her and she had to break his heart?

What if she fell in love with him?

She wouldn't. And too bad if she did, she would still walk away. An affair was one thing, marriage quite another. As a midwife she would be a helper of women, not a wife who served only her family. As frightening as the strike was, it had given her a chance to change her life. Also frightening, she thought as the realization set in.

The basket half full, she sat back on her heels, watching the sky edge toward indigo. The first stars winked into view, little miracles of light. How could anyone see them and not feel hope?

She dug again, reached into the dirt. Something stung the palm of her hand and she brought it to her mouth, a memory rushing back. The Labor Hall, Angelo's hand over her mouth, his skin warm against her lips. She wiped her palm on her skirt. *Basta*. She had more important things to think about now. She was to be a midwife. She prayed it would bring her joy.

That evening Carlo was walking the picket line with Gabriele and the twins and Angelo, his tenth or twelfth or sixteenth circuit, when Vittorio materialized at his side.

"Can I pull you away? I'll be brief."

Carlo handed his picket sign to Angelo. "I'll catch up to you."

"This way." Vittorio gestured toward the river, and the two men threaded past cranes and loaded train cars, the piles of slag surrounding the sheds made hazardous by the fading light.

At the riverbank, Vittorio put his back to the water and opened his arms. "This is it, the site of the new shed. We'll break ground next month, strike or no strike. However, I want you to know I'm not unsympathetic. Don't breathe a word of what I'm about to say or Lombardi will have my head on a platter."

Carlo agreed with a jut of his chin.

"If I was still cutting stone, I'd be siding with you," Vittorio said. "Even though I know it's folly. I know, I know, you want to make a statement, and I would too if I shared your idealism. However, I'm a realist, and if you ask me, this strike will do more harm than good. Trust me, if the shed owners had an inkling it was happening when it did, they'd have held the door open for you and kicked your asses on your way out."

"So instead we're supposed to lie down while they walk all over us? Say it's all right for men to die when they don't have to?"

"It's not forever, Carlo, I'm talking about now. Maybe with time—"

"We don't have time! We should have struck months ago, years ago. Now that Doc Carson says it's the dust that's killing us, our case is stronger than ever. They have to listen to us!" Carlo's face flushed with anger and frustration. He knew what his brother would say next, and he would be right.

"No, they don't."

Carlo groaned. Since when did the word *strike* make him think of defeat and despair? He couldn't give in to that kind of thinking. It was too soon, and there was too much at stake.

"You're reasoning with your heart instead of your head, like you always do," Vittorio said, not unkindly. "You can come at them with all the proof in the world that it's stone dust that's killing the men, and they'll shrug and say maybe so, and so what? Because for every man who dies, there are three men waiting to take his place. You know that. Please, Carlo, end it, I beg you. You've made your point. And the longer you're out, the greater the risk of violence. And I don't mean fistfights."

"You're worried about my safety on the picket line but not about the health of my lungs? What kind of logic is that?"

"You can walk off the picket line, Carlo. I can't snap my fingers and give you the equipment you want."

Carlo shoved his fists into his pockets. *Cristo santo*, the brutality of this world, the atrocities one man would do to another without blinking. Vittorio meant well, but Carlo wanted to strangle him all the same. If it hadn't been for him, so insistent, so convincing, he and Gabriele would never have left Viggiù. How their poor mother had cried when Vittorio left, then begged her remaining sons not to follow him. She didn't care about the money they would send, no money was worth losing a son, much less three. She broke their hearts. And they broke hers when they left, but how could they not? How could they choose poverty over a chance at a good life for their wives and children? Vermont had promised opportunity and wealth, and it had delivered—but at a price high enough to make him consider leaving after the first year. He knew now he'd never have done it. Vittorio was right, he was idealistic—determined to fight for what he thought was right and too stubborn to give up when the odds were against him.

"We never imagined this, did we?" Carlo said. "Back in Viggiù?"

"No, we didn't," replied Vittorio, sadness in his voice.

They walked back to the Labor Hall in silence and parted there. Carlo waited for the boys, still on the line, to circle around again.

How strange that right now he felt closer to his brother than he had in years. It was the power of memory talking, though, the shared grief over what they'd left behind. He felt a sudden desire to see his mother again, possibly for the last time. He and Gabriele should go when the strike was over. Better yet, all three brothers. Would such a reunion ever be possible? He could picture their mother's joyful face when they showed up at her door, all of them together again in the place they would always call home.

"Papà!" Paolo jogged his picket sign. "Over here!"

Carlo caught up with them. "Where's Angelo? He's got my sign."

"I've got it," Nico said. "He went to see what's happening at City Hall. A bunch of the men broke off over there to make a ruckus."

"Hang on to it for me," Carlo said. "I'd better go see what's what."

Angelo swung up onto the base of a lamppost to get a better view of the mob outside City Hall. Twenty or thirty men, mad as hell, shouting and stabbing the air with their picket signs, swarmed the entrance where two policemen stood guard. If he had to place a bet on how this mess was going to turn out, he'd favor the strikers.

"Dirty wops, get out of the way!" A woman pushing a baby carriage shook her fist. "Am I supposed to walk my baby in the street?"

"We ain't all wops!" one of the men yelled. "And we got a right to be here!"

"No you don't," a police officer said. "Not if you're blocking the right of way. Come on, fellows, move along." He made a sweeping gesture. When no one budged, he raised his voice. "You don't want to make me mad, trust me. I'd as soon arrest the lot of you as look at you."

"Arrest us, then!" shouted a young man wearing eyeglasses.

"Shut up!" said a gray-haired fellow standing next to him. "Spending the night in the hopper won't help us."

"Arrest the scabs, then," yelled the fellow with the eyeglasses. "They're the ones breaking the law. We're union workers, we got rights!"

"Yeah, and disturbing the peace ain't one of 'em." The officer jerked his head and another policeman stepped forward, club at the ready. "Move back, move back, you heard me! You want to strike, that's your business, but you've got no right to congregate here."

"We want to see the mayor!" the grayhair shouted. The crowd roared.

"And I want to fly to the moon," the officer said. "Get out of here!"

Shoving through the crowd, Carlo spotted Angelo and swung up onto the lamppost next to him. One elbow hooked around the post, he cupped his mouth and yelled. "Let's go, men, back to the line! Move along, let's go! We've got no business with the mayor. Listen to me! Everybody back to the line! I don't want any trouble here."

The mob rumbled with shouts and protests, stalled momentarily, then surged toward the doors, a river running high. Carlo kept yelling until other men took up the call. "Let's go, let's go! Move out, move along!" After a few tense moments that Angelo feared would lead to a free-for-all, the men closest to the doors eased back and those behind them followed suit, and on and on in a ripple effect until the surge subsided. The mob dispersed, trickling back to the line circling north on Main.

"There we go," Carlo said to Angelo, jumping off their perch. "Disaster averted."

For once Angelo wasn't sure he agreed with Carlo. If they did storm City Hall, the mayor would have to listen, wouldn't he? Barre was his city, so whatever happened there was his business, including the strike. He had power, and he listened to people with power and money. To businessmen.

Chasing after Carlo, Angelo considered what he was about to say if he had the balls to do it, then spoke before he could change his mind. "What about Vittorio? Couldn't he talk to the mayor and ask him to bring everyone to the table?"

"Why would he do that?"

"Well, because he's your brother. I thought—"

"It's no secret that we're on opposite sides of the fence here. You must know that."

"But he can't want you to die!"

Angelo prayed he hadn't crossed a line. Here they were, the two of them walking together and talking like equals, sort of, and now he'd probably ruined it. What went on between Carlo and Vittorio was none of his business.

"He doesn't," Carlo said, unperturbed. "We used to think alike when we were young, him and Gabriele and me. Back home you couldn't have told us apart, politically speaking. But that's changed now. We're proud men—not Gabriele, he's a goddamn saint, but Vittorio and I, we're proud. And stubborn. And pride is a brutal thing. It changes a man." He shook his head, his voice bitter. "You have no idea how much. I guess you wouldn't know this, but Vittorio wanted Gabriele and me to buy into the Milano with him, and he's never forgiven us for turning him down. That's when our troubles started. And now Gabriele and I are here and Vittorio is over there." He gestured toward the mansions on the hills. "It breaks my heart."

"I'm sorry." It was all Angelo could think to say.

"Me too, son."

Son. The word settled in Angelo's chest like a warm ember. It seemed like Carlo wasn't only being nice, talking to him like this, man to man. He was confiding in him, maybe even liked him.

"Anyway, for what it's worth, I'm on your side," Angelo said. "I'll be a union man someday, I promise. Nico's teaching me to carve. I like it." Though cutting was harder than it looked, like Nico had said, and Angelo had destroyed a fair amount of granite so far. Castoffs only, though, nothing Lombardi would miss. He'd get good at it eventually. One step at a time.

"Nico told me. But, look at this mess, son." Carlo swept an arm toward the horizon, putting the picketers on display. "Be careful what you wish for."

TWELVE

THE NEXT DAY, Rosina put on a white blouse and black skirt as Donata had requested, then tamed her hair into the most severe pompadour she could manage. The young woman she saw in the mirror appeared serious and capable, like someone a woman with child could listen to with confidence. She hoped so, because on the inside she was a vibrating bundle of nerves.

At Halliday's Pharmacy, she stopped just inside the door; Donata and the proprietor were deep in conversation. "No, I don't approve of violence," Donata was saying, "but I believe Miss Goldman made some valid points about women's rights, especially about the need for birth control." Rosina couldn't believe her ears. She'd never heard women discuss such a thing, much less with a man!

"Don't be shocked, Mr. Halliday," Donata continued, "it's something that must be talked about. If you saw what I do on a regular basis, what women go through when they have nine or ten babies in as many years, you might agree with me."

"My dear Mrs. Giudici, I'm the father of eight, and my wife is no worse for wear."

"I wonder if she would say the same," Donata said sweetly. She gestured to Rosina to step forward. "Do you know my niece, Rosina Bottinelli?"

"A pleasure!" Mr. Halliday beamed. "You're a lucky young lady, if I dare say so. Your aunt is the best midwife in town."

"You're very kind," Donata said. "However, you're wrong about Miss Goldman." As the shopkeeper opened his mouth to protest, she smiled and handed him a shopping list. "Why don't we continue our discussion the next time I'm here? Rosina and I must be on our way."

"Fair enough." Mr. Halliday began to collect the items on Donata's list. "I must say, I do enjoy a good argument with you."

Donata laughed. "As do I."

Rosina laughed too, surprised to see the two of them sparring cheerfully like youngsters. And how astonishing to learn that Zia Donata agreed with an anarchist's radical ideas! She had never heard her aunt say anything the least bit radical, which meant she must have kept her opinions to herself around the family. Which meant, as a child, Rosina hadn't known her at all. Who else didn't she know?

With her purchases stowed in her large black valise, Donata led the way to the Ambrosini home, relating the woman's birth history as they walked. They hadn't gone far when a running boy intercepted them.

"Signora Giudici, come quick! My mamma's pains have started and she needs you. Come now!"

"It's time, is it? Well then, off we go. Mrs. Ambrosini will have to wait. Young man, I'd like you to go to Washington Street, number 10, and ask the housekeeper for my birthing stool. *Vai, vai*, and be quick about it."

The boy took off, and Donata led the way uptown. They turned onto Third Street, commonly known as Strada delle Vedove, the street of widows, and Rosina crossed herself. A street reminiscent of death wasn't the best place for her first lying-in. She prepared herself for blood, panic, screams of pain, a warlike atmosphere. Yet inside all was calm. The small bedroom smelled of dried yarrow and sweat, the lone window was shuttered, and the walls glowed yellow in the lamplight. On the bed, a woman smiled weakly. She greeted them, then moaned, knotting the bedsheet in her fists.

"*Respira*! Breathe, Signora Monti!" Donata said. "*Brava*, there you go. As you see, I have a helper today, my niece, Rosina. She is learning to be a midwife." The woman nodded, eyes closed. Donata unpacked her valise, laying out bottles and cotton and scissors and thread next to the towels and basin already placed on a small table by the bed. She handed an apron to Rosina and slipped another one over her head. "Please fill the basin with hot water. We must wash our hands."

In the kitchen, five men sat around a table playing cards, smoking, and drinking wine as if no woman suffered in the next room. Rosina felt their eyes on her as she crossed to a steaming pot of water on the stove. Feeling terribly out of place and certain the men knew it, she filled the basin and crept back to the bedroom.

The laboring woman was on her side now, her nightgown a wet film across her breasts. She flung the sheet aside, breathing in quick bursts.

"*Bene*, *bene*. That's right, you know how to do it," said Donata. "Breathe, breathe. Good, now rest."

"How long has it been?" Rosina asked.

"A little more than three hours. I've examined her—you'll learn how to do that later—and she's nearly ready. This is her fourth baby, so it may come quickly."

Donata described the anatomical changes that happened during labor and the normal sequence of a birth while Rosina listened, gripping the footboard and watching Mrs. Monti suffer. When a knock at the door announced the arrival of the birthing stool, she scurried to get it, relieved to escape the mother's pain even for a moment.

For two more hours the laboring woman puffed and moaned. Following Donata's instructions, Rosina held her hand, wiped her face, and tried to encourage her during the contractions despite not knowing what to say. Things like *stay calm* and *you're doing very well* seemed inadequate, but to her surprise Mrs. Monti seemed to listen, and twice she stopped moaning when Rosina reminded her to breathe. It felt good to help her.

Finally Donata said it was time to push. "Do you want to use the birthing stool, my dear?" Mrs. Monti nodded, so Rosina helped her out of bed, averting her eyes from the blood pinking the wet sheets and striping the woman's legs. Seconds after she'd settled onto the stool, the next contraction hit.

"Rosina, kneel here, in front of her." Donata scooted back to make room. "I want you to see this. Gravity helps the baby drop."

Rosina knelt, her head inches from the woman's private parts, the birth canal a swollen slash in darkened flesh. She wanted to apologize for the invasion of privacy, though Mrs. Monti didn't seem to notice. Then she bore down and the top of the baby's head bulged into view, dark and slick.

"*Santa Maria, Madre di Dio*," Rosina whispered in awe.

The head disappeared. Mrs. Monti sucked in a huge breath and pushed again, possessed. This was her fourth baby? Rosina couldn't imagine anyone wanting another child after going through this torture even once. What about twins? Was it worse to deliver two babies at once, or better to get it over with? She would have to remember to ask her mother. And to ask her aunt whether women ever knew something was wrong, even before the birth. Because when her little brother Carletto was born, Rosina had been old enough to help, yet her mother had told her to tend to the men. Could she have known Carletto would be born dead? What if this baby was born dead too?

Mrs. Monti leaned against Donata, chest heaving. "How much longer?"

Donata patted her back. "You're almost there. The head was halfway out last time. Once more, *cara*. Rosina, take her hand."

As the next contraction swept in, Mrs. Monti pushed, head down and bellowing, her nails digging into Rosina's palm.

"Push!" Donata said. "There, the head is out! Once more and you can greet your little one. Push!" Mrs. Monti screamed, long and guttural, and the baby slipped into Donata's waiting hands. "Congratulations, you have a beautiful boy!" Donata held up a squalling, white-streaked infant, still tethered by the cord, with blood slicking his dark hair, swollen genitals, ten grasping fingers, and ten sweet little toes.

Mrs. Monti wept softly, her face bright with relief and joy. "*Grazie a Dio, grazie alla Vergine*," she whispered, and Rosina's throat tightened.

"Niece, help her to bed and then tell the father he has a son."

When Rosina opened the door she found the new father pacing in the hall. "It's a boy?" he said, then, "It's a boy!" From the kitchen came cheers of congratulations, whoops and whistles, the clink of glasses.

Donata wrapped the baby loosely and placed him between his mother's legs. "Bring that table closer," she told Rosina, "the one with the scissors and thread. Now pay attention." She looped the thread around the cord and knotted it tightly, told Rosina to cut it, then repeated the sequence a few inches from the baby's belly. "Good, now clean the scissors with the alcohol. The brown bottle." She pointed to a spot between the two knotted-off threads. "Now cut the cord here."

"Me? I don't know how!" Rosina looked pleadingly at Donata, whose expression said no excuses were allowed. "All right, I'll try." She positioned the scissors and squeezed. "It's like iron!"

"Try again."

This time the blades snapped closed. Rosina shuddered. How strange it felt to cut off a piece of someone's body. And how disgusting.

"Well done," Donata said. A few swift movements and the baby was bundled tight, an overgrown sausage. "Now he is ready for his mother. He may not nurse yet, but if he does it will hurry the afterbirth along."

Mrs. Monti reached for the baby, whose lips made little sucking motions. As she guided her nipple into his mouth, his eyes closed in a flutter of white and dark blue, then opened again to search for hers. She cooed and murmured, stroking her baby's head.

"Look how beautiful they are," Rosina said.

"Indeed," said Donata.

They had finished with the afterbirth—a vile, purplish blob that Rosina was distressed to learn must be examined to make sure no pieces remained in the womb—when Mr. Monti cracked open the door. Donata said to come in and he rushed to his wife's side. "He has strong hands!" he said happily as the baby gripped his finger.

"Now then, Rosina," Donata said, "after we clean up in here, why don't you make us some tea? I keep some in my bag. We'll stay for a few hours to make sure there are no problems. The mother could bleed if the womb doesn't tighten properly, and sometimes babies have trouble latching onto the breast, though this little one did fine. There can be other problems, especially infection. I'll explain all that later. One step at a time, yes?" She patted Rosina's arm. "You did well, niece."

By the time they'd tidied the room, Mrs. Monti and the baby were asleep. How ordinary she looked, Rosina thought, how peaceful. In truth, she'd been powerful in her labor, an unstoppable force. People always said childbirth was a miracle as if it simply happened, but that wasn't true. Women made it happen. They were the miracle workers. To see a woman become possessed, summoning her body's vast power to bring a life into the world, and then to watch her become this gentle creature falling in love with her child, the most pure, natural love there was—well, it was a marvel, there was no other word for it. *Una meraviglia.*

She went to put the kettle on. She couldn't wait for next time. She couldn't wait to be astonished again.

THIRTEEN

A WEEK INTO HER TRAINING, on one of those days when the sky pales to near white and the air stands still and everyone prays for a breath of breeze, Rosina plodded home feeling like an old, swaybacked nag. Exhaustion was her normal state now. Supposedly she would get used to the odd hours, the long nights that sometimes ran well into the next day, the routine visits that suddenly changed course. So far she hadn't. And the wicked heat didn't help. Nor did missing the trolley and having to walk across town. As one rumbled past, she watched the travelers with envy. Two steps later a harried-looking man brushed past her with an impatient glare, and she retaliated with one of her own. It seemed all of Barre was irritable today.

The day had been a long one. After running errands in the morning, she'd accompanied Donata on two home visits in the afternoon. The second one, which they'd thought would be brief, had taken hours, most of it spent trying to calm the distraught young mother. Stick-thin and malnourished, she cried when Donata said a wet nurse was needed. That the mother thought herself a failure was apparent in her slumped body and downcast eyes, and nothing Donata said convinced her otherwise. How depressing, Rosina thought, that a woman should judge herself by her body's ability to make milk.

Donata had told the young mother that she would bring her some soup later, proof that her aunt was more generous and kindhearted than Rosina was. Because all she could think about was pulling off her shoes and stockings and gulping down a glass of lemonade. Lemonade that she would, if she were as generous as her aunt, bring to the strikers swarming the sidewalks on Main Street. They walked for hours in this blazing sun while here she was, moaning about one trip from downtown to the North End. She should learn to be less selfish, more like her aunt. Had becoming a midwife made Zia Donata the generous person she was, or had she always been that way?

Rosina was crossing Granite Street when Angelo peeled off from the picket line and caught up to her. "Listen, there's a meeting tonight, a big one. Can you go?"

"I thought there weren't any meetings now. What about the picket line?"

"Some of the men will stay out there. You've got to come. Remember that Debs fellow who didn't get to make his speech on Primo Maggio? He's in Montpelier and sent a telegram saying he'd talk to us tonight if the Local kept it quiet. He doesn't want any more trouble. It's now or maybe never, because no one knows when he'll be back."

"I'll go if my aunt doesn't call."

"Your aunt? Why?"

"She's training me to be a midwife. I lost my job at the store."

"Oh, I didn't know. Well, you'll be good at it, no doubt about that. See you at your place, quarter to nine."

Rosina was almost home, pondering why Angelo would think she'd make a good midwife, when a big, bullheaded man rounded the corner and blocked her path. He eyed her from head to toe, his leer worse than Luigi Zucchelli's, and her skin crawled as she took in his pockmarked face, his mutilated ears like fists. She shuddered as if he'd touched her, then darted away, praying he wouldn't follow her.

"*Ehi*, you're Carlo Bottinelli's girl, aren't you? What's your hurry?"

She scurried on, holding her breath until he was out of sight, and minutes later she was home, the doorknob slipping in her sweaty hand. In the stairwell, the smell of simmering tomatoes and basil laced the air, familiar and calming. She shuddered again, remembering the man's greedy gaze, as if she were his to pluck off the street. And he knew who she was! She paused, gripping the handrail to steady herself. No, surely she was making an elephant out of a fly. Probably he worked with her father and was a perfectly decent sort. The strike was to blame. It made the whole town jumpy, what with the constant fighting at the picket line and everyone worrying about what might come next. It was exhausting and frightening, all the violence. Even childbirth was violent, she thought as she trudged up the stairs, though at least it brought life more often than death.

Clementina was in the kitchen, elbow-deep in dishwater. "*Com'è andata oggi*?" she asked.

"English, Mamma. You need to try, at least."

Clementina shrugged and Rosina dropped the subject, too tired to insist. "Everything's fine, Mamma. *Tutto bene*." For a moment she considered asking if her mother knew that awful man, in the hope of hearing that he was a good one. But her instincts told her he was dangerous, and too stupid to hide his brutality. Well, she'd seen it and she wouldn't forget it. God willing he wouldn't cross her path again, nor that of anyone she loved.

Evening arrived without a call from Donata, and at nine o'clock Rosina and Angelo stood pressed against the wall under the Labor Hall windows, where only a faint light shone. All the windows were closed and the curtains drawn, making it impossible to decipher what the men were saying.

"Of all the rotten luck," whispered Angelo. "I guess they're trying to make it seem like no one's there."

Without warning, the window above their heads flew open and they ducked, eyes locked together.

"Shut that damn thing!" someone yelled.

"It's an oven in here, we need air," said the man at the window. He stuck his head out. "All's clear."

"For now," someone grumbled.

"Leave it open," Carlo said. "No one who isn't already here is coming tonight. If word gets out somehow—and I don't see how, unless one of you goes running to the papers in the next five minutes—by the time anyone gets here Mr. Debs will be done talking. So let's let him talk. Mr. Debs, the floor is yours."

"*Madonna mia*, that man gave me a heart attack," Rosina whispered.

"Me too. Shhh!"

After a few words of thanks and introduction, Debs explained that he wanted to talk about the IWW, a new national union he was forming with Bill Haywood, a fellow socialist and labor leader. After clearing his throat, he said he would read from a speech he would give in New York City, and he hoped the men wouldn't mind. Then he began.

"In the evolution of capitalism, society has been divided mainly into two economic classes—a relatively small class of capitalists who own tools in the form of great machines they did not make and cannot use, and a great body of millions of workers who did make these tools and who do use them, and whose very lives depend upon them, yet who do not own them. And these millions of wage-workers are forced into the labor market, in competition with each other."

Going on in that vein, he explained that although workers produce in abundance, they can consume only as much as their wages can buy. And when they produce more than is needed, their employers close down. "And the workers find themselves idle and helpless in the shadow of the very abundance their labor has created."

A wave of applause, followed by a cry of "Capitalist pigs!"

"The capitalists own the tools they do not use," Debs continued, "and the workers use the tools they do not own. The capitalists appropriate to themselves what the working class produce, and this accounts for the fact that a few capitalists become fabulously rich while the toiling millions remain in poverty, ignorance, and dependence." He paused as a few men coughed.

"Andrew Carnegie is a type of the capitalist class. His mills are thronged with thousands of wage-workers who endure all the privations and make all the sacrifices of health and limb and life, producing thousands upon thousands of tons of steel, yet not having an interest, even the slightest, in the product. Carnegie appropriates the product, and the workers receive a wage that serves to keep them in producing order. And the more industrious they are, and the more they produce, the worse off they are. For when they have produced more than Carnegie can get rid of in the markets, the tool houses are shut down and the workers are locked out in the cold."

Debs glanced up and nodded for emphasis. "Now, what is true of steel production is true of every other department of industrial activity. You are inseparable from your labor power. This fundamental fact in modern industry you must recognize, and you must organize upon the basis of this fact. You must appeal to your class to join the union that is the true expression of your economic interests, and this union must be large enough to embrace you all, and such is the Industrial Workers of the World."

Applause, whistles, cheers. Debs went on to explain that capitalists and labor leaders, all of them wealthy or salaried, opposed the idea of a national union because they were looking out for themselves. After expanding on that thought, he quoted Karl Marx—whose portrait, by the way, he was glad to see prominently displayed in the Hall: "Workingmen of all countries unite. You have nothing to lose but your chains, you have a world to gain. You workers are the only class essential to society. You produce the wealth, you support government, you create and conserve civilization. You ought to be, can be, and will be the masters of the earth."

Thunderous cheering and clapping, so loud that Rosina covered her ears. "Masters of the earth," Angelo said. "I like the sound of that."

Carlo asked for quiet so Debs could finish.

"Never mind what others may say, or think, or do," Debs said, his voice rising with each sentence. "Stand erect in the majesty of your own manhood. Listen for just once to the throbbing of your own heart, and you will hear that it is beating quick-step marches to Camp Freedom. Stand erect! Lift your bowed form from the earth! The dust has long enough borne the impress of your knees. Stand up and see how long a shadow you cast in the sunlight!"

There was a rumbling of chairs and boots as the men stood, so that the room fairly shook with the noise.

"He's so passionate!" Rosina whispered. "How could anyone not believe every word he says? I couldn't have stopped listening if I'd wanted to."

"Me neither." Angelo smacked a fist into his palm. "The IWW will be our future, it has to be."

The ruckus inside died down, replaced by eager voices as the men shouted questions.

Rosina knew they should leave, but she felt rooted, still absorbing what she'd heard. *See how long a shadow you can cast*, Debs had said. Poetic words, powerful words, beautiful in their message and in their delivery. She laughed, her hand over her mouth. *Delivery*. What a perfect word! Debs's words were meant for the men inside, but he'd said them to her too. She too could cast a shadow, by bringing babies into the world, babies who might grow up to be artists, or scientists, or innovators who would bring about change of all kinds. Or simply loving sons or daughters. Even that would be enough.

She couldn't stop smiling.

"What is it?" Angelo whispered.

"I'm happy. He gives me hope."

"Me too."

A breeze kicked up and swept away the clouds. Angelo stared into Rosina's eyes, sparkling in the moonlight. He couldn't see the color, but he knew it well enough, a soft hazel that grew lighter or more intense depending on her mood. A color he could drown in. He thought again of their first time here, her lips against his hand. He'd barely slept that night.

What was she doing with Giorgio, that pathetic slug?

He should kiss her. Carlo always said that if doing what you wanted took guts and all you did was twiddle your thumbs, you were not only a coward but an idiot. Because if you sat around waiting for your luck to change, you'd find yourself with plenty of nothing.

He took her hand and waited, trying to read her face. Not a yes, not a no, as far as he could tell. She was watching him, maybe trying to decide if he planned to kiss her and whether she wanted him to. So before he could talk himself out of it, he did. She didn't kiss him back, but she didn't move or yell either, which he figured was as good as permission to do it again. This time he cupped her face, took his time. Afterward her gaze shifted, distant now, like she was reading and considering every thought in her head. Let them be good thoughts. Let her say *kiss me again*.

"Angelo . . . I can't."

"Then don't." He ran a finger along her cheekbone, and her lips parted. He kissed her again, a long kiss, the kind that leaves you confused about what's up and what's down.

When they finished, she smoothed her dress as if the gesture would undo what they'd done. "I should go," she said without conviction.

"You can't, the men are leaving now."

She couldn't think of anything else to say. She could feel every nerve, and something else too. A sense of rightness. They fit, somehow, the two of them. And that would not do. She hugged herself, trying to stem the urge to return to his arms, to deny that his kiss, though more gentle, made Marcello's seem chaste. She'd gotten it all wrong. Marcello, a shallow and fickle and proud man she could never care for, was safe. Angelo was the dangerous one. He would consume her if she let him, and then she would end up trapped in a kitchen with four children underfoot and an infant on her hip, as miserable as she'd feared.

"They'll be gone soon," Angelo said.

"Who?"

"The men."

"Oh. Yes, of course." Then, "Why did you say I'll be a good midwife?" Please, please, please, let his answer prove there'd been no meaning behind the remark, that he'd simply been making polite conversation.

"Because you will. I know it. Here." He tapped his chest, over his heart.

She stared at him, dismayed. Voices rose in the night air as the men left the Hall and filed past them, not six feet away. Minutes later the street fell silent.

"Let's get you home," Angelo said.

Yes, home now, quickly, quickly, before she made a terrible mistake. She must stay the course. If Marcello chose Isabella, then Giorgio would do fine. She could manage him, endure the boredom knowing that he bought her time. Either one, Marcello or Giorgio, was a means to an end. Angelo was not.

Side by side but not touching, they took Granite to Main, Main to Berlin, Berlin to Scampini Square, their paces matched, the silence between them intensifying the jangling of her nerves. He would expect more, surely. Let him think she would marry Giorgio, it was better that way.

They had reached her house. "Angelo, I have to say something."

"It's all right, I won't bother you."

"It's only that Giorgio . . ." She could hardly say his name.

"I know. Some guys have all the luck." Angelo lifted a tendril of her hair, tucked it behind her ear. "Sleep well."

She stared at him in surprise, half relieved, half disappointed that he didn't intend to fight for her. Seconds later he was rounding the corner without waiting to make sure she was safely inside, without looking back as she'd expected. She touched her lips, reliving his kiss. He wasn't what she'd expected at all.

FOURTEEN

IN THE FOURTH WEEK OF THE STRIKE, Carlo woke in the heavy hours of early morning to a sound ragged and raw. At first he thought it was a woman crying, then registered the sound for what it was: a bone-racking cough. It came from below him, filtering through the floorboards. Slowly his sleepy brain connected the dots. Below him was the room Gabriele rented from the Greco family. First alarm, then fear, a pain in his heart. It couldn't be his brother making that terrifying sound. Couldn't be. Yet he'd heard it too often over the last few months, a worrisome cough that Gabriele had brushed off. It was nothing, he'd said.

How long had he known?

Carlo rose and dressed, closed the door softly so as not to wake Clementina.

Downstairs, he rapped on the Grecos' door. The husband answered, knew right away why Carlo was there. "It wasn't bad at first," he said. "Now, I don't know."

"We'll move him to our flat," Carlo said. Greco nodded and retreated. At such a time, if a man lived near his family, only family would do.

Carlo eased open his brother's door. "Gabriele?" He was sitting on the bed propped on one hand, a handkerchief clutched in the other. He seemed dazed.

"*Da quanto tempo*?"

"Three months, four, I don't know. It crept up on me. Coughed a lot at work like we all do." Exhaustion in his voice. "It's worse at night."

"Is there blood?"

"Sometimes."

"*Cristo santo*. Why didn't you say something?" But he knew why.

Carlo sat next to his brother and together they stared at the wall. It was like being in a void, suspended in a place that wasn't real or recognizable, where time was meaningless. As the minutes passed, he couldn't have said whether the darkness was a deepening dusk or an approaching dawn. His thoughts arrived as if underwater.

"Have you seen a doctor?"

Gabriele shrugged. "No point."

Carlo could think of no argument to that. No one survived *mal d'america*.

"Don't tell anyone," Gabriele said. "I'm not ready."

Carlo nodded. "I know." He put an arm around his brother's shoulders, and together they wept.

Vittorio was at breakfast with the family when the doorbell chimed, insistent as a mosquito. "Who would come at this hour?" Marietta said. "Were you expecting someone?"

"No, whoever it is can come back later."

"Excuse me, Mr. Bottinelli." The housekeeper hovered in the doorway. "Your brother Carlo is here, I told him to wait in the parlor. He says it's urgent."

"Urgent?" Vittorio's thoughts went to strike violence. "Excuse me, dear."

"Should we come too?" Cosimo asked.

"No, I'll handle it. I'll see you boys at the Milano."

In the parlor, Carlo was pacing, hat in hand, sleeves rolled and sweat at his armpits. "You're here, thank God. I have terrible news."

"What is it? Sit down, you look like hell."

"Gabriele is sick." He felt sick too, saying the words.

"*Mio Dio*." Vittorio sank into an armchair. *Mal d'america*? It was unthinkable. "Has he been to a doctor?"

"No. He says there's no reason to go."

"That's ridiculous, he must be treated. I'll pay for it." Vittorio drummed his fingers, thinking. Then, "How long?"

Carlo shrugged. "A couple of months."

"All the more reason to see a doctor, then. It's early yet. He could be . . . helped." He'd started to say *cured*, but that was a cruel thought.

"Are you joking? There's blood."

"A treatment, then, a medicine, something to buy him more time. Surely they can do that."

"Since when? Name one person with *mal d'america* who's gotten more time."

"*Cazzo*!" Vittorio pushed to his feet and paced, rubbing his temples. How could this be happening to his brother? To them?

"If we had that vacuum equipment—"

"Don't start," Vittorio snapped. "You have no idea what I've tried to do. I'll have you know I pushed Lombardi about that and he wouldn't budge."

"You did?"

"Is that so surprising? I'm not heartless." Vittorio dug a cigarette case out of his dressing-gown pocket, held it out to Carlo. "Nearly ruined the partnership in the process, I might add."

Carlo ignored the cigarette. "You put your money behind Lombardi. Why him? I'd like to know."

"You know any other shed owners who are taking on a partner right now?"

"You've never forgiven us for the Milano deal, admit it."

"Don't you think I'd rather be in business with my brothers than with Lombardi? I can barely stomach the *coglione*. But I know a good opportunity when I see it. Tell me investing in a profitable business isn't a smart move." Vittorio threw up his hands, exasperated. "What am I saying? You wouldn't know a good opportunity if it bit you in the balls."

"Men judge you by the company you keep. Remember that."

"Did it occur to you that I might have chosen Lombardi because I thought I could do some good for my brothers?"

"Did you?"

Vittorio flushed. If only he had. But he still could. The fact that he hadn't swayed Lombardi didn't mean there wouldn't be other chances to try. And there would be other improvements he could fight for. He had money, and Lombardi needed it. All Vittorio needed was time. Time, along with his money, would give him power.

"No, I didn't think so," Carlo said in disgust.

"Where's the proof? No one knows for sure that the dust causes *mal d'america*."

"Will Gabriele's death be enough proof for you?"

"*Vaffanculo*!" Vittorio's blood surged and the room tilted. He steadied himself on a chair back, shaky and sweating under Carlo's icy gaze. "I'll speak to Dr. Bigonzetti. It could be pneumonia."

"He's a quack. Doc Carson sees this disease for what it is. Gabriele should go to him, for whatever good it will do."

"With rest and clean air, he might have more time," Vittorio said "There must be some hope."

"Then you admit the sheds are unsafe!"

"I admit no such thing. You're twisting my words. Look at Maurizio Ricci, twenty-five years in the sheds and healthy as a fish. And he's not the only one. All I meant to say was if Gabriele's lungs are weak, for whatever reason, breathing dust wasn't helping him."

"Fair enough. But you know he'll go back when the strike ends."

"Then he'd better get to work on a headstone," Vittorio snapped, and Carlo stared at him, speechless. "I'm sorry." Vittorio put a hand to his forehead. "I didn't mean . . . that was cruel."

"I have to get to the Labor Hall," Carlo said coldly, putting on his hat. "Do me one favor, I beg you. Keep this between us. Gabriele asked for my silence, but I thought you should know."

"Agreed. Thank you for telling me."

"Family is family, as much as you seem to hate being reminded of that."

"I didn't mean it, what I said about the headstone."

"No? But you said it." Carlo strode to the door. "Think about that, brother."

Vittorio fell into his chair, his body like lead, his mind stuttering with shock. Gabriele was only forty-two. He'd seemed healthy enough the last time Vittorio saw him. But that's what *mal d'america* did, it sneaked up on you. One day you were fine, or thought you were, and the next you had a cough. And before long you were hacking up your damn bloody lungs.

He lit another cigarette, cursing the tremor in his hands. Gabriele deserved better. Of course, people said that about any man who got *mal d'america*, but it was especially true for him. A gentle soul he was, nothing like his elder brothers. Even as a boy he was patient, an observer. He'd seen things, drawn things that Vittorio and Carlo had never bothered with, like a twisted persimmon tree near the cemetery or the skeletal cats that stalked their courtyard. He saw beauty in everything—rain-rippled window glass, broken roof tiles. Everything Gabriele drew or carved had life in it, a vitality Vittorio couldn't have achieved no matter how hard he tried. What cruel irony.

The door opened and he jerked upright. It was Marietta, asking what Carlo had wanted, if everything was all right.

"It's nothing, my dear." Vittorio cleared his throat, his voice rough. "It's only . . . more complaints from the union men. They're not happy that we'll break ground on the new shed during the strike."

"Thank goodness. I was afraid someone was ill."

She retreated, and it was all he could do not to chase after her, cry that she was right, the worst had happened. He needed her soothing voice, her reassurance. He groaned, head in his hands. He'd forgotten what despair felt like.

The next morning at ten, Vittorio parked the Oldsmobile in Scampini Square, his head foggy from too much brandy and too little sleep. He was in no mood for arguments. Gabriele needed to see a doctor and that was that. Dr. Carson had agreed to see him, though when Vittorio demanded to know what could be done, the doctor had demurred. "I'll tell you after I see him," he'd said. "However, as you know, there is no cure for *mal d'america*."

Even here the dust swirled, softening the Oldsmobile's shine. Trudging toward his brothers' building, Vittorio tried not to think of what the dust was doing to Gabriele's lungs. And Carlo's too, for that matter. And his nephews'.

Gabriele was sitting on the porch steps. He was thinner than Vittorio expected, drawn and pale, the skin under his eyes fragile. He wanted to embrace him, but they hadn't done that in years. Instead, he clasped his brother's shoulders, bent to kiss him. "Gabriele, *mio caro fratello*."

"Carlo told you, didn't he?"

"He did. I am distressed beyond words." Vittorio sat next to him. "I know you and Carlo think it's pointless, but I insist that you see a doctor. Dr. Carson is expecting you."

"So much for my privacy."

"I'm sorry." He touched Gabriele's arm, wishing the warmth of his flesh would disprove what they both knew was true. "Please, you must go. I will pay for it."

"I don't need your money, and I don't want it."

"It's too soon to give up! We must do everything we can. It could be something treatable. Bronchitis, pneumonia." Vittorio prayed for hope but found none.

"What gives you the right to tell me what to do? It takes illness to make you remember your family, does it? When was the last time you took supper or shared a glass of wine with us?" Gabriele wheezed, out of breath. "I don't want your charity, and I don't need a doctor to tell me I'm dying."

Vittorio stared at his clasped hands. The words cut, but they were true and honest.

"Thank you for the offer," Gabriele said, his voice softer. "I won't accept it. Money and doctors aren't penances that will ease your conscience, Vittorio. My work is my pleasure. It's all I have. Don't think for a minute I'll let you take that away from me." He went inside, leaving Vittorio squinting in the sunlight.

Vittorio wiped his forehead, his hand shaking, his heart bucking in his chest. If only he could lie down right here and sleep for days, wake up to the news that his brother would be fine, his illness transient. It had been years since he'd felt so helpless, so weak and inconsequential. He groaned. No, not inconsequential, anything but. Gabriele was in Barre because of him. Dying because of him. He doubled over, hands on his head, panic spiraling. They never should have left Italy. His own ambition was to blame, his lust for money and power, otherwise they would still be in Viggiù and Gabriele would be healthy, his lungs clear, and—

No. Vittorio forced himself up, straightened his waistcoat. It had been Gabriele's choice to come to America, as it had been his own, and Carlo's. And it had been Gabriele's choice to stay in the sheds when Vittorio had given him a way out. He could not, would not, blame himself.

Word was out by evening. The shed workers would have known soon enough anyway; when a man coughed as often as Gabriele did, with that familiar sound of guts ripping, they knew. Carlo told the family that night at dinner. Gabriele stayed downstairs to avoid the women's tears.

Three words told the whole story: "Gabriele *sta male*."

"Carlo, no," Clementina said, her face ashen. Nico sagged, his head in his hands, and Paolo swore and kicked his chair back, shoulders hunched and fists knotted.

"*Mal d'america*? No, it can't be true, Papà!" Rosina cried, though a cold knot of pain told her it was. She hunched over, weeping, until a movement made her look up. Her parents were embracing with a kind of fierce intimacy Rosina had never seen, her mother stroking her father's hair, whispering private words in his ear. Comfort, reassurance, love? She had never thought about her parents' marriage, whether it was good or bad. It was simply there, fixed, unworthy of contemplation. But that wasn't true, because what she saw here and now was proof of love, of a bond tenacious enough to survive raising three children to adulthood and losing one at birth, leaving their families to make a home in a foreign country, struggling to fit in yet remember where they came from. Her parents were in love, still. A realization that made the news about Zio Gabriele worse. Because as close as her father was to his wife, he was closer to his brother. They were blood. A loss this devastating would be like telling Nico or Paolo he would never see his twin again, an unimaginable divide.

Clementina kissed her husband, then took five small glasses and a bottle of grappa out of the cupboard.

"Gabriele will live with us," Carlo said, filling the glasses. "We must make him as comfortable as possible."

"He needs privacy," Clementina said. "He can't sleep in the parlor."

"He can have our room," Nico said. "We'll move downstairs. The Grecos won't mind." Paolo nodded in agreement.

"Papà, how long—" Rosina couldn't finish the question.

Carlo leaned heavily into his elbows, fingers digging at his temples. "God knows," he said. "No one knows."

For the next few days Rosina cried with everyone she spoke to, including Gabriele. It broke her heart to hear him cough through his tears, a horrifying sound like someone drowning. She considered it a blessing that the news had spread quickly because it meant she didn't have to explain her sadness. It would have been impossible to hide it and difficult to answer the same innumerable questions. Though she still had to endure everyone's well wishes and good thoughts, some mercifully brief but too many of them long, painful exchanges with people she barely knew. She saw Angelo one day, on the picket line. He saw her too and stopped to let the stream of men part around him. She thought he would come to her, but instead he put both hands over his heart and bowed his head. Rosina returned the gesture, grateful that he'd expressed his sorrow without asking anything of her.

Eventually, because no one can go on like that forever, she and her parents and brothers tucked away their anger and pain and went about their lives, weighted down yet with no choice but to remain upright. Rosina was glad, on those days when the telephone rang, to have the distraction of tending to women in labor, the pleasure of welcoming new life. If she had still been working at the store she would have cried all day.

Gabriele moved in upstairs and the twins settled in with the Grecos. For the first few weeks Gabriele kept to himself, walking the picket line for as long as his lungs would permit, then retreating to his room. Rosina would knock to ask if he wanted company, and he always refused, which distressed her no end.

"We should be with him," Rosina said to her mother one afternoon. "We don't know how much time he has left."

"It's good that you ask him." Clementina kissed the top of Rosina's head. "Keep trying. He'll say yes when he's ready. He needs to grieve in his own way. He knows the day will come when he can't care for himself, and that's a burden for a man like him."

"I wish he would go to the doctor."

"So would I, if a doctor could help him. Show him you love him, *non c'è nient'altro da fare*."

There's nothing else to do. Infuriating words, helpless words. Her dear uncle was going to die and no one could help him. How could life be so cruel?

The days passed, fleeting one minute, dragging the next. When there was no woman in labor to distract her, Rosina tried to find comfort in drawing, but her pencils stalled on the page and her charcoals crumbled in her fingers. The strike had prevented her from buying those watercolors she wanted, which was just as well. The world was colorless now. If she had managed to draw, she would have chosen the blackest charcoal and left not an inch of white on the page. Not a single ray of light.

FIFTEEN

A WEEK LATER ROSINA RAN INTO MARCELLO on Main Street. After inquiring after Gabriele, he suggested a walk. "It'll cheer you up," he said. "I'm darn good company and a very good distraction."

"For Isabella, not me," she said crossly.

"Not anymore. I'm a free man. Walk with me."

She was surprised, but in truth she didn't care if he wasn't the two-timer she'd thought he was. His reform, if real, gave her no pleasure. She was as reconciled as a person could be to the idea of Gabriele's approaching death, but she still thought about it every day. Courtship was the last thing on her mind, which even Giorgio seemed to understand. Three weeks ago he'd stopped by the house with a bunch of daisies and a note saying he was thinking of her, and she hadn't seen him since.

"*Dai*, Rosina." Marcello waved praying hands at her, back and forth. "Come on. You can't stop living because your uncle is sick. A walk will do you good."

Finally she acquiesced. Marcello went out of his way to be solicitous, insisting they didn't have to talk if she didn't feel like it. She was grateful and said so. They walked in silence, maintaining their distance, then sat on a park bench in the Common. Rosina took off her hat, letting the sun beat down on her face. How many more sunny days would Zio have?

Marcello grabbed her hat and put it on, waggling his eyebrows.

"Don't. I'm not going to laugh," Rosina said.

"Aren't you curious about me and Isabella? I'll tell you, it'll cheer you up. What happened was, I told her three months was too long to be apart and we'd have to see where things stood when she got back. I didn't mention you."

"Good."

"Then she wrote back, and I thought my fingers would fall off, her reply was so cold. She said we didn't need to see where things stood because we were finished. She said if she wasn't worth waiting for, then I wasn't the husband material she thought I was." His tone was disbelieving, as if he were guiltless and Isabella unreasonable. "We weren't engaged," he added.

"I know, but you led her on. And you kissed me. She probably read between the lines." She was being judgmental and she didn't care. So what if he wasn't a full-fledged two-timer? He was still a snake.

"Maybe so. Anyway, now what do you think? You and me?" He leaned in to kiss her and she pushed him away.

"Not now, Marcello."

He sighed dramatically and clutched his chest in mock anguish. "I'm wounded. Deeply. All right, let's meet on Sunday after church. My mother will want to see you again, and then we can go for a walk and I can show you off."

"Fine, but in a week or two, when I'm more myself. I'm sure your mother will understand." More likely she would take Isabella's side and blame Rosina for provoking her son's rejection. "I'll let you know when I'm free."

He frowned. "What do you mean? Zucchelli's is closed on Sundays."

"I have a new job. I'm training to be a midwife. I'm at the mercy of babies, you see. They don't care what day it is or what my plans are. When they're ready to be born, they're ready and that's that."

He was still frowning. "So you might not come? My mother will be offended if I tell her you'll be there and then you're not."

"I'm sure she'll understand. It's my job, we'll have to make the best of it."

"I suppose so," he grumbled. "For now."

There it was: *for now*. Good. He wouldn't want to marry a midwife. After all, how could someone whose work was unpredictable cater to his every whim? She would enjoy his attention and bide her time—hopefully a long, long time—until he figured out she didn't want him, or vice versa. The thought flashed through her mind that she was being cruel, leading him on like he had Isabella. Still, it wasn't cruel if their so-called courtship was merely a dalliance, which it certainly seemed to be.

"I should go. I have to visit a mother and her new baby."

He caught her hand. "Not yet. The carousel is up at Depot Square, what do you say we ride it? One ride, that's all. Come on, it'll be fun."

She was about to say she was too sad for such frivolity, then agreed. If she wanted him to court her, she'd have to meet him halfway. "One ride. But only because I'm going that way."

Ten minutes later Marcello was buying tickets. "Choose your steed, my princess," he said with a sweeping gesture. "Wait! Better yet, a royal carriage." He hopped into a giant swan car and patted the seat. "Come on, get in."

Rosina hesitated, then slid onto the seat next to him. She and Giulia preferred the horses, always racing to see who would get to their favorite one first, a white charger with its front legs tucked up, ready to leap. If Rosina lost the race, she would ride the roaring tiger Zio Gabriele had chosen for her the first time they'd ridden together, years ago. He had climbed on a giant rabbit, sitting sideways with his legs crossed and nibbling a pretend carrot to make her laugh.

Those days were gone forever. Now riding in circles surrounded by shrieking children seemed like a senseless waste of time.

"It's cozy, isn't it," Marcello said, looping his arm around her shoulders.

"Don't," she said, trying to extricate herself. "People still think you're with Isabella. They'll talk."

"Let them," he said cheerfully, and kept his arm firmly planted.

Whether it was the dizzying whirl or the weight of his arm and the press of his thigh, soon enough Rosina forgot about Isabella, even forgot, for a time, that her uncle was sick. For those suspended minutes—one ride, then another—she felt happy with Marcello beside her, his body sending heat waves into her skin.

Afterward, hurrying off to meet Donata, she told herself she would have to talk to Giorgio soon. Once he knew she was seeing someone else he would understand that they had no future. Still, he would be hurt, and she hated that. Angelo would be hurt too. She'd nipped his interest in the bud by claiming she was with Giorgio, so what excuse could she have for taking up with Marcello instead? Still, it didn't matter how Angelo felt. She'd told him she wasn't available, which was true, and which man she'd chosen was none of his business. She'd made her decision, and it was the right one. Angelo wasn't, and couldn't be, part of her plan.

Within minutes of leaving Marcello and arriving late at the Vitale residence, Rosina wished to be back on the carousel. Donata was none too pleased with Rosina's tardiness, which wasn't the worst of it. Mrs. Vitale had given birth two days before and had had a rough time of it, twenty hours of labor and a breech baby that Donata had miraculously turned head down. Both mother and baby were fine now; it was Mr. Vitale who wasn't. He sat in the parlor coughing, a blanket wrapped around his gaunt frame despite the heat, bloody spittle in the basin by his side. Whenever Rosina walked by, he watched her with dark, pouched eyes, and she had to remind herself that he was in his thirties, early forties at the most, not the ancient man he seemed to be. Imagining Zio Gabriele in his place, she struggled to keep her composure.

"It's so sad," she said to Donata after they'd left, "all these men dying. It's not fair. Why is money more important than men's lives?"

"A good question without a good answer," her aunt said.

"And then I think about some of the women we see, the horribly poor ones or the ones whose husbands beat them. They're trapped. They don't even have a chance to take care of themselves. It's all so sad."

"You have a kind heart, niece. Come, let's sit for a few minutes." Donata eased herself onto a low stone wall and stretched her legs discreetly. "*Uffa*, my knees aren't happy with me today. My dear, seeing what goes on behind closed doors is a part of midwifery no one can prepare you for, isn't it? There's a lot of hardship in the world."

Rosina nodded, blinking away tears.

"Many years ago, I was like you, young and emotional. For a long time I was angry about things I couldn't change. Then I decided to forget those things and do what I could instead. Midwives do more than deliver babies, you see. If we choose to. We can educate women, help them understand that they do have some choices in life. Though I admit those choices are limited when there are ten mouths to feed."

"Do you mean birth control? I heard you talking to Mr. Halliday about that. And you mentioned Miss Goldman. I've read about her ideas. I'm surprised that you agree with her."

"I do to some extent, yes. She is quite extreme, isn't she? Many people don't want to hear what she has to say. I think it's because the thought of a changing world frightens them."

"Not me. I want it to change."

"It will, but slowly. Miss Goldman knows that, and she knows she has to keep trying even when her efforts seem in vain. She's passionate, and I believe she won't be stopped. She says women should have control over their bodies, their very existence, that it's their right, and I agree. I know it's shocking to talk about birth control and abortion, but if women aren't educated they'll continue to let the Church think for them. Shouldn't they be able to make their own choices?"

Rosina smiled. "You're as political as my father, Zia. I had no idea."

"True. I'm on the side of common sense. I understand the Church's thinking, theoretically, and I agree with it, theoretically. However, in practice there should be exceptions to the rule. Can a woman be a good mother if her life is nothing but drudgery and deprivation? I say no. She suffers and her children suffer. And in my opinion, it's immoral to force a woman to carry and raise a child after she's been assaulted or when her life is in danger."

Rosina thought of Mrs. Giordano, who'd delivered her ninth baby recently. She was exhausted and old at thirty-seven and there wasn't a part of her that didn't sag. She didn't seem to care that her house was filthy and her children rarely bathed. People said her husband stayed out until all hours drinking and carousing. What must her spirits be like, getting up each morning knowing she'd be worn to the bone by dusk and her husband didn't give a fig?

"We won't see birth control in my lifetime," Donata said, "almost certainly not in yours. But I will say to anyone, man or woman, that I support it. And if they'll listen, I'll explain why."

"It's confusing," Rosina said. "Birth control seems wrong and right at the same time, doesn't it?"

"Agreed. There is one battle I believe can be won in your lifetime, Rosi. The vote. We have a long road ahead of us, but I believe it's worth the journey."

"You truly think it's possible?"

"Some states have it, so I have hope. It will take a lot of work and determination, but there are women willing to do it. I've been a member of the Vermont Woman Suffrage Association for years. You should come with me next time there's a meeting in Montpelier." Donata stood, wincing as her weight settled into her knees. "I'll have to put a mustard plaster on these old joints this evening. We are done for today. Go on now, enjoy your young, healthy knees."

Rosina said she did want to go to a meeting, very much, then set off for home. Walking up Main, she lingered at the storefronts, admiring pretty silk scarves and silver pocket watches, imagining what she'd buy when her family didn't need every cent she earned. Those watercolors, for one thing. And a gift for Zio Gabriele, not that he would want anything. Something small and beautiful and thoughtful that would bring him pleasure. A painted tile, perhaps, like the ones housewives in Viggiù often kept in their kitchens. He could keep it next to his bed, a reminder of home.

Abandoning the shop windows, she strolled north to the Maple Street junction, where the road led uphill to Hope Cemetery. She hadn't been there in ages. She and her mother used to go often to tend the family plot, scraping lichen off the stones and pulling weeds. Hope was a peaceful place, comforting even. She liked to think that the dead knew that their families remembered them with love.

Why not go there now? It would be a fine walk, and surely there was weeding to be done.

The road to Hope rose softly at first, then grew steeper, a long mosaic of dried mud, a crazy pattern of wheel tracks and hoofprints. She was halfway up the hill when the sun disappeared and the sky descended, threatening rain. Every so often the clouds parted, letting in shafts of light like luminous roads to heaven. What a silly, overly romantic idea. She was no longer sure heaven existed.

Finally she reached the cemetery's entrance, devoid of any sign to announce its name or welcome visitors. It made sense in a way, because believers in the certainty of salvation didn't need a sign reminding them to have hope. Rosina wished she were one of them. When she was young she had accepted the teachings of the Church, believed without question. Now, when the kindest, most lovable man was waiting for death, no promises of salvation and eternal peace could comfort her, though she prayed her uncle would have both.

Up ahead, two funeral horses stamped and shifted, waiting for a dozen black-hatted mourners encircling a new grave to finish their sad task. Averting her eyes, she hurried past them toward a towering sculpture of an angel carrying a young woman to heaven. The entwined figures rose into the sky, heads and eyes lifted. Even though she knew the angel was supposed to be a comforting companion on the dead woman's journey, she'd found the statue frightening at first. Now she saw neither comfort nor fear, no religious meaning—only the stonecutter's skill.

Passing the angel and his prey, Rosina descended the gentle slope to the Bottinelli plot where baby Carletto and Gabriele's wife lay. For the first time, she saw the expanse of grass surrounding the two markers as a reminder that more graves would come. Tall weeds and skeletal remains of flowers edged the stones, and creeping lichen blurred the carvings of lilies and broken branches. She brushed away debris and pulled weeds, her mind settling with the work. Only the chatter and call of birds, the occasional distant voice or soft snort of a horse broke the peace. She was almost done when the grassy swish of approaching footsteps announced a visitor.

"Angelo! Whatever are you doing here?"

"I saw you at the foot of Maple." He flopped onto the grass. "Who's Carletto?"

"My little brother. Born dead, poor little fellow."

"I didn't know. I'm sorry."

"Why didn't you say something when you saw me?"

"It took me this long to decide if you'd want company. Being sad about Gabriele and all."

"That's sweet of you." She gathered the weeds, piled them behind one of the stones. "I hope the birds will find them for their nests. I didn't know I was coming here, so I didn't bring a bucket."

"They will." Angelo plucked a dandelion gone to seed and blew the white fluff into the air. "Death to life."

"In a way." Rosina sat, wrapping her skirt around her legs. "It's peaceful, isn't it?"

"Yeah." He puffed on another dandelion and tossed the stem aside. "I saw you and Marcello at the park. I guess you're seeing him now?"

Rosina ducked her head, embarrassed. "I don't know, he—"

"It's fine, honest. Like I said." Angelo stood, brushed off his trousers. "Listen, I have to get back to the line and I want to stop at my mother's grave first."

"I'll go with you." He offered a hand and she pulled herself up. "I've been meaning to thank you for that. Being on the picket line, I mean. It means a lot to Papà, and I'm sure to Zio Gabriele too."

"It didn't seem like much of a choice."

They walked north to a crabapple tree loaded with blossoms, where a rectangular stone lay flush to the ground. *Antonetta Lucci, Beloved Wife and Mother, 1856–1898.*

"It's a beautiful spot," Rosina said. "I'm glad this tree keeps her company."

"Me too." Angelo's voice caught.

"You must miss her terribly."

"I try not to think about it."

He wanted to tell her the whole story, that it wasn't only her death that pained him, it was having to leave school because of it. That after his mother died, his father took to drink in a deliberate way, lost his blacksmithing job and couldn't stay sober long enough to look for another one. That Angelo had dropped out of school to do whatever work he could find, it didn't matter what, as long as he went home with a few coins in his pocket. That he got good at stealing eggs and raiding gardens, and when his pants got too short and his shirts threadbare, he'd find new ones on someone's clothesline. He couldn't tell her any of that, though. Couldn't admit he'd been nothing more than a common thief.

He kissed his fingertips and touched them to his mother's stone. "A storm's coming. We should go."

The first raindrops hit long before they reached the road, painting the pale granite stones in dark streaks and spatters. Rosina held her skirts higher, the other hand clamped on her hat. The cemetery was growing fast, she thought as they passed dozens of new graves filling its southern reaches, some of them still damp earth. No doubt many of the graves belonged to the lucky dead, old men and women who had lived full lives. Still, too many belonged to the unlucky, the younger men who hadn't.

"Angelo, what if . . ." She let the question die.

"What if what?"

Did he ever wish his family had never come to America, like she did sometimes? Like she wished today?

"Never mind."

How cruel life could be. She said a prayer for her father and brothers, Angelo too, all the men laboring in the dust.

SIXTEEN

VITTORIO AND LOMBARDI BROKE GROUND on the new shed on the fifth of July, an event better attended than the trickle of a Fourth of July parade had been. Barre hadn't been in the mood to celebrate Independence Day, not with the strike infecting everyone with fear and uncertainty. A more exciting spectacle drew the townsfolk to congregate in Burnham Meadow, where hundreds of striking union men ringed the construction site and taunted the workers with obscenities and jeers. Though they could barely be heard over the growl of the steam shovel, that didn't stop them from hurling the most expressive insults they could invent, in any language at their disposal.

The strikers' issue with the new shed was that its construction signified more than continuity and survival, which was, typically, the most employers could aim for during a strike. Scabs were expected.

Attempts to fulfill orders coming in from around the country were expected. Attention to bottom lines was expected. But with this new shed, Lombardi was taking a step forward; even worse, he was taking it without the men who'd worked for him for years. The shed meant expansion, and coming now as it did, it was an insult too far, a nose-thumbing with a very clear message: The strikers didn't matter.

Carlo stood watching, his face grim. The men's picket signs, made for the occasion in English and Italian, were equally clear in their messages: "Fuck off!" and "No Suction, No Shed!" and "Shame on you!" and "My kids are hungry!" Carlo wanted no part in this particular protest, not when family was involved, but he might not have a choice. The strikers were as angry as he'd ever seen, already wound tight at eight in the morning. The curious townspeople stood in packs and clusters, the women watching in worry and fear, the men loudly vocal in defense of one side or the other. If a showdown was going to happen, no one wanted to miss it.

Carlo feared it would. The anarchists saw violence as a means to an end, and they were at the site in numbers. The proof that he had reason to worry was written in big black letters on their picket signs: "COSTRUITELO, LO BRUCEREMO!" You build it, we'll burn it. No doubt they were ready to make good on the threat. He'd tried to reason with them as they'd arrived that morning, even begged them to leave things be. But they wouldn't listen, and now there they were, standing arm in arm, a wall of furious men shouting the words that bobbed above their heads.

Surveying the scene for signs of imminent danger, Carlo saw Vittorio inside the flagged perimeter of the future shed, standing with hands on hips and disgust on his face. In a surprising twist to the day, Daniele and Cosimo were with him. Though they privately supported their father in whatever he did, they rarely took a public stance. Carlo was searching for Lombardi when someone yelled "Now!" and the union men hurled tomatoes and rotten fruit plucked from their pockets. Vittorio and the boys ducked and spun, shouting and swearing as red and brown pulp splattered their clothing. The men watching went wild with jeers and laughter, women gasped, and boys ran shouting about the thrilling turn the day had taken. And all the while the excavator bit into the earth again and again, unstoppable.

Carlo was about to go tell the men to stop the attack—he knew damn well that when the fruit was gone, rocks would come next—when the crowd shifted.

"Move aside, coming through!" Lombardi shouted, marching toward the construction site with two dozen policemen behind him. Once there, the officers ringed the site's flagged perimeter, one man every six feet, stances wide and clubs ready.

"*Cazzo*," Carlo muttered. Some people might find the police presence comforting, but he did not. Barre didn't have two dozen officers, which meant Chief Brown had brought in reinforcements. Which meant he, like Carlo, expected real trouble. "What a fucking mess."

"I was thinking the same thing," said Gabriele, landing at Carlo's side.

"What are you doing here? Go home, for God's sake."

"It'll take more than lung disease"—a wheezing breath—"to keep me away from this circus. Do you have a plan?"

Carlo shook his head. "Spooked horses would be more willing to listen to what I say."

"What's Paolo doing over there?" Gabriele jerked a thumb toward the excavator.

"Where? Damn it, he falls in with the anarchists and I'll wring his neck."

"He does like a fight, that one," Gabriele said. "I'll go have a word with him."

A fit of coughing racked his body and he steadied himself on Carlo's shoulder. Carlo felt the choking cough slice through his brother's muscles and bones. He was useless, goddamn it. Couldn't help his brother, couldn't stop the anarchists. He spat into the dust.

When the fit had passed, he insisted that Gabriele go home. "I'll find Nico. He's the only one who can talk sense into Paolo. And don't come back tonight, you look like hell."

Carlo trudged toward the picketers. All he could do to calm them was to talk to them man to man, appeal to their sense of decency without the pressure of political conformity staring them down. He might as well save his breath, though. They were as bullheaded as he was, every last one of them.

When the lunch whistle blew at the sheds and the excavator shuddered into silence, the onlookers drifted away and most of the strikers returned to the picket line. Carlo assumed Vittorio and his sons had gone home to clean up because Lombardi was alone at the site, leaning against the excavator and exchanging malignant stares with the anarchists, who hadn't budged.

He found Paolo and Nico in the picket line near the Hall, told Nico to keep his brother in check, then skirted the line to find his organizers. "Pray," one of them said when Carlo asked what they thought he should do about the anarchists. "Not much else we can do."

Carlo lit a cigarette, smoked it down to a stub, ground it out with his heel. Pray. Nothing we can do. In other words, in dealing with the anarchists, he was useless, a word that described him every day lately. A useless piece of shit, unable to control what he'd started. The men had listened when he'd urged them to strike. Now some of them, too many, thought he was soft.

He strode back to the site. Lombardi saw him coming, spit tobacco juice in his direction. "This gang here isn't my doing," Carlo said, "and I'm trying to call them off. Anything happens, I don't condone it. You should know that."

He stalked off before Lombardi could reply, walked through the Meadow to the Hall and kept going. The anarchists had better keep a lid on their bullshit for a lousy goddamn hour, because he was sick to death of it. He needed Clementina's soothing voice in his ear, the warmth of her soft body in his arms. He was going home.

Thirty minutes after nightfall an explosion lit up the sky. Carlo was at the Labor Hall, where the floorboards thundered as if the granite core of Millstone Hill had been yanked out whole and catapulted into the Meadow. He ran outside and stood watching, hands to his head, while smoke billowed twenty feet above the construction site and faltering flames licked the damp earth. Men came from all directions, the night shift picketers falling out of line at a dead run. All across town, stonecutters and quarrymen and townspeople bolted from their homes, grabbing knives and pistols, hammers and wrenches, sticks and canes, whatever was at hand. No one knew what they'd find, what need there would be for self-defense.

There was no need. When Carlo reached the site it was empty of men save one, likely dead. Probably the poor wretch who'd lit the fuse and failed to run fast enough.

"Carlo!" Angelo dashed up to him, breath heaving. "What the hell?"

"Go get Doc Carson," Carlo said, then joined the men who'd run past him to huddle around the fallen man. "He's dead?" he asked them. He couldn't see the man's face, if he had one. "Who is it?"

"Giacomo Gatti," one man said, shaking his head. "Poor damned fool."

"A young damned fool." Carlo's body sagged. "I'll tell his mother."

By the time the fire brigade arrived the flames had flickered out. The firemen stomped around the periphery obliterating embers with heavy boots. A few minutes later Chief Brown arrived with his team of policemen armed with lanterns. "Back off now, all of you," he said to the firemen. "I don't want anyone destroying evidence." He signaled to his men to fan out, then turned to Carlo. "You're thinking I should have kept my men here overnight, aren't you? Well, I got a whole city to take care of."

"You think you're going to find evidence in that hellscape? You won't, and you don't need it. You know as well as I do who did it, and they'll say so themselves in tomorrow's papers. The dead man's a known anarchist."

Chief Brown glowered at him. "Goddamn strike. Happy now, Bottinelli?" He stomped off.

On his way to the Gatti house, Carlo ran into Angelo and Doc Carson. "False alarm, he needs a coroner instead. I'm on my way to tell the family."

"I'll go with you," said Angelo.

"This is mine to do, son. Go home."

Outside of City Hall a few of the strikers were milling about, smoking and swearing about the turn things had taken, their picket signs tossed against the wall or flung on the ground. "Go home, all of you," Carlo said. "A few hours with no one walking won't be the end of the world."

"It's the beginning of it now, ain't it?" one man said. "No telling what those fucking anarchists will do next now that they got their first taste of big trouble, but I'll bet you the paycheck I don't have that they'll want more. Me, I'll cross the line if anyone else dies. You heard me, Carlo." Echoing him, the others picked up their signs and left.

Their voices faded and Carlo was alone, his footsteps loud in the empty street. Prospect Street wound uphill from City Hall, a long way, too long, to the Gatti house. God, he was tired. His shirt stuck to him and he stank and he could taste his breath. Not that it mattered. Mrs. Gatti wouldn't notice, and if she did she wouldn't care.

It was his fault, this violence. He knew about the anarchists' penchant for trouble, knew it wouldn't take much to set them on that course. Still, he'd done what he had to do, chosen the lesser of the evils. He had to keep telling himself that. Men would die with or without a strike, and *mal d'america*'s reach was longer. If only his choice hadn't led to this, what he was about to do now—speak words no mother should ever have to hear.

SEVENTEEN

A WEEK AFTER THE EXPLOSION, Rosina was up to her elbows in dishwater when the telephone shrilled at nine p.m., the sound drifting in through an open window. Grabbing a dish towel, she dashed into the stairwell in time to hear Mrs. Calcagni shouting into the receiver. Then she hung up. "Rosina! Rosina Bottinelli! *Sei a casa*?"

"*Eccomi*!" Rosina leaned over the railing. "Was it my aunt?"

"No, it was the Pope. Go to North Seminary, number 28. Tell me everything when you get back."

Rosina changed into her midwife's clothes, relieved to have a reason to get out of the house. She was sick to death of listening to her mother, who had been in a snit about Marcello for days. First she had complained that he wasn't Catholic. She had been snapping green beans, winging them into a metal bowl with unnecessary force.

Then she reminded Rosina that Carlo didn't like the Battaglia family's politics.

Rosina had replied in an equally impatient tone, which only made her mother's snit worse. "Yes, I know, and yes, Papà said that. Cheer up, Mamma, our courtship might not last."

Clementina's eyes had drilled into Rosina's head as if mining her thoughts, a skill she was uncannily good at. "*Ma cosa stai dicendo*? If you mean you're throwing over Giorgio for a man you're not serious about, you're not the sweet daughter I raised."

"I'm not serious about Giorgio either, so what's the difference?"

At that, Clementina had announced that she didn't trust Rosina to let the poor man down gently, so she'd gone to the Marellis' house that same day to break the news to his mother. Rosina was insulted but also relieved, though she dreaded the inevitable day to come when she would run into Giorgio on the street.

At least Giulia was on her side. She always was, ever since high school, even though they were complete opposites. Giulia and her sweetheart, Davide, would marry in December. She was a romantic, dreaming of her wedding day and a large family, talking incessantly about dresses and flowers and cake fillings. Rosina retaliated by wailing about missing the frescoes in Italy and describing in great detail the recent articles she'd read in the *Daily Times*. Though they didn't share each other's interests, they listened anyway and cheered each other on.

"Marcello is *bellissimo*, and much more interesting than Giorgio," Giulia had said. "I do feel sorry for Giorgio, though I suppose he's better off being jilted now than later, seeing as it was going to happen. Poor thing, he was very devoted." Rosina said if she wanted devotion she'd get a dog, and they both laughed.

Her uniform on, Rosina told her mother she was leaving and not to wait up, then rattled down the stairs to freedom and fresh air. Finally, she could breathe. Was every mother as opinionated and pushy as hers? Maybe she should get a dog after all, a puppy to distract her mother from the tiresome topic of men.

When she knocked on the door at number 28, all was quiet. It must be early in the labor, she thought.

Donata opened the door. "Come in," she said quietly, and something in her voice made Rosina hesitate. "Quickly."

The flat was dark, silent. No welcoming lamp burned, no anxious father paced in the parlor, no children scurried underfoot. "What's going on? Oh no, did the mother—?"

"No, no, she lives. You must be strong, my dear. What we must do tonight is difficult."

"It's a stillbirth?"

"If only it were." Donata lowered her voice further. "The mother has drunk pennyroyal tea for two weeks to no effect. She's very young, barely fourteen."

"Pennyroyal . . . oh, I see." Now she understood the quiet, her aunt's somber tone. "And unmarried?"

"Yes. The baby is her brother's. He doesn't know about it and he must not know."

"Her brother!" Rosina's voice rose. "He should be arrested!"

"Quiet, the girl is frightened enough. Our secrecy is to protect her, not him. I've spoken to a couple near Waterbury who have offered the child work and board on their farm. And now we must do our part to keep her safe. If you're willing. Not all midwives will end a pregnancy. If you wish to leave, I understand. But you must know that the girl is desperate, and if I turn her away she will go to someone else, perhaps someone with less knowledge and skill. Or she will try to end the pregnancy herself and most likely die from infection."

"I . . . I don't know what to do."

"We must begin now. We have use of this house tonight, no longer."

"Who lives here?"

"You do not need to know." Donata went into the bedroom, leaving the door ajar.

Rosina moved to follow her, then stopped, started again and stopped again, her body vibrating with rage at the brother, sorrow for the girl and her child. And terrible, terrible doubt. Right and wrong, neither and both. If she thought about abortion as a tragic thing that unknown women did for unknown reasons, it seemed so clearly wrong, a crime and a sin. Yet the girl here in this house was real, and young, and she had suffered horrific harm. What life did she have now? What hope could she possibly have if she was forced to be a mother when she was only a child herself, trapped in the very home where she was in danger, living in fear? How many of her brother's children would she be forced to bear? Could she love a child born of such a union?

Rosina wavered, shifting foot to foot. Her gut told her to stay, but if she did, she would help to take a life. Yet women died giving birth while their babies lived—was it wrong to instead save the mother and sacrifice the child? Could she be that kind of midwife? Or would she send girls like this one away, possibly to their deaths? Two deaths, mother's and baby's both.

But she need never know what happened. It wouldn't be her burden to bear.

No, that wasn't true. She would always wonder whether she'd made the right choice, whether blood was on her hands. Either way, the burden was hers.

Her eyes locked on the open door. In or out?

Fourteen years old, this girl was. She deserved a chance at a decent life. It was their duty to help her. Rosina moved swiftly, closing the bedroom door behind her.

"I'm here, Zia. What can I do?"

They stayed all night to make sure the bleeding stopped and no fever rose. At five in the morning a farm truck pulled up and the girl got in, shaky and weak. Rosina went home with Donata, for some food to fortify her, her aunt said, and a private place to talk or cry. Nothing about what they'd done had been easy, and she didn't expect her niece to walk away untouched.

They settled in the parlor with a pot of coffee and a plate of toast. "Cry if you need to," Donata said. "Let it out here, because when you leave, it's over. You may tell no one, do you understand?"

"Yes." Sitting on the brocade sofa, Rosina felt sad but oddly calm. Would she be willing to do it again? She couldn't say. What they had done would take weeks if not months to sink in, and only then would she know the answer.

"I'm all right. We did the right thing for her, I do believe that. But for her to suffer because of that terrible man, and lose her family—it's wrong. I do hope she'll be better off. How sad that we'll never know."

"You may feel differently tomorrow. It's normal to have doubts, even regrets. But if you do, remember that you gave that young woman a future. Even after all these years, I need to remind myself of that from time to time."

Rosina mounded raspberry jam onto a slice of toast, suddenly ravenous. "I laugh now at how naive I used to be. I thought midwives delivered babies and that was that."

"Some do," said Donata, pouring the coffee. "As I told you, for others it's much more. A calling. It's not for everyone. But it is your calling, of that I have no doubt."

"The fellow I'm seeing doesn't like it. He thinks I'm standing him up if I have to work when we've made plans to go out."

"It does take a certain kind of man to put up with our comings and goings. Do you love him?"

Rosina hesitated. The truth would make her seem either shallow or mature enough to know her own heart. "Honestly, no." Donata didn't flinch, only sipped her coffee, listening. "Can I tell you something in confidence?"

"Of course, always."

"I don't want to marry. Not now and maybe never. Mamma doesn't know, it would break her heart."

"You're right about that."

"I used to think I could be an artist, did you know that? I mean make a living at it. I want to do something important with my life. I can imagine being daring like Emma Goldman, but not being stuck at home taking care of a house and children."

"You're young yet. Marriage can wait if that's what you want, no matter what your mother says. Of course she wants to see you settled, but the choice is yours, dear. And who knows, you might fall in love and change your mind."

"I don't want to."

Donata smiled. "It's not always a choice. Did you know I had a child? A son, Roberto." Her voice thickened. "Don't mind me, I always get teary when I talk about him. My little angel. He died of fever at three months."

"I'm so sorry, Zia, I didn't know. That's terribly sad."

"You wouldn't know, it was before you were born. My dear, I can't counsel you about love. You see, my husband and I had to get married." She spoke without embarrassment. "We grew to love each other, but it took time. He would have preferred me not to be a midwife, but he knew better than to press me about it. I have always known my path, and being married didn't change that. I was fortunate. If I had refused to marry him, or left him afterward, or if he'd left me, I would have been destitute. Who would want an unmarried woman with a child to be her midwife? No one."

The door opened and Marietta stepped inside. "May I intrude? Rosina, dear, I had to say hello. It's been far too long."

As Rosina rose to kiss her aunt, Vittorio walked by the open door, hat on and obviously in a hurry. He seemed thinner than she remembered. Older too.

"Is Zio well? He looks drawn."

"He doesn't sleep, poor dear. He's terribly worried about Gabriele, as we all are. And now after that explosion—you know he's gone into business with Mr. Lombardi, yes?" Rosina nodded. "The violence and that young man's death are tearing him apart. And then there's the cost of replacing the equipment those men destroyed. I do worry."

"I worry about Papà too."

"Let's look forward to better days, shall we? Now, please forgive me, but I must go out. Stay as long as you like, and do come back to see me, won't you? You are always welcome here, no matter what those cantankerous men think. We women have to stick together."

"Yes, we do! Like suffragettes!"

"Speaking of that," Donata said, "there's a meeting in Montpelier on Monday. Shall we go?"

"Yes! Zia Marietta, come with us!"

Marietta laughed. "Oh dear me, I don't know about that, Vittorio would have heart failure. I choose my battles carefully, niece. You see, I prefer to win."

The coffee and toast finished, Rosina headed home. *We women*, Zia Marietta had said, as if welcoming Rosina to a secret society of women who lived life on their own terms. As tired as she was, she wanted to document this strange day. Illustrate it. How? What would she draw? The exhausted young girl with grief and gratitude written on her face? Perhaps. Her thoughts flitted from the girl's beast of a brother to Paolo and Nico, fortunately both of good character. From Nico her mind jumped to Angelo, then to the Labor Hall and Eugene Debs's inspiring words.

Yes. She knew what she would draw tonight—a young woman like herself, standing next to the girl's bed, her shadow too long for the page.

EIGHTEEN

THE DAY AFTER THE SUFFRAGE MEETING, Clementina surprised Rosina by wanting to hear all about it. Washing vegetables for dinner, Rosina described the Montpelier schoolroom where the meeting was held, on State Street not far from the gold-domed statehouse; the group of about twenty spirited women who sat on folding chairs watched over by an American flag; the singing of "Battle Hymn of the Republic" and how she'd hummed along because she didn't know the words; the need for volunteers to hand out flyers at events and parades and markets. Rosina had volunteered for all the Barre events, of course. Most impressive were the leaders, four women who spoke with confidence, holding out hope for Vermont despite the failed suffrage vote in New Hampshire the previous year.

"Women have the vote now in three or four states, I don't remember which ones. We can do this, I know it! Someday women in Vermont will have the vote, and I'll be one of them. You will too! We need to file for citizenship as soon as possible so we'll be ready. And I know you're tired of hearing me say it, but you need to work on your English."

"We'll see," Clementina said. "I'm not sure I agree with this line of thinking, but you keep telling me what you learn."

"Did you know Zia Donata has been a member of the Vermont Woman Suffrage Association for years?"

"That doesn't surprise me one bit," said Clementina. "She has never taken the common path." Just then someone pounded on the door. "I'll get it," she said, wiping her hands on her apron.

It was Angelo, standing hat in hand. "What a nice surprise!" Clementina ushered him in. "You must be exhausted. *Vieni, vieni.* Come in and sit for a while."

"*Grazie.* I've been walking since six this morning. I did a double shift to cover for the man that was killed."

"*Una vera tragedia,*" Clementina said. "Come, Rosina is in the kitchen."

Angelo hoped he hadn't made a mistake in coming, but he saw Rosina so rarely these days that it drove him wild. He wasn't about to try to woo her away from Marcello—she knew her own mind and he was pretty sure she wouldn't change it for him or anyone else—but he could stay underfoot, and one of these days she might want to kiss him again. And then who knew what might happen? Marcello might find himself tossed aside like the rubbish he was.

Rosina returned his greeting politely and pulled out a chair. Angelo sat, hat on his lap. He was skinnier than ever, his beard scraggly, she thought as she put the coffee on to boil. He looked older too, like her father and brothers did. How long could the men go on like this?

"You'll stay for dinner, won't you?" asked Clementina. "It's only the two of us. Gabriele eats in his room."

No, no, no! Rosina busied herself with cups and saucers so her mother wouldn't see her dismay. She could manage coffee with Angelo, but a meal? Could she sit next to him that long without her mother noticing that the air vibrated between them?

"I'd be glad to stay if you've got enough. I brought you these." Angelo dumped wild strawberries from his hat onto the table. "There's more along the river if you want them. I found a big patch across the bridge past the Labor Hall."

"You're kind to think of us," said Clementina, gathering the strawberries into a bowl.

"I had to get away from the line for a while. It's pretty awful out there, policemen all over the place and a fight every five minutes. Mostly yelling and a few black eyes, that kind of thing, but it brings you down. It sure doesn't feel like we're all in this together anymore."

"Nico says the same thing," Rosina said.

Dinner was a thin pastina with beans, carrots, and wild chicory. Angelo forced himself to eat slowly, savoring every mouthful. "Best meal I've had in weeks," he said. When Clementina served the strawberries mixed with bread chunks and honey, he could have died happy right then and there.

When they'd finished, Rosina put some strawberries in a bowl for Gabriele. "I'm going to read to Zio now," she announced.

"Go with her, Angelo," Clementina said. "Gabriele will be happy to see you."

"It's our—yes, of course he would," Rosina said. It would've been rude to say this was her private time with her uncle, even though it was. She'd begun to read aloud to him only recently, as a way to spend time together without him having to talk too much. Back in Viggiù, they'd read together on rainy days or played card games that he'd let her win. He would tell her stories about Viggiù in the early days, and about Italian explorers like Amerigo Vespucci and heroes like Giuseppe Garibaldi. In exchange, Rosina would make up stories about princesses and buried treasure that surely bored him, and he would listen as if they were masterpieces written by Dante. Her throat ached. And now too much time had passed and however much time was left would be too little.

"It's *Gulliver's Travels*," she said, hoping Angelo wouldn't be interested.

"Can't say I've heard of it, but that's all right. I'd like to see him. If you don't mind."

"Of course."

They knocked, and a frail voice said to come in. Gabriele was sitting by the window, soft light from a table lamp failing to hide the hollows at his collarbones and the sunken bruises under his eyes. A basket at his feet held bloodied handkerchiefs.

"Excuse the mess," he said as Rosina kissed him. "Angelo, it's good to see you. How are the men's spirits?"

Angelo considered lying, then decided Gabriele would want the truth. "Pretty bad, to be honest. No one's got the stomach for it anymore. A lot of the men don't show up for their shifts, and today a bunch of them ditched the line and sat around playing cards. I've heard talk about crossing the line if Carlo doesn't call a vote soon. But I guess he's told you."

"My brother tries to—" Gabriele coughed, wet and rasping. "Tries to shield me . . . from all that. He means well."

He was wheezing now, an alarming whistling sound that Rosina didn't seem to notice. She must be used to it, Angelo thought. He hadn't been in a sickroom since his mother died. Should he sit or stand? It didn't seem right to sit on the bed, but there was nowhere else. He settled on leaning against the wall, hands shoved in his pockets.

"I haven't been there . . . since the explosion," Gabriele said. "That morning. Wanted to go back . . . after, but couldn't . . . make it. Angelo . . . you're still . . . walking the line? Walk . . . for me too."

"I do, every time. We all do."

What he didn't tell him was that things had gone from bad to worse since the explosion. Carlo and his helpers had their hands full trying to keep things under control, which they mostly didn't manage to do, like a week ago when a Scottish shop owner wouldn't extend credit to the Italian strikers and they burned the place down. Meanwhile, the anarchists still kept a presence at the new shed site, at least three of them there every day, sunup to sundown, standing with arms crossed, giving the *malocchio* to the construction workers and the new excavator Lombardi had brought in to replace the one they'd blown up. They were probably thinking of blowing this one up too. So much for solidarity. So much for the singing and marching on Primo Maggio, the atmosphere of brotherhood. These days Barre felt like the kind of place where men would sell their mothers for a cigarette or a beer.

"Are you all right?" Rosina had little furrows of worry between her brows.

"Yes, sorry, thinking about the strike, that's all. Say, Gabriele, it looks like you've been busy here." Angelo jutted his chin toward the bed, strewn with pencils and stacks of drawings.

"Yes. Designing . . . my stone."

"Oh, sorry, I didn't mean . . . I'm an idiot."

Gabriele smiled weakly. "No harm done. I've finished it. It's the one . . . on the pillow. Bring it here. I'll show you."

He held the sketch in trembling hands, his fingertips tinged blue. Inside a frame of twisting wisteria was his name in elegant capital letters, and underneath that, his birthdate followed by a blank space. Across the top, bigger than his name, were the words "*L'arte è la vita, la vita è l'arte.*" Three parallel lines running across the bottom edge represented the colors of the Italian flag, Gabriele said. He handed the sketch to Rosina. "The rest . . . you'll understand."

"Zio, it's beautiful." Rosina willed herself not to cry. *Art is life, life is art*—her uncle believed that with all his heart. And what faith he had! Instead of dried pods or barren vines, or a broken column or tree, all traditional symbols of death, he'd drawn flowers, a symbol of growth, of life. Of a long life, because wisteria bloomed year after year, often for decades. Each spring, a rebirth.

He was coughing again, hunched in his chair against the pain. Panting and sweaty, he pulled a clean handkerchief from his dressing gown pocket, then gripped the chair arm. Ready for the next one, Rosina thought. And the next and the next, on and on for how much longer?

"Can I get you some water?" she asked.

Angelo jumped up. "I'll get it!"

"No. I'm all right." Gabriele pointed to a cupboard. "Put those . . . drawings in there . . . will you?"

"If you don't mind my asking," Angelo said, gathering the sketches, "do you have other work I could see? I know you're the best sculptor in Barre, but do you draw much?"

"Was the best." Gabriele coughed again, a mercifully brief spell. "I won't . . . get back to it."

"Don't say that, Zio!" Rosina clutched his arm. "After the strike—"

"No. Let's not pretend. Angelo . . . the top shelf. Yes, there. What I've done . . . since I got sick."

Angelo handed the first sketch to Rosina, then the next, working through the stack. Each one depicted a tiny portion of the natural world in magnified detail, as though Gabriele had shrunk to the size of an ant. Curving lines and marching geometrics seemed at first like something imagined, then flashed into recognizable form. An abstract sea, its undulations curving beneath a broken surface, became the body of a leaf if studied long enough, and a repeating pattern of coarse ridges shifted into the bark of a pine tree.

"Wow," said Angelo. "These are like nothing I've ever seen before."

"Me neither," Rosina chimed in. "I couldn't draw something like this no matter how much I tried."

"You can . . . if you look hard enough. Always something—" Gabriele coughed again, then caught his breath, eyes closed. "Something new to see. If you try." He wheezed, his face pale. "Rosina. Keep them. When I'm gone."

"Of course I will, Zio, I'll keep them forever." Her throat knotted again, and if she didn't start reading right then she would cry, which would do her uncle no good. "Well then, let's see what trouble Gulliver will get himself into this time."

Angelo helped Gabriele into bed, then sat on the floor while Rosina took the chair and began to read. Angelo listened with his eyes closed. He liked the story well enough, and at first he followed along, picturing the Lilliputians, the Tramecksans and Slamecksans with their high- and low-heeled shoes. After a while he found himself paying more attention to Rosina's voice than the story, which sent his imagination in another direction, one that would get him in trouble if he didn't nip it in the bud. He sat up straight, eyes open. Think about Gulliver, not her.

After half an hour Rosina closed the book. "We'll leave you now, Zio. Don't forget to eat the strawberries. Sleep well." She closed the door gently.

Angelo said goodnight to Clementina, and Rosina followed him out into the stairwell. "Is there always blood like that?" he whispered.

"Almost always. It breaks my heart."

"Mine too." He fidgeted, then shoved his hands in his pockets. It was overwhelming, this desire he had to take her in his arms. Not the time, not the place, he told himself.

"You're sweet to say so." Rosina shooed him onto the stairs. "Go on, then, I know you need to get back."

"Walk me out?"

She hesitated. "All right, the air will do me good. It's terribly stuffy in his room."

Downstairs, they stepped into night air thick with damp and insects. "Not much better out here, is it?" Angelo said. "Wow, look how many stars there are tonight! How would Gabriele draw this sky, do you think? I bet he'd lie on his back so the treetops would frame it. Like this." He made a window with his hands above his head and peered through it.

"He'll never draw the sky again, will he?" Rosina burst into tears.

"Hey, I'm sorry. I didn't mean—"

"No, it's all right." She sat on the steps, hugging her knees and sniffling. "I'm not always like this. It's just that every time I see him he looks worse."

Angelo sat next to her and she leaned into him, warm tears soaking his shirt. He put one arm around her, then the other. The most natural thing in the world, the two of them together, her hair soft under his chin, her body sturdy and warm.

After a few minutes she quieted and sat up, wiping her face. Dear, dear Zio. How much longer would he be able to see the stars? If he could draw them, would he make those faraway spots of light appear to be something else only inches away? His close-up views of the world were beautiful but sad, as if he wanted to see only what fell within arm's reach. As if he were afraid that by looking up, into the distance, he would see an end to his life.

They sat, arms lightly touching, gazing upward until the moon rose above the trees and whitewashed the stars. Angelo stayed on after Rosina went inside, watching the moon creep across the sky, mentally shifting the balance of light and composition in his imagined sketch. As soon as he got the chance, he'd draw that starry sky the way Gabriele would have done, and he'd give it to her. Then she would know he understood her grief.

NINETEEN

THE FOLLOWING SUNDAY Rosina put on a pale yellow dress with pearl buttons on the bodice, one of her favorites to give her confidence. She would need it, having agreed to meet Marcello and his mother after church. How well could she act the part of an enamored young woman? She would find out today, because there was no harsher judge than a hawkeyed mother. Lifting her chin, she turned her head side to side, studying her reflection. She'd done her hair perfectly today, and her skin was clear, if a little too brown from the sun. It made her look healthy, she decided. Vigorous.

At breakfast, Clementina called Marcello a few choice names under her breath. She still refused to accept him as a substitute for Giorgio, whom she was determined not to give up on. "He's gotten taller," she said, as if he were a boy still growing into his oversized feet and height was an essential asset in a husband. When Rosina laughed, Clementina dug in. "He has. Some young men get a late growth spurt, you know." When Rosina reminded her that Giorgio was twenty-five, Clementina warned her that he might set his sights on someone else. Rosina responded with a cheerful "I hope so!" and Clementina gave up the battle. Thirty seconds later she declared Angelo Lucci a good alternative.

"Why, because he brought us strawberries? I don't think of him that way, Mamma. Not at all."

"No?" Clementina's voice dripped with doubt. "You should. He's Catholic and he's a good boy. He likes you. You'd have to be blind not to see that."

"Wishful thinking, Mamma. Why don't you play matchmaker for Nico? He isn't seeing anyone."

"Watch that sharp tongue of yours, Rosi. Men don't like it."

"I learned it from you. Ask Papà."

Clementina harrumphed, failing to hide a smile.

Rosina had decided to skip Mass to keep her dress unwrinkled and fresh, provoking more disapproval from her mother. On the streetcar going downtown she sat next to a young couple who seemed to think that taking their eyes off each other would cause immediate death. They looked unrealistically happy, as if they believed the future held nothing but goodness. After a home visit the day before to a mother whose baby was unlikely to live and to whom Rosina could offer only useless consolation, she found it painful to watch this young woman and her sweetheart. What lay ahead for them? Uncertainties of health and trust, certainties of pain and sorrow, arguments about money spent or time lost. Their romantic fantasies would fade, certainly. If they were blessed with the children they probably wanted, every new arrival would mean more clothes to wash, more meals to cook—and, if the family was very large, more teenage girls forced to mother their sisters and brothers. No mother could care for ten or twelve children by herself. Rosina had seen enough women depleted by domestic lives to know that however much joy their children and husband provided, it wasn't always enough.

She turned away as the lovebirds nuzzled. Since when had she become a cranky disbeliever in romance, in true love? After all, her parents loved each other. She didn't *not* believe in romance. In fact, she envied this couple in a way. How much simpler her life would be if all she wanted was to gaze into a man's eyes with the rapture of this young woman, to treasure his words, dream of her wedding day, the tidy home she would keep for their growing family. To be happy like Giulia, who would have the life she wanted. Still, romance faded, and loving someone didn't solve all the world's problems.

Standing to get off at the next stop, her gaze fell on another couple, a grim-faced woman with gray hair seated next to a fat, florid old man, seemingly oblivious to each other. So much for rapture.

Marcello was waiting near the bandstand, arm in arm with his mother, who wore a feathered hat more suited to Easter than to the heavy days of summer. Still at a distance, Rosina pasted on a smile. Mrs. Battaglia leaned over to say something to Marcello. Judging by her beady-eyed gaze it was probably something along the lines of "My dear, she's no Isabella, is she?"

No, she most certainly was not.

"Signora Battaglia, how nice to see you. What a lovely hat." Rosina pecked Marcello's cheek. "And you are very handsome in that suit."

"I told him the pinstripe was a good choice," Mrs. Battaglia said, then pursed her lips. "I'm sorry to hear your uncle is ill. Those stone sheds are terrible places, aren't they?"

Rosina went rigid. Marcello looked at her in alarm as his mother barreled on.

"Marcello tells me you're a midwife."

Rosina forced a civil tone. "Yes. That is, I'm learning to be one."

"You do know that the better women are using doctors now? Indeed. Isabella told me she plans to have a doctor deliver her babies, didn't she, Marcello? There won't be much need for midwives in the future, you know." Mrs. Battaglia waved a dismissive hand, then launched a cloying smile at Rosina. "Of course it won't matter once you have children of your own."

Rosina was speechless. How dare this woman disparage the Bottinellis' livelihood, then presume that having children would deprive her of ambition! And that remark about Isabella's babies was shockingly rude.

Marcello clamped a hand onto Rosina's arm as if he knew trouble was coming. "I'm sure Rosina has—"

"Thank you for your concern, Signora Battaglia." Rosina mimicked the woman's smile. Oh, but why had she interrupted Marcello? Exactly what was he so sure about on her behalf? "However, you're quite mistaken. I enjoy being a midwife and I'm sure I'll do it for a very long time."

It was hard to believe the woman had ever given birth. She probably considered it unladylike, the old witch. Obviously she didn't know that a midwife's work was an act of intimacy, as personal as the confessions heard by a priest. What did doctors, meaning men, know about childbirth and a woman's needs? Midwives saw women's vulnerability and strength. They witnessed the love, or lack of it, that defined a couple's marriage, shared in the delight of children who wanted a brother or sister and comforted those who cried to think of another hungry mouth sharing their food. Most of the women talked and talked during the postpartum visits. Rosina knew which babies were wanted and which were not, which had been conceived with love and which hadn't, which husbands beat their wives, which women dreaded the thought of the next baby. And which had contemplated ending their pregnancies despite the risk and shame. Mrs. Battaglia was ignorant, and a fool.

"Well, we must be off!" Marcello said brightly. "I'll see you at home, Mamma." Then, as he steered Rosina toward Elm Street, "Never mind her. I doubt there's a woman in Vermont, or probably anywhere, that she thinks is good enough for me."

"Except for Isabella."

"She does like her, I admit it. Don't worry, give her time and you'll pass her test. You've already passed mine."

"Is that so? Do you think you've passed mine?" The words came out snippier than she'd intended.

"I'd say I have. We could kiss right now and find out."

She tossed her head. "As if kissing is all that matters."

"You like it well enough."

"Change the conversation, please."

"All right. Guess what I did this week."

"I don't know, sold some pork chops?" Snippy again.

Marcello laughed. "You've got a swell sense of humor. Yes, I did, in fact, but I also rescued a kitten from a rooftop and chased a bat out of a chimney. I'm starting to think I should be a veterinarian instead of a fireman."

From Elm Street they looped back to Main, ending up at Dodge's Creamery. Rosina balked at the cost, knowing the Battaglias' business was suffering, but Marcello insisted. "Strike or no strike, sometimes a fellow has to treat his girl," he said, ushering her into a booth. After ordering two strawberry ice cream sodas, he took her hand. "We get along, don't we?"

"I suppose we do. I'm afraid I can't say the same about your mother. She dislikes midwives, doesn't she?"

"She thinks they don't want to have families of their own."

"And what do you think?"

He shrugged. "She's probably right." Noting her steely gaze, he added, "About some of them, anyway."

And he was afraid she was one of them. Maybe she was, maybe she wasn't. He had no idea about the war going on in her head. Marriage and children, no marriage and no children—neither choice seemed right. The third option—yes to children, no to marriage—was too self-destructive to consider. She would be shunned, unable to work, a destitute burden on her family, and her children labeled bastards, taunted into shame.

Their sodas arrived and Rosina dove in, satisfied that Marcello was proving to be exactly who she thought he was. He wouldn't tolerate a wife who was called to work at all hours of the day or night, often on a moment's notice. He would think feeding their children, bathing them and putting them to bed, was women's work and only women's work. He was old-fashioned, happy with the inequality between men and women. How typical.

"It would make it hard to have a family, though, wouldn't it?" Marcello said.

"My aunt Donata was married." She could almost hear him thinking, *Was married. Meaning she's a widow, meaning her husband, poor, long-suffering fellow, had put up with a midwife for years and years and now he was dead.*

"Did they have children?"

"One." Grudgingly she added, "He died very young."

"Well, there you go." He finished his soda. "Shall we?"

"Yes, I've had enough." Rosina pushed her half-empty glass away.

Outside, Marcello looped her arm through his, chaining her to him. "Anyway, don't worry, I don't think you'll be that kind of midwife."

Which kind? The kind who gave up working or the kind who didn't?

"By the way," he went on, "I want you to know I'm not courting anyone else. In case you thought I was. Since when I was with Isabella, you know . . ."

"You kissed me? Don't worry, I didn't suppose you were. After all, your mother would be exhausted if she had to keep track of more than one woman's faults at a time." Spoken as if she was kidding, which she was not.

Marcello laughed. "I'll say it again, you have a good sense of humor."

"I'm glad you think so."

She ducked her head as if blushing. How did they appear to passersby? Happy, like the young couple on the streetcar? Would women and men watch them with envy, thinking each had made a fine catch? Would they think them enamored, devoted, inseparable? In truth, he was a shallow, fickle man. And she? An opportunist who was, God forgive her, using him. For one desperate moment she imagined choosing to be a nun. At least that would stop all this courtship nonsense for good. Though she had no intention of remaining chaste her whole life, husband or not.

They had arrived in Scampini Square. Marcello bent to kiss her and she tilted her head, eyes closed. At the touch of his soft lips and prickly brush of mustache, her body flared. At least she didn't have to pretend about that.

Whether it was because Marcello was kinder than Rosina had thought or he'd gotten one too many black looks from Clementina and hoped to win her over, he began to bring her gifts of meat from his family's shop. Rosina wondered if the generous gifts—she knew the shop remained empty for hours at a time—meant he truly did care for her. Clementina, despite her pride, couldn't say no. For weeks on end the family ate no meat unless the twins managed to shoot a rabbit or pheasant; even chicken was a luxury because they needed the eggs from the laying hens and the roosters had gone under the hatchet long ago. On those occasions when Marcello arrived with a heavy sack of whatever the shop could spare, Clementina returned the favor by inviting him to stay for a meal.

One such day in mid-August, after a lunch of sausages and white beans, Rosina invited Marcello to go downstairs to the garden with her. "You've been very generous to my family," she said. "I'd like to thank you by sketching your portrait. Will you pose for me? The light is nice at this hour."

"No kidding! I didn't know you drew. Are you any good?"

"You'll have to wait and see."

She chose a grassy spot in filtered sunlight. "Sit over there, please."

He sat with one knee bent, an arm hooked around his shin. No hat, gaze confident, eyes warm, head tipped so that the light caught his cheekbones.

"Look past me, over my shoulder," Rosina said. The warm light caught the rich texture of his tight curls, the angular bridge of his nose. Roughing in his head and upper body, she drew quickly, confidently. Thanks to her uncle, she'd gotten much better at drawing people.

"You're adorable when you concentrate," Marcello said. "You've got a sweet little frown. Makes me want to come over there and kiss you."

"Please don't talk, it's distracting."

For half an hour more she worked, until he complained of cramped muscles. "Can I see it?"

"Not yet." She stopped to appraise her work. Though the likeness was good enough, recognizably Marcello, she hadn't captured *him*—his possessive gaze, his ease and confidence, his belief that the world was his. None of that was in her drawing. What was worse, she'd filled the page with his upper half, leaving no room for the rest of him. She'd drawn half a man.

Marcello got up to peer over her shoulder. "Look at that, you're good! Can I keep it?"

Rosina glanced up at his lively face, then back at her lifeless sketch. "Yes, of course, when I've finished. I'm glad you like it." She wasn't glad, though. The half man she'd drawn was as beautiful as Marcello yet as blank as the white marble eyes of a Greek statue. Clearly she lacked the skill to capture who he was beyond his sculpted face. Then again, maybe lack of skill wasn't to blame. Maybe she'd drawn the real Marcello, blank and empty because he *was* blank and empty. A false front, like their courtship.

"You're something, you know that?" He sat next to her, pulled her into a long, lingering kiss.

She had never felt so guilty in her life.

TWENTY

SEPTEMBER ARRIVED WITH AN OVERNIGHT COLD SNAP, painting the maples in rich reds and rusts and the birches in golden yellows. Mild evenings followed still-sultry afternoons, warning of summer's end. Rosina was half awake early one morning, shivering in her muslin nightgown, when she was called to the Basso household.

Stepping outside into the thinning light of near dawn, she wondered what the day would bring. She'd learned so much, seen all kinds of homes, all kinds of lives. Poverty beyond imagining, and comfortable, spotless homes where the children were clean and well fed. Babies who refused to nurse and little gluttons who screamed when there was no nipple in their mouths. Mothers with mastitis and piles and sagging bellies, mothers delirious with joy when their babies were born, mothers who sobbed in despair. She had fetched water, held the hands of laboring women and wiped their sweat. She had cut umbilical cords and shut doors firmly in fathers' faces with promises of soon, very soon. All told, being a midwife meant appearing unperturbed when everything she touched was bloody, sweaty, infected, awful, or disgusting and remaining calm and pleasant when women screamed in pain or husbands panicked.

And yet she liked the work, liked feeling needed and knowing she helped women through difficult times, loved sharing their joy. She had learned to think on her feet, had proved to have good judgment and common sense. She knew how to turn breech babies, even if not always successfully, and what to do when a blue baby wasn't breathing. She had offered comfort for losses of all kinds, tragic and not, to mothers whose babies were born deformed or dead and to fathers whose longed-for sons turned out to be daughters. She had learned to endure, with compassion, a mother's or father's anger and grief.

Because of the strike, Donata had farmed Rosina out to two other midwives to speed up her training. The sooner her niece could make a midwife's full wages, she said, the better. Rosina appreciated the extra work, though both women were less pleasant than her aunt, and far less capable. One did as little as possible and grumbled at the slightest delay or complication, and the other was efficient but lacked Donata's sensitivity and concern. Rosina suspected her aunt had farmed her out for another reason—to show her that not all midwives were exceptional or even competent, and to remind her that she must choose what kind of midwife she would be.

At the Basso residence, a young boy opened the door. "Papà! *L'altra signora è arrivata*!"

Rosina stepped inside. Two little girls played with rag dolls on the sofa while another small boy and an older girl shot marbles in the corner.

Mr. Basso came into the room at a fast clip. Sweat ringed the armpits of his white shirt and his eyes were wild like a spooked horse's. "Thank you for coming quickly. Your aunt says the baby will come soon." He gestured to a door. "She's in there."

"Very well. Don't worry. After birthing five children, I think your wife knows what to do, don't you agree?" Mr. Basso, pacing, frowned as if she'd spoken gibberish.

Mrs. Basso had prepared well. Sunlight filtered through worn but spotless lace curtains, and the iron bed frame shone with fresh white paint. Stacks of baby blankets and diapers crowded the bureau alongside a basin of steaming water.

"I think this one is in a hurry." Maria Basso spoke lightly, as if the midwives had come for coffee.

"Rosina, check her, please," Donata said.

"A quick look, yes, Signora Basso? Oh, you're right, your baby will come very soon. She's fully dilated, Zia."

"Very well, what's next?"

"I'll check the baby's heart." Rosina placed a Pinard horn on the woman's belly, moving it around until she found a heartbeat. "Regular and strong. The head is down. Shall we move her to the birthing chair?"

"Is that what you advise?"

"If she's agreeable, yes. It's almost time to push."

"I think . . . ," Mrs. Basso huffed through a contraction, "I think I'd like to stay here."

"Rosina?"

"It's fine, but she should lie on her left side. Are there any extra pillows, Signora Basso? We need to raise your head."

"They're in the cabinet," Donata said. "Very good, proceed. She is in your hands. I'm here if you need me."

Rosina paused, surprised, then helped the woman onto her left side. She took her place at the foot of the bed, her heart beating as fast as the baby's. Then there was no more time to be nervous because Mrs. Basso took a deep breath and pushed.

The baby crowned and receded, crowned and receded, until finally a warm, sticky little head filled Rosina's palm. She held her breath, shocked as always by this first touch of a new life, the warmth of two bodies creeping from her hands to her arms, into her chest, a soft glow of happiness. Cradling the little skull with one hand, she felt for the cord around the neck. Free and clear. *Grazie, Maria santissima, grazie.* She waited for the next push, then eased one shoulder free. Seconds later, the slippery body settled into her hands. "Look at you, you perfect little thing," she murmured. "*È perfetta*! Signora Basso, you have a beautiful baby girl!" She slapped the soles of the baby's feet, provoking a satisfying wail.

"Another girl? I knew it!" Mrs. Basso beamed, her face wet with sweat and tears.

"Yes, and a hungry one, it seems. She's trying to eat her hand!" Rosina cut the cord, cleaned the baby's mouth and nostrils, and wrapped her tightly, each move unhesitating. Then she settled the baby onto her mother's breast.

Donata called to Mr. Basso to come and meet his daughter and he charged into the room with the children behind him. He kissed his wife, let the children admire their new sister, then whirled over to kiss Rosina and Donata too. "Thank you, both of you!"

"My pleasure," Rosina said around the lump in her throat. How wonderful that this baby had been born in a place of love, of hope and possibility. And into her own hands! How satisfying it was to have knowledge, and to use it.

"You did well, niece," said Donata. "It's clear that you don't need me anymore. For the next month or two you will be the midwife and I will assist you. I will do and say nothing unless you ask me to, or if there's an emergency." Rosina threw her arms around her aunt. "Oof, this is good news, I see. Let me breathe, dear."

"Sorry!"

"I have something for you." Donata pulled a long chain from inside her blouse, a small silver saint's medal hanging on the end. "This has served me well for many years, and now it's your turn. Raymond Nonnatus is the patron saint of midwives. Pray to him for protection and he will watch over you."

"Thank you, Zia." Rosina hugged her aunt again, then slipped the chain over her head.

"There's something we need to do tomorrow," Donata said. "I'll see you at Halliday's, five o'clock. Now go and share your good news."

Rosina left the house floating, lightheaded with joy. She was a midwife! On her way home she stopped at the butcher shop to tell Marcello the news. She expected him to feign enthusiasm for her new independence, this step toward a future he would want no part of. Instead, he leaned across the counter to kiss her.

"A real midwife, imagine that! We'll celebrate this weekend. How does a glass of spumante in the bandstand sound?"

It sounded heavenly. Rosina floated out of the store and over to the tailor shop. Giulia raced out from behind the counter to hug her. "When the time comes, you must deliver all my babies, every single one. I promise I'll keep you busy," she said, laughing.

"I'll give you a discount, two for the price of one. Like bottles of liver pills!"

Giulia kissed her. "It's a deal!"

"Marcello and I are celebrating on Saturday. I need to figure out what to wear."

"I have the perfect dress," Giulia said. "I'll bring it over tonight."

The dress was a wonder, a sheen of pale lavender over an underskirt of pearl gray, and it fit well except for the length, which Clementina said she could shorten in no time.

"It used to be my favorite," Giulia said mournfully, "but now it's too tight in the bust. It's perfect on you though."

"Are you saying I have the chest of a boy?" Rosina laughed.

"No! Only that yours are teacups and mine are bowls. Or something like that."

Rosina stood straighter, pushing out her chest. "I like my teacups." A parade of tiny pleats marched across the bodice, curving in strategic locations. The squared-off neckline flattered her, she thought, swishing the silky skirts. Though the color wasn't one she would have chosen, it complemented her eyes nicely. As did a pale gray hat accented with violet feathers.

"*Che bella*," Giulia breathed. "Marcello's eyes will pop out of his head."

"Now, who will go with you?" Clementina said. "Giulia? Or should I?"

"No one, Mamma, I don't need a chaperone. I've been alone with Marcello plenty of times."

Clementina crossed her arms. "At night? In the park? Wearing that dress?"

"I'll go! Davide and I both will," Giulia said. "Don't worry, Signora Bottinelli, I've got an eagle eye. Davide does too."

"*Va bene*. Rosina, take off the dress. I'll put in a new hem right now."

When Clementina had left the room, Rosina flopped onto the bed. "A chaperone! My mother is so old-fashioned!"

"Better me and Davide than her. I promise, you won't even know we're there. We'll wear black and hide in the bushes if you want us to."

"No you won't, I'm going alone. Try to avoid my mother for a while afterward so you won't have to lie. When she sees that I'm fine, she'll forget all about it."

The next afternoon Rosina had barely opened the door to Halliday's when the proprietor boomed his congratulations. "Well done, Miss Bottinelli. And your bag is ready"—he gestured toward a large black valise on the counter, identical to Donata's—"with everything you'll need." Donata beamed.

"Zia! No, it's too much."

"Nonsense. You must have the means to get started. Look inside, dear."

On top of all the supplies she would need, including a Pinard horn made of polished wood, was a book covered with Florentine paper in swirling blues and greens. "How beautiful," Rosina murmured.

"It's your midwife's diary, the first of many, I hope. Keep a record of the women you tend to, and their health, the length of their confinement, how the babies present, whether boys or girls, healthy or ill or stillborn—anything important. It will help you learn, and later to remember all the women and babies you have helped. Write down their names and, God willing, you'll watch them grow."

Rosina was thanking Donata when a frazzled-looking Mr. Basso raced in. "Please! Something for fever, and quickly!"

"For your wife or the baby?" Donata said as Mr. Halliday sprang into action.

"For my son, he's burning up. He was fine last night, now he's barely moving. He says his throat hurts something awful."

Rosina and Donata exchanged glances, fear in their eyes. "Have you called a doctor?" Rosina asked. "Yes? And your son, is he with the other children?" Mr. Basso nodded.

"Let's go see what's what, Signor Basso." Donata took the medicine Mr. Halliday had set on the counter, then marched toward the door. "We'll stay with you until the doctor arrives."

The boy was semiconscious when they arrived, his skin speckled and aflame. Donata took one look at him and told the father to take his other children into the parlor and stay with them. "Is there someone who can take them for a few days? We must keep your son isolated."

"My mother," Mr. Basso said as he ushered the young ones out.

"Good," Donata said. "Now, Rosina, tie a handkerchief over your mouth and nose and sit with the mother and baby. Try to keep her calm, we don't want her milk to dry up."

"He was in here with us for only a few minutes," Mrs. Basso told Rosina. "My son. That's good, isn't it? He was more interested in his marbles, bless his heart." She brushed away tears.

"Yes, that's very good. Try not to worry."

When the doctor had examined the boy, his face was grim. "Scarlet fever," he said. "I've seen three cases this week."

"Any deaths?" Donata asked quietly.

"One. I've got another call to go to. Can you stay until I can find a nurse?" Donata said she would. "Give the boy cool sponge baths and aspirin," the doctor said as he left, "and hope for the best."

By morning, the children had been sent to stay with their grandmother and a nurse had arrived. The boy's fever was down and he was breathing more easily.

"Everything went so well with the birth," Rosina said as she and Donata left the house, "and then this came with no warning. You never know, do you?" She took a deep breath and the Nonnatus medal moved against her skin. Someday, inevitably, there would be an emergency and she would need the saint's protection like never before. She prayed that day would take its time in coming.

The celebration with Marcello didn't happen on Saturday after all. Rosina was called to a lying-in that afternoon, and the next day Marcello had to go to Rutland with his father to settle some financial matters. Over the next few days a flurry of births kept Rosina busy. Though most of them were her aunt's customers, Donata intervened only to make suggestions as needed. She had spread the word that Barre had a new midwife, and Rosina had posted notices of her availability in shop windows and on church bulletin boards. When the first call that her aunt hadn't orchestrated came in from a woman in St. Monica's Parish, Rosina was thrilled. And when she walked home after the birth five dollars richer—the fee Donata had suggested for a lying-in and as many home visits as needed—she was lightheaded with pride. She was on her own, an independent businesswoman. The future had arrived.

The next Saturday evening, a week later than planned, Rosina took the 7:10 streetcar downtown to meet Marcello. She felt like a lady in her finery, and the bandstand, painted white with vine-covered trellises, was the perfect place for dressing up and drinking spumante like city sophisticates. The perfect place for romance, even if she was only playacting.

Giulia had been correct in her prediction. Marcello didn't take his eyes off Rosina from the moment she stepped off the streetcar until she stopped at the foot of the bandstand steps, at which point he took her hand, kissed it, and led her with great ceremony to the bench where the promised bottle and two glasses waited. He kissed her, then poured, kissed her and made a toast to the new midwife—"*Alla nuova levatrice*!"—kissed her, drained his glass, and started over. After the second glass, Rosina couldn't stop giggling and Marcello wouldn't stop kissing her.

"You do know," she said, coming up for air, "that we're in a very public place?"

"So let's go somewhere else," he murmured, his mouth on her neck.

"Marcello! What are you saying?"

Of course she knew perfectly well. And the truth was, she was curious—and almost giddy enough to cross the line her mother and the Church said she'd go to hell for if she did. Almost. She had often wondered what sharing a bed with a man would be like, the intimacy that would come with bared skin. It seemed impractical to limit that expression of love to marriage. Wouldn't a marriage suffer if the man and woman had different ideas about what should go on in the bedroom? If their ideas were very different, then someone would have to compromise, and she doubted very much that it would be the man. Certainly not if that man was Marcello.

When the time came, with the right man, she would do it.

"I'm saying that sometimes kissing isn't enough," Marcello said, inching his fingers around her neckline.

"This time it will have to be." Rosina pushed his hand away and struggled to sit upright. It was nearly dark now, the passersby few and the birds silenced. The air hummed with the rhythmic scrape of katydids.

"Oh, all right." Marcello rolled to his feet, drank straight from the bottle, then fell back on the bench. "Have another glass," he said, offering it to her.

"No, thank you."

"Come on, we're just getting started." He swigged the bottle, then filled her glass. "Drink up. *Cin cin*!"

Rosina took tiny sips to placate him. It was dark now; she should have let Giulia and Davide come with her. No, it was fine, Marcello had taken no for an answer, wasn't even trying to touch her now. She should leave, instinct told her. But why? He was being sweet, saying how impressed his mother was with his portrait, how they'd propped it on the mantel and would frame it when business picked up. A few more minutes, then she would go. It was a lovely night after all, breezy yet warm enough to be comfortable in her elegant dress.

Another sip. "Are you truly happy for me?"

"What, that you're a midwife? Sure. Why wouldn't I be?" His words were slightly slurred. He took a last swig, turned the bottle upside down, then tossed it aside. "Should've brought another one." Sliding closer, he draped a heavy arm across her shoulders.

"I didn't think you approved. Your mother certainly doesn't."

"She likes to talk, that's all. Doesn't mean anything."

"All right." Another sip.

His arm was off her shoulders now. He took her hand, stroked it gently. "You have pretty hands." He kissed her palm, his tongue making small, warm circles.

Rosina caught her breath, heat flooding her body.

"You like that?" His tongue moved to her mouth, urgent, insistent. "Yeah, you do." His hand was at her breast, probing. "*Maledetto corsetto*," he muttered. "What's in this thing, metal?" Giving up on the corset, he reached under her skirts, grazed the top of her stocking.

She swatted his hand. "Stop it!"

"You know you want it."

"I said no!" She pushed him hard, kicked at his shins.

"Okay, okay." Releasing her, he took her hand again, gently, as if to kiss it, then forced it down to his crotch. "See how much I want you?" He was panting now, thick-voiced, his free hand unbuttoning his pants. "Touch me."

"No! Let me go!" His grip loosened as he fumbled with a button and she grabbed his hand and bit it.

"*Cazzo*!" Roaring with pain, Marcello rolled away, cradling his hand. "What the hell?"

Rosina stood, shaking. "I said no and you didn't listen! You're a pig!"

"I listened! Plenty of fellows would have taken what they wanted." He inspected his hand. "There's no blood. Hurts like hell, though."

"Good. You're a pig and I'm leaving."

"And you're a tease. Can't blame a fellow for trying."

Rosina hurried across the park, across the street, to the trolley stop under a streetlight. She hated to wait knowing he was watching her, and she would have walked if she hadn't worried that he would follow her and try again. Not that she would let that happen. She waited ten minutes, maybe more, glancing at the bandstand every few seconds. A man walked by on the other side of the street, igniting a flash of fear. How many times had she walked across town in the dead of night? Her mother always warned her to be careful, and Rosina was, though maybe not careful enough. She thought of that horrible man she'd seen on the street a while back. Imagine running into him at night!

Another glance back. Marcello was gone and the trolley was coming. She was safe.

At home, she slipped inside with hardly a sound, and a good thing too, because her mother was dozing in the parlor. If she ever found out what had happened she would tell Papà and he would beat Marcello up, or the twins would. One more act of violence that would accomplish nothing. She had handled Marcello herself. Not that biting him wasn't violent too.

People were animals, herself included.

So much for her sophisticated evening. If trying to take advantage of her was what Marcello considered romantic fun, he was an ass as well as a pig. Fumbling with buttons and hooks, she undressed in a hurry, pitching dress, corset, stockings, garters, all of it, onto the floor. The dress lay there next to the bed, empty and crumpled, a hollow reprimand. She'd been stupid. She fell onto the bed, suddenly exhausted. Terribly stupid. And very, very lucky.

Which was what Giulia said the next morning when Rosina told her what had happened. After a fitful night she'd risen early to catch Giulia before Mass. Giulia took one look at Rosina's face and banished her two younger sisters from the bedroom. "And don't listen outside the door, you hear me? I'll know if you do, and you don't want to find out what I'll do then!" She slammed the door, ignoring her sisters' protests. "Now tell me everything."

Standing guard at the door, Giulia listened, her expression flickering from shock to disgust to fury. "I never should have let you go alone!" she said when Rosina had finished. "Why did I listen to you? Davide and I could have had a nice evening in the park together, and then he would have been there to give Marcello what-for. Stupid, stupid, stupid."

"Please don't feel bad. It was scary, and of course I was furious, but he wouldn't hurt me." Said to make Giulia feel better, because she only half believed it herself.

"That's not the point! He's a boor to have even tried, especially when you hardly know him! Davide didn't try anything like that for months, and only after we were engaged. I told him I wanted to wait and he respects that!"

"Because he knows if your father found out he'd break him in half like a twig and toss him into a quarry." That made Giulia laugh. "Please, I don't want to think about Marcello anymore, so can we talk about something else? What's the latest on the wedding?"

"Nothing!" Giulia flopped onto the bed. "This strike had better end or I'll never get married. It's very depressing."

Rosina stretched out next to her. "The strike is ruining everything. And Zio is getting worse. He hardly talks anymore because of the coughing."

"It's all depressing." Giulia bounced to her feet. "Come on, let's go to Mass early. We have a lot of praying to do."

"I need to go to confession. Do you think I should say I bit Marcello?"

"I should say not, you were defending yourself."

"I never did confess to kissing him before he threw over Isabella."

"Tell the priest that, then."

They left the house arm in arm. Confession would be a comfort today too, as would Mass. The Church had always been a comfort, its rituals and expectations constant and predictable. It still was, even though Rosina didn't believe everything the Church taught anymore. She would go to confession, make her penance, light a candle for Zio Gabriele. She would chant the Latin prayers, kneel and stand, cross herself, and take communion. And for that brief time, that hour of quiet scented with incense, she would find peace.

She pulled Giulia closer, kissed the side of her head.

"What's that for?"

"For being my friend. I'm glad we met." Glad, too, that her parents hadn't given up Catholicism when they came to Barre, like so many of the Italians had. Like the Battaglias. Like Marcello. Marcello the pig.

TWENTY-ONE

ON THE SEVENTEENTH DAY OF SEPTEMBER, in the seventeenth week of the strike, Gabriele died. No one expected it to happen so soon. Clementina said she'd never forgive herself for not paying enough attention to the uneaten meals, the bloody handkerchiefs and pillowcases, the coughing that interrupted his speech and stole his breath. She saw them, heard him, but all of it had become normal, expected. Gabriele had time yet, they all said. *Mal d'america* didn't move fast, not usually. But this time it had.

Dr. Carson said they shouldn't blame themselves, Clementina in particular. It was true that sick men often lingered for years; however, complications arose at times. Any number of possibilities. It was possible that a blood vessel had burst in Gabriele's lungs and killed him quickly, possible that he'd had another condition, undiagnosed, that hastened his death. The family couldn't be blamed for overlooking his decline, not with the strike sapping their energy, dulling them and distracting them in the endless days and weeks, one running into the next.

Clementina found him. She woke before dawn to a house too quiet. Careful not to wake Carlo, she put on a dressing gown and stood outside Gabriele's door, waited for the coughing that split each hour of the day and night. Silence. She knocked softly, entered. No sound, a still shape in the bed. She knew before she touched him that he would not stir. She closed her eyes, palm to her heart, thought of her husband, how the coming day would devastate him. Sat in the chair by the window where faint moonlight seeped in. Waited for her eyes to adjust to the darkness. Saw something white on the nightstand—a piece of paper, perhaps nothing, perhaps everything. She went to the kitchen, unfolded the page.

> My beloved family,
>
> Forgive me. I have felt death coming on and said nothing. I am ready, but I know you are not. I cannot bear to warn you and see the pain in your eyes. Instead, each night I leave this letter on the table beside me. One day you will find it come morning.
>
> I love all of you deeply.
>
> Marietta, Daniele, and Cosimo, we have been strangers of late. I regret all the meals we did not share and the circumstances that have kept us apart. I wish you long, happy lives.
>
> Donata, time slipped past us. Please know that not a day has passed without some thought of you. I carry with me memories of our childhood together, our life in Viggiù. There is no one kinder or more thoughtful than you, or stronger. I know you will comfort our brothers.
>
> Clementina, you have been as loving and true as any blood sister. That has meant the world to me.
>
> Paolo and Nico, my dear nephews, I watched with pride as you grew into men and fine artists. Remember the good times we shared and help your father through this time.

Rosina, my dear niece, you know what a special place you hold in my heart. I wish you years of happiness and love, and many children. Tell them about me. Tell them how much I would have loved them. Talk to them about art and never give up on your own. Keep my drawings and give one to Angelo. He is a good man with a big heart and an artist's soul.

Carlo and Vittorio, you know me better than anyone in this life, and I pray you will make peace with each other. Go forward with love between you as brothers should, I beg you. Carve my stone and bury me, both of you, together. I want no funeral Mass, only a burial at Hope with you and my dear sister and the rest of the family there to bid me farewell.

All of you, remember me as I was before this terrible time, in health and good spirits. I kiss you goodbye and carry you in my heart.

—Gabriele

On the day of the burial the barren sky shone pale and cold as if lit by moonlight. The procession of mourners stretched from the North End halfway up the hill to Hope, a mile away. The women prayed as they walked, their hands working rosaries. The men left a skeletal picket line in place and marched for Gabriele instead this day, their hands filled with wreaths and flowers as if the strike hadn't emptied their pocketbooks.

Carlo walked behind the hearse, an open wagon pulled by a spotted gray horse, both loaned by Gabriele's close friend Camolli the grocer. Carlo's eyes and throat ached, his heart too, with a pain deep but muted, as if he moved beneath a blanket with too tight a weave to allow grief to see the light of day. The horse plodded, setting a pace so slow it resembled a standstill, the climb to Hope growing steeper and longer with each dragging step. Paolo led the horse with Nico and Angelo at its flanks. Behind the wagon, Donata walked with Carlo, Clementina with Rosina. With their arms linked, Rosina felt the weight of her mother's slow steps, the burden of her mother's grief.

At last—and too soon for Carlo, because he had hoped never to arrive—they reached the grave site. Rosina stepped forward to brush away the freshly dug dirt that spilled onto her aunt Agnese's grave, but Carlo stopped her. It was fitting, he thought, that earth from Gabriele's grave touched his wife's, a sign that they were about to be reunited in eternity. Because today Carlo believed in God, in forgiveness and eternal life, with all his heart.

As he and Donata took their places next to the open grave, the mourners assembled. "He will come, won't he?" Carlo said to his sister, his voice barely audible.

"He said he would." Donata glanced toward the cemetery entrance, her eyes worried behind her black veil. "Should we wait?"

Carlo cleared his throat. "Dear friends, my family and I thank you all for coming." His voice sounded distant, unrecognizable even to himself, and his English, needed for the mourners who weren't Italian, seemed stilted and strange. "I ask for your patience. Apparently my brother has been delayed." He bowed his head.

A flush of low voices and shifting bodies. The stonecutters would rather not wait for such a man, no longer one of their own.

Five minutes passed, filled with shifting bodies, whispers, tears. A few small brown birds began pecking at the mound of fresh earth as if to say life and death were one, an endless circle. Rosina saw Isabella and her mother among the mourners. Hopefully Marcello wouldn't come.

When ten minutes had passed with intolerable slowness, Carlo addressed the mourners again. "Thank you for your patience. We will have to begin without him." Moving to the wagon, he signaled to the twins, then asked Angelo to step in for Vittorio. "The cowardly bastard," he muttered under his breath as the four of them hoisted the pine casket off the wagon and onto the ground. The three boys stood quietly next to the pit as Carlo stepped forward.

"I have dreaded this day," he said, his voice rough. "I have no speech prepared. I know Gabriele would understand. All he would want is a few simple words and the promise, from all of us, not to forget him." He paused to wipe his eyes, and when he spoke again it was in Italian. If anyone didn't understand him, so be it, because today he needed his own language. "I don't need to tell you he was the best stonecutter in Barre. And one of the best in Viggiù. Or that he was a fine man, you know that too. Our mother called him an old soul because even as a boy he had more wisdom, sense, and compassion than most men. He deserved to live a long life. You men know this, and maybe you women too—Gabriele designed his stone. My sons and I will carve it." His voice was shaking now, and he couldn't control it, couldn't stop this pain that wanted to kill him. "It's as beautiful . . . as his soul. *O Dio mio, Dio mio.*"

He dropped to his knees and would have collapsed if Clementina hadn't knelt with him. They stayed like that, bent together, while Rosina sobbed quietly, arms wrapped around her body, half crushing the purple flowers she'd brought.

It was all Angelo could do not to go to her. She shouldn't be alone, but he could do nothing about that. Carlo had asked him to step in and he had, and Carlo needed him more than Rosina did. Quietly, he took four shovels from the wagon and placed them next to the grave.

Donata asked for volunteers to help lower the casket, and as several men came forward Carlo struggled to his feet. "No." He had to be strong. Had to bury his brother. Not a chance in hell he'd let anyone stand in for him. "I can do it." He gathered himself, then nodded to the boys, and they took their places.

When the coffin was in the ground, Carlo scattered in handfuls of dirt. Donata pulled off a glove and did the same. Both bowed their heads. "Rest in peace, *mio caro fratello*," Carlo said. "May God welcome you into his kingdom." Then he and the twins and Angelo filled the grave with dirt as weighted and immovable as granite.

Rosina spread the purple asters she'd gathered on the mounded earth, then knelt to pray. Rising afterward, she came face-to-face with Marcello. She greeted him curtly, then moved away.

"Rosina, wait! I'm sorry about your uncle." Marcello opened his arms in a pleading gesture. "And about what I did that night. Honest, I am."

"This isn't the time or place for that," she said. "Now please excuse me, I need to be with my family."

One by one, the mourners filed past the family to pay their respects. So many of them had brought flowers that the mounded soil bloomed with color, and bouquets and wreaths covered the grass nearby. Rosina was thanking Giorgio, who was last in line and clearly hoping to linger, when she noticed an approaching figure. Abandoning Giorgio, she said, "Mamma, look over there, it's Zia Marietta."

Clementina put a hand on her husband's arm, a warning to be civil. "Carlo, Marietta is here."

She arrived out of breath, her eyes bright with tears. "Oh dear, I'm too late. I'm so sorry. My deepest condolences." She hugged and kissed the women, and she would have kissed Carlo if his voice, low with fury, hadn't brought her up short.

"And your husband, where is he? He can't be bothered to come to his brother's funeral?" Trembling, he ignored Clementina's nails digging into his arm. To hell with decorum.

"I am deeply sorry," Marietta said. "You have every right to be angry. I apologize for my husband. He intended to come, but he was simply too distraught. I hoped to convince him or I would have arrived sooner. We are all devastated, truly. Daniele and Cosimo send their condolences."

"Too distraught?" Carlo snorted. "Too heartless is more like it."

"Thank you for coming, Marietta," Donata said.

"You must know I loved Gabriele very much, and I have missed him these past few years. All of you." Marietta took an envelope from her purse. "Please take this for the funeral expenses."

Carlo's eyes cut her. "Has my brother lost his mind? He sides with the people who could have saved Gabriele, doesn't have the decency to come to his funeral, and now he dares to offend me by giving me money? *Non ci credo*, it's beyond belief!"

Marietta paled, trembling.

"Carlo, please," Clementina said, "you're being unfair. Vittorio couldn't have saved Gabriele, you know that. Try to—"

"Try to what?" Carlo shouted. "Calm down? I don't want to calm down! My heart is breaking and I'm livid as hell that the only brother I've got left couldn't bother to mourn with his family."

"It's not Marietta who deserves your anger," Donata said.

"No, it's our brother, *quel figlio di puttana*!" As Marietta cringed at his vulgarity, Carlo felt the fight drain out of him. He was so tired, so goddamn tired. Of the strike, the fighting, the violence, of beating his head against the wall. Of being stupid enough to believe that men would do the right thing when they could, even if it cost them.

He took Marietta's hand. "Forgive me, I spoke in anger. I know Vittorio isn't responsible and I know you mean well. Thank you, but the Mutual Aid Society paid for the casket and half of the undertaker's services. They would have given more, but with the strike lasting so long..."

"Take it, Carlo," Clementina said.

"No. I had hoped for my brother's presence, not his money."

"It's not his," said Marietta, and everyone went silent. "It's mine. Years ago, when every dime we had was going toward the Milano, I took in sewing to help pay our expenses. I put some of the money aside in case we needed it later. As it happened, we didn't." She lifted her chin. "Vittorio doesn't know about it. It's mine to use as I wish."

"How kind of you!" Rosina hugged her aunt. "Papà, Zia is being very thoughtful and generous. It would be rude not to take her gift."

Carlo turned to Paolo and Nico, who exchanged glances, then nodded in unison.

"All right, then," Carlo said. "It appears I'm outnumbered."

Clementina accepted the envelope from Marietta. "It's truly kind of you, my dear. Will you walk back to town with us?"

"I believe I'll pay my respects and rest for a little while. It was a long walk up the hill."

Carlo was about to make a nasty remark about Vittorio forcing his wife to walk to the cemetery instead of escorting her in his car, but Clementina's eyes pierced him.

"I'll stay too," Angelo said, stepping forward. "If that's all right. I don't mean to intrude. I thought I'd fix up these flowers here on the ground."

"That's very kind of you," Clementina said.

"When you're ready, I'll walk back with you, ma'am," he said to Marietta. "I've got a strong arm to lean on."

"I'll keep you company, Zia," said Rosina.

"Let's go home," Carlo said to Clementina. "Donata, are you coming?"

Arm in arm, the trio set off across the grass. Carlo was bone-tired, his body aching like an old man's. If his luck turned out to be better than Gabriele's, he might live long enough to find out what true old age felt like. Luck was only half of it, though. If he wanted to live to see his grandchildren, better yet watch them grow up, he had to keep fighting for what he knew was right. The stonecutters, especially his sons, deserved no less. But not today. Today he had no fight left in him.

Angelo began to sort the flowers and wreaths, figuring out how they'd look best encircling the grave. Rosina and Marietta settled on the grass, shoulder to shoulder, watching.

"He has a good eye, doesn't he?" Marietta said.

"I have to choose one of Zio's drawings for him. He asked me to."

"Let the boy choose it himself."

"You're right, I will."

Rosina leaned her head on her aunt's shoulder, grateful for her companionship. Seeing Marcello, today of all days, had shaken her, more than she'd like to admit. She'd avoided the Battaglias' shop since the evening at the bandstand, and until now it seemed Marcello had been avoiding her too. Would his apology be the end of it, or would he bide his time, then come crawling back, confident that he could charm her? She'd be happy to fizzle his confidence.

And then what? Must she endure Giorgio again? If so, at least she knew he would never lay a hand on her. Why weren't there more sweet, kind men like Zio Gabriele in this cruel world? She missed him terribly. How empty the house felt, how devastating it was to want to tell him something and then remember she couldn't. Never again.

"Oh Zia, I miss him." Rosina wept. Marietta murmured comfort, smoothing her niece's hair.

When Rosina looked up again, Angelo was surveying his work.

"What a beautiful display," said Marietta.

"It is, truly," Rosina said. "Like a blanket of colors to keep him warm."

Angelo beamed. "That was the idea."

"Are you ready to go, Zia? I am."

Angelo offered a hand to Marietta, then to Rosina. "Thank you," she said. "Will you walk Zia home? I'm sure Mamma needs me." She kissed her aunt goodbye, nodded to Angelo. *How kindhearted he is*, she thought as she hurried off. He acted like he was part of the family, taking Vittorio's place and arranging the flowers.

The thought made her stop, stock-still.

Well, he wasn't. She marched on. She couldn't think about him now, couldn't worry about men at all. Forget Angelo, forget Marcello and Giorgio. She had an uncle to grieve for, work to think about, money to earn. That was enough.

The next morning Vittorio drove to Hope, dread mounting. The thought of his brother's fresh grave renewed his loss, which he could not have prevented no matter how desperately he wanted to, and the shame of his absence the day before, which he certainly could have.

The previous evening had been hell. Marietta had arrived home from the cemetery hours later than he'd expected, dismissed the housekeeper, then sat in the parlor all evening with a bottle of sherry. This from a woman who never drank more than a thimbleful at a time. After nine o'clock had come and gone, he'd inquired about dinner. That was a mistake.

"I'm sure you can find some bread and ham," Marietta said, her voice filled with disdain. "After what you did to your family today, I have no appetite." The implication, Vittorio understood quite clearly, was that he shouldn't have one either.

"Carlo was a wreck and rightfully so," she continued. "I can't imagine he'll ever forgive you. And I know Donata was hurt, though she'd never say so."

"You're wrong about that." Vittorio rubbed his temples, wondering if he dared ask where his wife kept the pain tonic. "She came to my study this evening and spoke her mind. Rather colorfully, in fact."

"Good." Marietta refilled her glass. "I'd like to be alone now. I had Miss Simpson fix up the guest bedroom. Your things are in there."

Too stunned to argue, Vittorio had retreated. Never had his wife been so cold and unforgiving. He'd spent a miserable night feeling like a beaten dog, and now he was about to visit his brother's grave, alone. His own doing.

Leaving the path, he trudged across the damp grass to the family plot. Flowers carpeted the fresh mound, cascading onto the ground in streams of color. Proof, he thought, of the abundant love for a good man. He was glad no monument stood there yet; for now, at least, he could avoid the reality, the permanence, of his brother's death carved in stone. On a marker of his own design, which—shame rising again, sickening, smothering—Vittorio hadn't seen. He hadn't even asked Gabriele what he'd had in mind, though, in his own defense, it had seemed a question best left unasked.

The cemetery was quiet, offering a sense of refuge that Vittorio rejected. Perhaps in a year or two or twenty he would come here and feel at peace, but not today. The heavy air choked him, floral scents mixed with the tang of damp earth in a perfume so thick he could taste it. His eyes watered. Dear Gabriele. How could he be gone when they had been boys not long ago?

He stood next to the grave, head bowed, measuring his loss, acknowledging his regret. No words could capture the layers of emotion and conflict in his heart. What would he have said about Gabriele at his graveside yesterday? Did he have knowledge Carlo wasn't privy to, some tale only he himself could share? How well had he known his brother? When he thought of him, he pictured a quiet child, a naive young man, the brilliant artist he'd become. Could he honestly say he knew what his brother had held dear in his heart and mind?

Gazing at the grave, he noticed a rolled-up paper tucked into the flowers. He bent over to retrieve it and lost his balance, his fingers sinking into the soft earth. He snatched his hand back, horrified to think of what lay beneath the imprint left behind.

He unfurled the paper. It was a portrait, a charcoal likeness of Gabriele so true it kicked at the heart. Wearing a stonecutter's hat and leaning on a block of granite, he looked as animated as he'd ever been in life, his eyes alight as if telling a story he loved to share. And now that light, that spirit, was gone. Choking back tears, Vittorio surveyed the grounds, hoping to see a friend, a stranger, anyone at all. What was he doing here alone? He should have endured the cold shoulders from the stonecutters, paid his respects to Gabriele, to his family. Kept his dignity. He'd been selfish, monstrously so.

Dropping heavily to the ground, he wept. He had driven a wedge between himself and his brothers, distanced himself. Christ, he'd even made his home on the opposite side of town. He hadn't realized his choices could destroy their family. He'd been blind. Stupid. And self-righteous to think it was up to Carlo to come to him or for Gabriele to intervene when the right thing, the honorable thing, was to meet Carlo halfway. And then the strike had made everything worse. He was exhausted, worn out by all the conflict, the anger, the waking up in the morning wondering what harm or hurt the day would bring. What harm or hurt he himself would cause. It was unthinkable that he and Carlo would spend the rest of their lives at each other's throats. He couldn't lose both his brothers.

He struggled to his feet, rescued the sketch from the damp grass. A beautiful tribute, it belonged here, yet he couldn't leave it to be ruined by dew and rain. Carlo should see it.

The steps creaked under Vittorio's feet, two flights of claustrophobia in the narrow stairwell. On the first landing he wiped his palms, on the second he took off his hat. Steeled himself and knocked.

An unsmiling Clementina opened the door. "I'll get Carlo." She gestured him in.

He barely remembered the place. Jackets and shawls hung from hooks by the door, and a horsehair sofa stood beneath windows framed by simple white curtains. A table in the far corner held a few coins, a crumpled stonecutter's hat, a deck of cards, a pocketknife. He stepped toward the mantel to look at a framed photo of Carlo and Clementina, smiling in their wedding finery. Viggiù, a lifetime ago. Marietta, Agnese, and Donata stood on one side of the bride and groom, Vittorio, Gabriele, and Pietro, Donata's husband, on the other. Eight smiling, hopeful faces. Eight young people who couldn't wait to see what the future would bring. And now three of them were gone.

"Vittorio." Carlo stood in the kitchen doorway, suspenders hanging at his waist.

"Carlo." Vittorio opened his arms, then let them fall. "I'm here to apologize."

"The person who should hear your apology is dead."

Vittorio flinched. "Please, may I sit?"

Carlo gestured toward the sofa but remained standing. Clementina reappeared to ask if the men would like coffee, and Carlo crossed his arms. "No," he said, "my brother isn't staying long."

Though the rudeness irked Vittorio, he let it go. He would say his piece and get out.

"I was wrong. I hurt you and Donata, the whole family, and I'm sorry. My wife barely speaks to me. I won't humiliate myself further by making excuses. I want you to know I'll regret not burying my brother for the rest of my life. For not sharing that burden with you. And for not closing the Milano so my sons could be there too."

"Good."

Vittorio handed him the drawing. "Have you seen this?"

"What is it?" Carlo unrolled the paper and his face crumpled. "Who did this?"

"I don't know. It was on his grave. Please, keep it."

Carlo stared at the drawing, his jaw working. Something gave way deep inside him, a further softening of his resolve. Enough was enough, the strike had to end. They had failed. He had failed. He thanked God that Gabriele would never know it.

"I'm going to call a vote."

Vittorio didn't reply. He was gazing at the ceiling as if his thoughts were written there.

"Did you hear me?"

"I think," Vittorio said, shifting his gaze to his brother, "you should wait."

"What are you talking about? It's what you want."

"Allow me a last-ditch effort, if you would. Please." Too little too late. Still, he felt compelled to try. "Some of the shed owners are complaining about having to turn down orders that are beyond the scabs' ability. They do a good enough job, but good enough isn't sustainable. Cutters like you and Gabriele don't grow on trees. Let me see if I can get the shed owners to discuss the possibility of a settlement. Bear in mind that even if I can convince them to negotiate, I can't promise terms you'll like." Vittorio put on his hat. "Give me a week. And not a word to anyone, I beg you."

"Not a word."

Carlo followed him to the door, and for a moment Vittorio thought he might call him back, offer him that cup of coffee. Wishful thinking. Reconciliation, he knew full well, wouldn't come that easily.

TWENTY-TWO

VITTORIO HAD KEPT HIS WORD. Two days after his talk with Carlo, the shed owners convened in a meeting that went nowhere. No negotiations, no compromise.

No surprise, thought Carlo when Vittorio came to him in defeat.

The next morning the boys were gone when he got up, Rosina too. Carlo hoped that meant a birth, another few dollars in the family till. After bolting his breakfast, he kissed Clementina goodbye without telling her his plan. No need to get her hopes up, though he was confident the men were ready for a vote. On his way out of the house he nearly went to check on Gabriele, reigniting loss like a hand gripping his throat.

The hours before dawn had brought rain and thunder, but the storm had passed, leaving only occasional showers. Despite the sunlight filtering through the clouds, Carlo couldn't shake off his sense of foreboding. He had no reason to worry more than he did any day, yet the feeling persisted that he would regret setting this day in motion.

At quarter to seven the Meadow was quiet apart from the usual shed ruckus and heave of machinery at the construction site, now a mud pit due to the rain. He found the twins and Angelo sitting on the Labor Hall steps under umbrellas, smoking. Their picket signs lay on the ground, wet and torn. These days no one had the will to make new ones.

"Heard anything?" Carlo said.

"Nah, all quiet." Nico ditched his cigarette.

"I'm calling a vote. Spread the word, tomorrow at noon."

"It's time," Paolo said. The four men picked up their signs and fell into step. Man by man, the skeleton night shift crew peeled away.

By midafternoon, the last threat of rain gone and the air so thick you could touch it, Carlo knew something wasn't right. The premonition had barely kicked in when a dozen stonecutters arrived outside of their shift, armed with clubs and walking fast and deliberate to a sitting train car loaded with stone. Some climbed aboard, others ringed the car with clubs at the ready. One fellow, name of Pierantonio Montanara, sat himself on top of a granite block. Their presence prevented the scabs from looping chains around the stone, which meant a crane couldn't lift it and the stone would remain uncarved. Carlo didn't like it, but at least it was a peaceful form of resistance. For now. He hoped the scabs had enough sense to know those clubs were intended for their heads.

An hour passed, then two. Someone handed out beers to the train car men. Whenever a scab came within ten feet of the car, one of the men took a well-aimed piss. Pierantonio sang from time to time, mostly ditties with filthy lyrics, and sometimes the other train car men joined him. Mostly they didn't. Too much effort, and besides, who had the heart?

The picketers plodded, muddy and sullen and bored, in a ragged line that no longer made it as far as City Hall. No one took lunch—again, too much effort. The train car men hung on, clubs dangling. Pierantonio stood and stretched. It occurred to Carlo that all the men might feel like he did, their empty stomachs twisting with worry. From time to time he tried to talk the train car men down and got laughed at or spat upon, or told to mind his own fucking business because they'd had it up to here. If a man wanted to carve this piece of rock, he'd have to do it with a broken head.

The hours inched by. One minute before five o'clock, time stopped, the way it does in those split seconds before a gathering storm unleashes its power. Then a shot pierced the air and Pierantonio was dead, face down on the bleeding stone with a bullet through his head. The picketers spun around, tried to make sense of what they saw. From all sides, dozens of men came running, each one armed, each one ready and eager to give Pierantonio company in whatever hell or heaven he'd gone to. Screaming at the men to abandon the train car, they took aim. An odd quiet fell as work in the sheds ground to a halt, broken seconds later as the scabs poured outside, their faces either appalled or triumphant. Message sent and received.

Trapped in a web bristling with guns, the men on the car dropped to the ground, hands up. The mob—hired guns, not a familiar face among them—marched them out of the Meadow toward City Hall, at which point the Meadow became a mass of movement and sound. Some of the strikers were frantic with rage, others wept, others collapsed in despair, heads in hands. Nico was on the ground, Angelo kneeling beside him. Paolo stood, bowed and pale faced.

Carlo wasn't the first to reach Pierantonio. Four men hauled his body down while another ran to get the coroner. One man took off his shirt and covered the dead man's face, then sat next to him as if he needed protection.

Numbed with shock, Carlo sagged against the train car. Acid burned his throat. It would be a wife who received bad news today, and she would hear it, as she must, from him. For the love of God, he was sick of the suffering and the futility. Sickened that another man was dead, and for nothing.

He went to his sons, embraced them. The next day, they would vote.

That night, close to ten o'clock, Rosina left home to tend to Mrs. Riva, who'd gone into labor with her first child early and fast. From the first instant there was blood, so much that Rosina sent the husband to fetch a doctor, and hopefully Donata too. The placenta was blocking the birth canal, tearing as the canal widened. The mound of scarlet towels, sheets, and blankets grew quickly, blood coating Mrs. Riva's legs and Rosina's hands. Ghost white and breathing fast, Mrs. Riva seemed barely aware of the baby inside her or her body's relentless work. When Donata arrived, her face revealed that she had little hope for this mother and her child. By the time the doctor got there, Mrs. Riva and her baby were dead.

"Placenta previa, a perilous condition," the doctor said, covering the body with the bloodied sheet. "My sister died of it. Nothing you could have done, but you know that. I'll notify the coroner."

When the doctor had gone, Mr. Riva sat weeping next to his dead wife and child. Donata spoke to him quietly, a hand on his shoulder, and he nodded, face buried in his handkerchief. "Let's give him some privacy," she said to Rosina, and they went into the parlor to wait for the coroner.

Rosina sat on the sofa, then stood, too agitated to keep still. "It happened so fast. And all that blood! I've never been so terrified." She wiped away tears. "I keep thinking we could have done something."

"I won't tell you it gets easier, *cara*. As difficult as it is to accept what happened, you must remember that you did everything that could be done. Midwives are not miracle workers."

"I'm afraid the next birth will be the same."

"Learn to put your fear aside or it will do you in, and the mothers you attend as well. If you're afraid, they'll be afraid, and that's not good for anyone. No more tears now. The coroner should be here soon and you must be strong for Mr. Riva. I'll be at home if you need to talk."

After the coroner had come and gone, Rosina set about cleaning the bedroom. She offered to take the bedding home to wash it, but Mr. Riva said no, he would burn it. She understood. He needed no reminders of this day, especially not when he was alone at night in his bed.

Walking home, her mind in turmoil, she thought about her aunt's warning to put fear aside. She had known women could die in childbirth, or weeks later from infection, but contemplating the possibility of death wasn't like seeing it happen. Only once had she seen a woman die, and she had been in Donata's care, an older mother of six children and already sick, weakened by influenza. This was different, a healthy young woman, her first child. Rosina squeezed her hands into fists, choked with grief. The way clean white towels could wick dark with blood within seconds—how was it possible that a human body held so much blood and that it could come out so fast?

Her legs trembled but she couldn't stop, for if she did she would never move again. Two human beings in her care were dead. She could put aside her fear but not her sense of responsibility, not her conscience. How could she go to another lying-in with this carnage, this tragedy, this dead mother and child forever burned into her memory? How could she, knowing it could happen again and almost certainly would? Her worries about marriage, about children coming at too high a price, seemed shallow and petty now. Compared to the suffering of the Riva family, they were nothing.

She stopped, realization cutting to the bone. In truth, what came at too high a price was being a midwife.

She forced herself onward, one step, then another. The doctor and Zia Donata were right, Mrs. Riva and her baby couldn't have been saved. Still, she had failed them. She hadn't been herself since the funeral, had gone to the lying-in with grief clouding her mind. A midwife couldn't let her own life get in the way of her work. She wanted to help women, not play a part in their deaths. She gasped as the knowledge sank in. She would have to find another way.

She dropped her birthing bag, took off her Nonnatus medal. The chain lay coiled in her palm, its medal as useless as slag. She considered tossing it into a row of bushes but dropped it into her bag instead.

Walking again, one foot after the other. Was there no end to grief? To loss? Zio Gabriele, this mother and her child, her own future that she wanted so badly. How quickly she'd come to think of herself as a midwife, and now she would never be one again. Who was she, then? No one. A young woman without hope.

PART III

LIFE

TWENTY-THREE

FOURTEEN HUNDRED UNION MEN, GIVE OR TAKE, streamed into the Labor Hall to cast their votes—*yes* to return to work, *no* to maintain the strike. When the tally was done, 1,383 men had voted *yes*. The strike was over. Carlo was so relieved that his legs failed him and he sat where he stood, right there on the floor. Dear God, how good it would feel to get back to work, to create beauty instead of watching families suffer. He would give written notice to the shed owners that evening.

Paolo hauled Carlo to his feet and slapped his back. "We did it, it's over. Come on, chin up!" He forced his father to look at him, said the words he knew his father needed to hear. "We did what we could, the best we could, you hear me? We're with you, Papà, this time and next time. We're not done by a long shot."

Next time? Next time was beyond imagining.

Once he'd gotten his voice back, Carlo spoke forcefully to the men, warning them not to carry their hostilities with them. No one knew who'd hired the thugs who shot Pierantonio, and no one was going to find out, so it was best not to go around casting accusatory looks at any shed owner they thought seemed guilty. Carlo didn't state the obvious, that the ringleader was most likely whoever the train car's stone had been destined for. He did say that the train car sitters who'd been dragged down to City Hall had gotten off with a reprimand, so no one should have a beef about that. As for Pierantonio's funeral, donations were welcome, and he expected to see every last goddamn one of them at Hope Cemetery the day the man's body went into the ground. And if anyone so much as breathed the air near the site of the Lombardi-Bottinelli shed he would personally rip their lungs out.

As they left the Hall, Angelo said to Nico, "It's the right thing, isn't it? To end the strike?" He wished like hell he could have put a big *YES* on one of those slips of paper. "We'll have another chance when the IWW—"

"If we don't die first." Nico cut him off, then slapped him on the back by way of apology. "Hey, I'm a little short-fused these days. By the way, I'd stay away from my father for a while if I were you. He's going to need some time."

The next morning, five months after the men had traded their tools for picket signs, the seven o'clock whistles blew and the workers strode into the sheds past the scabs milling around the doors. Carlo was prepared for some last-minute violence if the scabs dragged their feet, prepared too for tension and high tempers as the shed owners and the union men returned to sharing their turf. What a relief, then, that the scabs kept quiet and the Barre men kept their fists to themselves.

Vittorio had arrived at the Meadow early, as concerned as Carlo that the transition wouldn't go well. Instead, the men came back to work with their dignity intact, or as much dignity as a bunch of roughnecks could have. It was enough. If Lombardi hadn't been there he'd have applauded them for their determination and commitment, for standing up for themselves and, in the long run, every stonecutter in America.

Wait, he thought as he followed Lombardi into the shed, was this pride he felt? Good God, his stonecutter's blood must run deeper than he realized. Something had to be done about *mal d'america*, and *would* be done; it was a matter of time. Hell, if he got somewhere in this town, if he gained enough clout to have the ear of the health commissioner, he'd insist on some action. And if Lombardi didn't like it, he could find himself a new partner.

An hour later Vittorio was at the bank, tasked with picking up cash to pay the scabs. As the teller counted out stacks of bills with maddening slowness, he drummed his fingers. Lombardi was back at the shed, stationed outside at the desk they'd hauled from the back office and planted outside. Two armed men flanked the desk, ready for any scabs who didn't take kindly to the news they were out of work or for any union man who wanted to give them a going-away present. Vittorio had tried to talk Lombardi out of the show of force, but the man wouldn't listen.

Finally, cash in hand, he joined Lombardi at the desk, checking off names as the pay envelopes went out. Only sour looks and a few insults interrupted the morning's peace. Vittorio bestowed some sour looks of his own on the line of scabs snaking away from the table. Good riddance to them, these men who'd put their own needs first, who had no interest in the common good. Then he burst out laughing. First he'd sounded like a stonecutter, and now a goddamn socialist! Had the world turned upside down?

"What's funny?" Lombardi said.

"Nothing. I'm glad the strike is over, that's all." It was the truth, though only part of it. There had to be common ground. There had to be a way to secure the needs of businesses and protect the workers at the same time. It bore thinking about.

A man stepped up to the table, eyes downcast. "Name?" Vittorio checked him off the list and pointed at Lombardi. "Get your money from him. The next train leaves at quarter past eleven. I don't care where you're going, make sure you're on it." He hoped the man heard the contempt in his voice.

The end of the strike. The end of one chapter in the history of Barre and the beginning of another. An idea was taking shape, growing with surprising speed. It wasn't going to be easy and Marietta might protest, but his gut told him he was on to something.

"Next!" Vittorio lifted his chin, filled with newfound pride to be part of the granite industry again, this time wearing a different hat. And pleased as punch that Lombardi had no idea what color Vittorio's next hat would be.

By the time the noon whistles sounded, word had spread about a back-to-work celebration at Rebuzzi's place a week from Saturday, with beer and wine and cockfighting, the chance to fill one's pockets or empty them. Rebuzzi lived on an isolated stretch of South Main, a few blocks from the firehouse and a stone's throw from the city limits. A hard-packed patch of dirt behind the shoebox house had seen plenty of cockfights, plenty of money lost and won. Rebuzzi took a cut because he took the risk. Cockfighting was illegal, as was the gambling. Not that anyone gave a damn. The men were eager to throw their first week's wages away on drink and chance, no matter how much their wives and sweethearts might complain. It had been a long haul, this walkout, and they needed to blow off steam, have some laughs. No better way than a drunken celebration to rebuild the bonds that had been stretched thin to breaking.

As if the strike ending wasn't excitement enough, that evening the men would turn out in force for another event, this one at the Opera House. The timing set Carlo on edge, but there was nothing to be done because the date had been fixed months before. Half of Barre, anarchists and socialists and capitalists, stonecutters and quarrymen and business owners alike had marked their calendars for the big event—a speech by that outspoken anarchist Emma Goldman, a ball-breaker if ever there was one. Carlo prayed no one would cause a rumble.

At quarter to eight that evening, Rosina perched on the edge of her seat at the Opera House, buzzing with excitement at the prospect of hearing Emma Goldman speak. Sandwiched between her two aunts, she tried to ignore Donata's chilly demeanor.

It hadn't been easy to tell her aunt she was giving up midwifery. She had gone to Washington Street to break the news, begged Marietta to stay with her for moral support. Donata looked wary while Rosina made small talk, her nervousness in plain view. Finally Marietta suggested she get on with it and Rosina blurted, "I don't want to be a midwife anymore," then kept going, talking too much, explaining that the decision had been difficult but it was for the best, and she was grateful for everything Donata had done for her, and for having faith in her, and she'd never forget any of it, ever.

Donata had said nothing except "I see," her gaze biting enough to wither grapes on the vine.

Marietta had escaped then, going to the kitchen for tea and cookies, and Rosina used the interruption to retrieve her birthing bag from behind the sofa where she'd hidden it. "You should have this. Everything is there, the Pinard horn and plenty of supplies. Except the notebook. I've written in it." She smiled halfheartedly.

Donata regarded her icily and said nothing.

"You've been so generous. I hope you know how grateful I am, for everything you gave me and taught me." She was repeating herself, a stupid squawking parakeet. Staring at the pattern on the rug, she added, "I'm sorry to disappoint you. Truly."

At that Donata softened. "I know you are. And you're free to make your own decisions, of course." Her voice was sad and her face weary, which made Rosina feel worse than ever. "But please, keep the bag. I don't expect you to return a gift, and you may find that you need it after all."

"Here we go!" Marietta said cheerfully, bustling in with a tray of tea and cookies. Behind her lumbered Carmela, enormously with child.

"Oh! I didn't know!" Rosina said. "Congratulations to you and Daniele. When is the baby due?"

"Early next month." Carmela popped an entire cookie in her mouth. "I don't like to say the date, it's bad luck." Avoiding Donata's eyes, she busied herself with another cookie. "Dr. Samuelson will deliver him. We're sure it's a boy," she added emphatically, apparently pleased with her body for obeying her wishes.

So, Carmela was one of those women Marcello's mother had mentioned, convinced by their doctors that midwives were dirty and ignorant. How could she be like that, living in the same house as Zia Donata and knowing how respected she was? Rosina wanted to snap at Carmela, but Donata didn't react at all.

Later, as Rosina was leaving, Marietta tried to reassure her that the news was understandably difficult for Donata to accept, coming as it did on the heels of Gabriele's death, but with time she would come around. Rosina made Marietta promise to accompany them to the Opera House. She and Donata had made their plans long ago, but given the circumstances Rosina dreaded being alone with her. Finally she'd escaped, relieved that neither of her aunts had asked her what she planned to do for work. She had no idea.

The auditorium was overstuffed with men in suits or shirtsleeves and women in their Sunday best. Rosina tapped Donata's shoulder and pointed. "Look over there, it's Mrs. Tompkins and Miss O'Flaherty from the suffrage group," she said with false gaiety. "There are quite a few women here. At least fifty, wouldn't you say?"

Donata murmured polite sounds that might have been agreement. Rosina sighed and went back to watching the crowd. Daniele and Cosimo were there, surprising given their stouthearted allegiance to their father and his politics. Not that she'd ever heard them express a political opinion of their own. They were more like Zio Gabriele, God rest his soul, preferring to listen while everyone else spewed opinions left and right. Vittorio wasn't sitting with them, which she assumed meant he wasn't coming. Angelo caught her eye and waved. He looked happy. Her father and the twins too, everyone. Now that the strike was over, the whole town seemed lighter.

She made another survey of the room and ended up back at Angelo. He was talking to Nico now, both of them animated, exuberant as puppies. When Angelo laughed his whole face lit up. She'd never noticed that before. And his hair was longer now, his curls looser. The length suited him. She made herself look away, certain he knew she was watching him. Did he know she'd quit midwifery? Not unless Nico had mentioned it, and why would he? What would he think of her if he knew? He'd had such confidence in her. Probably he'd be as disappointed as Zia Donata was. That was all she'd done lately, disappoint people. First Giorgio, then Marcello (who didn't matter), then her mother when she learned that even though Marcello was out of the picture (no explanation given), Rosina refused to see Giorgio again. Then, worst of all, Zia Donata.

"Rosina, are you well?" Marietta said, startling her.

"Oh! Yes. Only I wish they'd start. I can't believe Emma Goldman is here."

"Who were you waving at over there?" Marietta peered in Angelo's direction.

"Oh. Angelo Lucci. Remember him from the cemetery?"

"Indeed I do. He's a fine young man, isn't he? Your mother likes him."

"You're as bad as she is! Don't get any ideas, Zia. We're friends, that's all." Who never saw each other anymore. Who had kissed. Twice. Rosina flushed.

"Indeed." Marietta's eyebrows rose into delicate arches of doubt.

Another wave of arrivals pressed into the auditorium and soon the walls were lined with standees. "We're ready for you, Miss Goldman," one fellow shouted, and his friends laughed, egging him on. "Come on out here and try to convert us to your infidel, anarchist ways!"

When Miss Goldman finally took the stage to applause and shouts and jeers, Rosina noted with surprise how petite the woman was, except for her head, which was far too large for her narrow shoulders.

Her fame had made her seem bigger than life. She knew how to make people listen, though, because everyone had an opinion about her. The crowd was fired up, the room vibrating, and the woman hadn't even opened her mouth yet.

After being introduced by Luigi Galleani, the publisher of *Cronaca Sovversiva*, Goldman welcomed everyone and said she was honored to speak in the labor-strong city of Barre. Given the recent strike, she would address the issue of workers' rights, a core concept of anarchism. If time permitted, she would touch on women's rights as well, in particular the question of marriage.

"Is marriage a question?" Rosina whispered to Marietta, who laughed and said apparently it was. She would have made the joke to Donata too, if she hadn't been a grumpy gargoyle.

Emma Goldman put on a pair of spectacles and began. "Anarchism, to the great teachers and leaders in the spiritual aspect of life, was not a dogma that drains the blood from the heart and makes people zealots, dictators, or impossible bores. Anarchism is a releasing and liberating force because it teaches people to rely on their own possibilities, teaches them faith in liberty, and inspires men and women to strive for a state of social life where everyone shall be free and secure."

"Free or a free-for-all?" shouted one of the Main Street shopkeepers. "That's what we'd have without a government to give us structure." A few other men called out in support, and Goldman waited for them to quiet down before continuing.

"There is neither freedom nor security in the world today. Whether one be rich or poor, whether his station high or low, no one is secure as long as there is a single slave in the world. No one is safe or secure as long as he must submit to the orders, whim, or will of another who has the power to punish him, to send him to prison or to take his life, to dictate the terms of his existence."

A man in the front row jumped up and yelled, "Or send him to an early grave by making him breathe stone dust all day!" His friends clapped him on the back as he sat. The crowd rumbled, voices raised, and an edge of unrest rippled across the room.

Luigi Galleani stepped to the podium. "You're entitled to your opinions, but tonight it's Miss Goldman's turn to speak. Those who want to hear what the fine folk of Barre have to say can do so on their own time."

After that, Goldman continued for a good thirty minutes without interruption. "Anarchism rests on faith in humanity and its potentialities," she said. "Nowadays most people believe that the stronger the government, the greater the success of society will be. It is the old belief in the rod. We have emancipated ourselves from that stupidity. We have learned that freedom in the development of the child secures better results, both so far as the child and society are concerned."

She paused to survey the room. "That, ladies and gentlemen, is anarchism. The greater the freedom and the opportunities for every unit in society, the finer will be the individual and the better for society. Anarchism is not a cut-and-dried theory. It is a vital spirit embracing all of life. Therefore I do not address myself only to the workers. I address myself to the upper classes as well, for indeed they need enlightenment even more than the workers."

Freedom and opportunities for everyone, Rosina thought. For us too, we women. She squeezed Marietta's hand.

"Enlightenment? That'll be the day!" shouted a man in shirtsleeves. "Why don't you try telling the shed owners to get enlightened?" With that, a scuffle erupted in the back of the room. The shouting and shoving and crashing of overturned chairs lasted less than a minute before six policemen hauled the unruly bunch outside.

Galleani suggested it was time to wrap things up, seeing as the crowd was so rowdy. Goldman insisted on saying a few words about marriage first, to expand on the idea that anarchism strives to maximize the individual's—meaning men's—possibilities without the confines of an oppressive government. "Therefore," she said, "women should be granted the same right to those possibilities without the confines of a marriage based on the need for financial security. Some people believe that marriage is the only security for the woman, for the child, the family, the State. But it is no security to love, and without love no true home can or does exist. Without love no child should be born, without love no true woman can be related to a man. I believe when a woman signs her own emancipation, her first declaration of independence will consist in admiring and loving a man for the qualities of his heart and mind and not for the quantities in his pocket."

At that, the crowd erupted in applause and shouts and catcalls. Galleani announced that the event was over and asked everyone to leave peaceably. "Miss Goldman thanks you for coming tonight and hopes her ideas will . . ."

His words were lost in the clamor. As her aunts stood to go, Rosina sat there, stunned. What Goldman said about women and independence, about not being bound to a man because of his money, about loving him for his heart and mind—it was as if she had seen inside Rosina's heart.

"Are you coming, dear?" Marietta said.

Rosina stood. "She gives me hope," she said with wonder.

"Indeed," said Donata, whose mood had brightened. "I'm glad she mentioned emancipation. It will only come when women have the vote."

"You're right, Zia." When women were heard, change would come, bringing the freedom they deserved. "How brave she was to talk about women's independence in a roomful of men! I don't think she cares if her ideas cause a riot."

On the sidewalk, Rosina linked arms with her aunts, filled with determination and hope. It was true that she needed to find work, but until then, and later, whenever she wasn't working at whatever dreadful job she found, she would devote her time to the suffrage effort. There was no need to wait for picnics and parades to hand out flyers and sign up new members of the suffrage association. The time was now. Every day. Always.

"Zia Donata, listen! I have an idea."

TWENTY-FOUR

EARLY IN THE MORNING on the Saturday after Emma Goldman's speech, Rosina and Donata set up a table next to the bandstand and stocked it with dozens of flyers and a clipboard with an enrollment sheet. Across the front of the table, Rosina draped a banner she'd made that said, "Let Your Voice Be Heard! Join the Women's Suffrage Movement!" Her plan to advertise the Vermont Woman Suffrage Association at points around Barre several times a week had returned her to Donata's good graces, and thank heaven for that. She hoped to do the same in Williamstown and Graniteville and Montpelier, and any other town reachable by train in one day.

By lunchtime, two tall stacks of flyers were gone, the names of fifteen potential new members had been added to the enrollment sheet, and an old woman had berated Rosina and Donata for a solid ten minutes, calling them immoral and a disgrace to good women everywhere.

"I hope she complains to everyone she knows," Rosina said. "She'll help us get the word out."

"We're doing quite well without her," said Donata. "I'll need to print double the flyers for next time."

Rosina was chatting with a young woman trailing three children when Marcello approached. He glanced at one of the remaining flyers, then stuffed it in his pocket. Then he paced, glancing at Rosina repeatedly as if he had something urgent to say. She avoided making eye contact, happy to make him wait.

Finally she bade the young woman good day and marched over to Marcello. "Why are you here?"

"I never see you anymore. Can we talk?"

"About what?"

"Anything. I miss you. I apologized, didn't I?"

"Hush." She pulled him away from the table, out of Donata's hearing. "Saying you're sorry doesn't change anything. You didn't respect my wishes, which means you don't respect me."

"I do! I'm crazy about you. I made a mistake, that's all."

"Rosina," Donata called, "why don't you and your young man take a walk? I can finish up here."

"Please?" Marcello touched Rosina's arm.

"Oh, all right. Zia, I'll be back soon."

Marcello started up Washington Street toward Currier Park. "No," Rosina said. "I'm not going to the park with you. We're going to stay on the street where everyone can see us."

He held up both hands. "I won't touch you, I promise."

"You're right about that." She pointed toward Church Street. "That way. We'll make a quick loop, then I'm coming back to help my aunt clean up."

"What's all that about, anyway?" Marcello said, matching Rosina's brisk pace. He pulled the crumpled flyer from his pocket. "'Women, your voices need to be heard! Emancipation is our declaration of independence! Help us get the vote and become equal members of society!' Do you believe this stuff?"

"Yes, I do. It's the future. It *will* happen." Rosina marched along, chin lifted.

"I don't get it. You'd rather hand out flyers than spend time with me? I apologized, doesn't that mean something? I'm fond of you, I've said so. I told you I wasn't seeing anyone else, and I'm not. Including Isabella. I haven't so much as said hello to her."

Rosina whirled around. "Did you try to have your way with her too? Oh, don't bother answering, I can see it on your face. You're a fool to think she would let you when she wanted a ring. Go back to her. Maybe she still loves you."

"I don't want her, I want you."

They turned onto Averill Street, where a huge maple with yellow-tipped leaves stood in an open lot. "Please, let's sit over there," Marcello said. "No touching, no kissing. I want to talk to you without running, all right?"

He seemed so forlorn that she felt sorry for him. "For a minute." Tucking her skirts, she sat with her back against the tree.

"Speaking of a ring," Marcello said, "I've been thinking about marrying you since I met you."

"You have not."

"Why wouldn't I? You're pretty and smart and you make me laugh. You'll be twenty-one next year, and our shop is doing well again. And we're good together, or we were before. I promise that won't happen again. I can wait, honest."

"What about love, Marcello? And respect? Trust me, you don't want someone like me. I'm interested in politics and art and suffrage, and"—she threw up her hands—"I don't know, so many things! It's fine for women to stay home and raise a family if that's what they want, but they shouldn't be forced to give up everything else. I don't know if I'll ever marry, but if I do I'll still want to work. Would you want that? Would you help with the children and the chores, or pay for a housekeeper when I wasn't home?"

He blinked. "You want to be a midwife forever?"

"Yes!" Said without thinking. "I mean no. I, I'm not a midwife anymore."

"Why not?"

"It doesn't matter."

"Please tell me."

"I don't want to. Leave it alone, please."

"Okay, okay. But don't you see, that's good! If we marry you won't need to work. My father is making plans to expand, and when that happens I'll move up to manager. I could provide for us."

He was serious! Imagine that: He wasn't the unfeeling cad she'd thought he was, someone she could toss aside without guilt because he'd do the same to her. She'd let him down, maybe even broken his heart. How sad. She took a deep breath, let it out slowly. It pained her, but it changed nothing. In the ways that mattered most, he was who she thought he was, the opposite of what she wanted. He wanted what was familiar, what he'd grown up to expect. He would have no trouble finding a young woman eager to have his babies and clean his house and cook his meals. For him, that would be a good marriage.

"No," Rosina said gently. "You and I want different things, Marcello. I'm sorry to disappoint you. I have to go, my aunt is waiting. *Arrivederci*."

She left him sitting under the tree, his dejected face burned into her mind's eye. It had to be this way. He would never understand her. She couldn't explain to him what Emma Goldman had allowed her to understand, that having a traditional family life wasn't the necessary result of love. That she could have love and children, either or both, with marriage or without it, if she had the strength to bear judgment. And that being a workingwoman didn't mean she couldn't choose marriage or children, if the father of those children were enlightened enough. She could be like her aunt, a wife and mother, a workingwoman, a suffragette—an exhilarating thought, until she remembered she had no work. No laboring mothers awaited her help, no babies would give themselves into her hands. What else could she possibly do that would bring her the same joy and satisfaction? Art, certainly, but nothing else she could think of.

Up ahead, a maple towered above its neighbors, etching the sky with leaves blood red. If she narrowed her view to only the branches patterning the sky, it looked like one of her uncle's drawings. *Carissimo* Zio Gabriele, he had perceived the world differently from most people, and so did she. She would find a way to fit into this society made by men, for men. It was hers too. A woman's world.

We women. *Noi donne insieme*. *Grazie*, Zia Marietta.

And she still had her art, even if only for herself to enjoy. As soon as she found work she would buy those watercolors she wanted and then she would paste paintings of orange and red and yellow flowers all over her walls.

At the park, Donata was chatting with Mr. Halliday, who despite his wife and eight children seemed more than happy to indulge in good-natured argument with a single woman, albeit a widowed one. Was Zia a spark in his life, a safe way to revisit his flirtatious youth? Or a comfort, someone who expected him to be no more and no less than who he was? The opposite of Marcello, who saw only what he wanted to see.

Rosina arrived home from the park to find Angelo sitting on the porch steps. "What's the matter, my mother wouldn't let you in?"

"I didn't ring. I've got something to show you." He thumped a sketchbook perched on his knees.

"Can it wait? I'm late, and Mamma's expecting me to help with lunch. And I'm tired."

"Hey Angelo, how'd you get here so fast?" said Paolo, rounding the corner with Nico and Carlo. "I swear you were at the shed not two minutes ago."

"Stay and eat with us," Nico said.

"Nah, thanks. Your mother invited me for dinner before we go to Rebuzzi's."

"She did?" Why she was surprised, Rosina didn't know. In fact, she wouldn't be surprised if Giorgio would be there too. Her mother was relentless. She probably didn't sleep at night because of all her scheming.

"See you later, then." Nico pointed surreptitiously at Rosina, eyebrows waggling. Angelo pretended not to notice.

"I only have a minute," Rosina said, sitting next to him. "You decided out of the blue I had to see these now? You could have shown them to me at dinner."

He flipped the book open to the middle. "This one here, I was trying to draw like Gabriele. What do you think?"

A mass of deep, shaded lines and pocketed swirls angled across the page. Rosina let her vision blur, refocused and looked again, then closed her eyes. When she opened them, she saw that the mass rose and narrowed toward the top corner, disappearing into the distance.

"I know! It's a road. With wheel tracks and hoofprints." Like Maple Avenue, all dried mud and crazy patterns that day he'd followed her up the hill to Hope.

"That's right! I knew you'd see it." He turned the page. "This next one isn't right yet, it's too realistic. But you'll get the idea."

It was the starry sky he'd framed with his hands the night they'd read to her uncle, a dizzying spray of tiny dots set in translucent black, surrounded by irregular puffs in a deeper, velvety black. The puffs, she realized, were the encircling trees, leafed out and full. The stars, impossibly, seemed to move the longer she looked at them, swirling and spinning inside their frame.

"It's perfect, exactly like what Zio would have done." Rosina bit her lip.

He set the book in her lap. "Start at the front now. That's my regular stuff."

There was Mr. Camolli in his grocer's apron, weighing onions. Next, a derrick crane swinging a block of granite off a train car while four men reached for it, frozen in time. Then a flock of geese strutting at river's edge, and after that a gang of little boys playing stickball, short pants showing their dirty knees. There were dozens more, drawings of people she knew, all of them coming alive as she gazed at them through Angelo's eyes.

"These are wonderful. Zio would have loved them."

"This is the best one." Angelo flipped to the back of the book, to a loose sheet of paper with pinholes along the edges.

Rosina caught her breath. It was a portrait of a young woman, thoughtful, confident, even beautiful. A portrait of herself. She was sitting on a park bench, one elbow hooked over the backrest, one hand on the hat in her lap, her loose hair framing her pale face. Her gaze was distant, as if she were daydreaming, but her lips were parted as if in that instant she'd had the most thrilling idea, as if in another instant she would jump up to tell someone about it. She didn't recall sitting in the park alone like that, and if she had been, her hair wouldn't have been loose like a little girl's. Which meant this was Angelo's vision of her. It was her, yet not her, yet more than her. Then she laughed, because he'd read her mind. She was always tempted to let down her hair at the park, to tear off her shoes and stockings and feel the breeze and the sun on her bare skin.

"I don't know what to say." She couldn't get over it, this vision of herself that saw beyond her face and eyes and hair, deeper, into who she was. Exactly what she hadn't managed to do with her sketch of Marcello.

"Don't say anything, then."

"It's only charcoal, but I look so alive. I swear I can see the colors that aren't there. But you made me prettier than I am."

"I draw what I see."

Would he kiss her now, after so obvious a declaration of, if not love, admiration at least? Why not, when he'd kissed her already without any declaration at all?

But no, he was standing, taking the book from her. "I'll give it to you someday. Maybe. See you tonight at dinner. Don't sit there, go help your mother!"

He was on his way before she could reply. There was a jaunt to his step, a kind of delight, as if he knew what she'd been thinking. How irritating! But she couldn't help smiling.

"See you tonight," she called. But nothing would happen tonight because he wouldn't dare touch her under her parents' noses, and then the men would be off to Rebuzzi's to celebrate.

Wait, did she want something to happen? *Mamma mia*, she needed a nap to clear her head. A dalliance with Angelo was no more possible now than it had been before, even less so. His drawing wasn't admiring, it was romantic, idealized. She saw desire in those charcoal lines, yes. But what if what she saw was more than desire? What if it was love?

She jumped up. There was work to be done, and a good thing too. She needed to silence the quickening of her body, now, before dinnertime came. Then she could face Angelo as if she'd never seen his drawing, never thought about what it meant.

TWENTY-FIVE

ANGELO ARRIVED AT THE BOTTINELLI HOME at seven that evening. The men were in the parlor, Carlo reading and the twins playing cards. "Rosina *è in cucina*," Nico said, angling his head toward the kitchen.

"*Va bene*," Angelo replied nonchalantly, resisting the urge to bolt in there. He feigned interest in the card game for a while, then wandered over to the fireplace to look at some framed photographs on the mantel. That was when he noticed his sketch of Gabriele on an adjacent wall, framed in dark wood like a real work of art.

"*Ehi*, you found my drawing! It sure looks good framed like that."

Carlo lowered his newspaper. "You did that?"

"Yeah. I wanted him to have it, but he said I should keep it to remember him by. It didn't seem right, though, so I put it on his grave."

"Clementina!" Carlo bellowed. "The portrait of Gabriele, Angelo did it."

"Imagine that! It's a beautiful likeness," Clementina said from the doorway. "Come and eat now, dinner is ready."

The meal passed quickly—too quickly for Angelo, who couldn't help watching Rosina as she passed platters of food or jumped up to replenish the breadbasket. It was like no one else was in the room, only the two of them, and she moved in a circle of warm light only he could see and feel. Though maybe she felt it too, because when she set a coffee cup in front of him, her fingers trembled. He was trying to think of a good excuse to stay there instead of going to the party when Carlo and the twins pushed back their chairs and it was time to leave.

"Those poor birds," said Clementina. "I don't understand how anyone can enjoy watching animals kill each other."

"I hate it too," Rosina said.

Angelo decided then and there to have nothing to do with the cockfights. A few beers and some laughs, that would be enough.

The men had been gone barely an hour when a frantic hammering sent Rosina to the door. "Cosimo! *Che c'è*? What's wrong?"

"It's Carmela," her cousin said, out of breath after running up the stairs. "Her pains have started and she's in a bad way. Can you come?"

"Me? I'm not a midwife anymore, and besides she doesn't want one. She wants a doctor."

"Yes, but the baby is early and Dr. Samuelson has lumbago and she doesn't trust the other doctor. And Donata is in New York." Cosimo wiped his brow. "You know what to do, right? Please come."

"There's a midwife on North Seminary, you should ask her."

"That witch? They don't want her," said Clementina from the kitchen doorway.

"Carmela trusts Zia Donata and Zia trusts you," Cosimo said. "I can't say the same about the other midwife. Please. Daniele is panicking and even Mamma can't calm him down."

"When did her contractions start?"

"I don't know, I think a couple of hours ago, but she's screaming like a pig with its throat cut. I brought the car. Hurry!"

"Rosina, you must go," Clementina said.

"Surely another midwife could—"

"There's no time!" Cosimo grabbed her shoulders. "Please!"

She gave her mother a pleading look, then gave up. "Give me a minute."

She hurried off to get her bag. She wasn't prepared. And to be responsible for the birth of Vittorio's grandchild—no, impossible, if something went wrong they'd never forgive her. It would be one more thing tearing the family apart. But Carmela needed someone. Needed her, plain and simple. She dug her Nonnatus medal out of the bag and slipped the chain over her head. The saint had better listen to her prayers tonight.

Bag in hand, she returned to the parlor. "Let's go." She was as ready as she'd ever be. Which meant not ready at all.

Rebuzzi's yard was a mass of bodies shape-shifting in the flickering light of a dozen lanterns. At least forty or fifty men, Angelo thought, shouting and swearing in a mix of languages and laughing loud enough to wake the dead. And every last one of them hell-bent on getting drunk if they weren't already. He wove through the crowd to the cockfighting area. He'd take a peek, that was all. Where a ragged circle had formed around two strutting birds, bloodstains marked the hard-packed dirt and smoke rose from cigarettes, cigars, and kerosene lanterns. Aroused by the noise and blood, the birds circled and dodged and struck, quick and vicious as vipers. Angelo had never thought of a bird's eyes as murderous, but these were, shiny black and rimmed with savage red.

An hour passed without his realizing it, filled with roars of bloodlust, shouts of victory or loss, accusations of cheating, insults involving wives or mothers. Then, during the time it took to get a new bird into the ring, the words "strike" and "vote" and "motherfuckers" sparked from the ebb and flow of voices and a scuffle broke out. Angelo moved away, wondering where Rebuzzi had put the beer. Shouldering through the crowd, he passed a big, pockmarked fellow with ears like pine cones, curled up at the edges and thick, as if he'd grown up talking with his fists.

"No one'd be dead if that *stronzo* Carlo hadn't forced the vote in the first place," the pockmarked man said to the fellow next to him, short and barrel-squat. He swigged his beer. "Never should've struck in the first place, but goddamn it, after we went that far we shouldn't've caved. That was Carlo's doing too. Went soft after his dear little brother died."

Angelo froze, listening. Who were they? Granite men or they wouldn't be here, but he couldn't remember seeing them around Burnham Meadow. Quarrymen, maybe, or cutters at the sheds at the north end of town, out toward Montpelier.

"Well, no one would be dead if the fucking shed owners gave a fuck," said the barrel fellow.

"Damn right," said the pockmarked guy. "But I still say Bottinelli thinks he's God, telling us what to do all the time. Strike, don't strike, stay away from the scabs, give money to the widows, do this, do that. Needs to be taken down a notch or two, you ask me."

"*D'accordo*." The barrel fellow nodded. "You and me, we'll take care of him. But not tonight. Too many Carlo worshippers here, you know what I mean? Right, Rico? Right?"

Rico. Angelo said the name under his breath so he'd remember it. He needed to warn Carlo that these idiots were talking shit about him. He had no doubt they'd go after him, soon if not tonight. Best to keep an eye on them.

Rico picked his teeth. "Maybe. I need another beer."

"Get me one too."

Rico slapped hand to elbow, his kicked-up fist telling his buddy where to shove it. Hell of a guy, Angelo thought, following him into a hole of a kitchen at the back of Rebuzzi's house, packed with men and bottles and smoke. He grabbed a beer and made himself disappear—one of the crowd, a fellow enjoying a drink, laughing at jokes he didn't listen to. No one would notice him watching Rico.

Rosina fretted all the way to Vittorio's house, imagining one dire childbirth scenario after another. She had half a mind to insist that Carmela let the available doctor deliver the baby. What did it matter if she didn't like him? Then Cosimo swung the car to a halt and ran around to grab her bag. Fighting a sense of doom, she followed him to the house. She could do this. She had to. Carmela needed her.

Daniele was pacing on the front walkway, running a hand through his hair every few steps. When he saw Rosina he threw down his cigarette and ground it into the stone. "Damn that doctor, I don't like this at all. You'd better know what you're doing."

"You could thank her for coming, you know," Cosimo said.

"Take me to her, please." Rosina marched past both of them into the foyer.

Carmela was screaming as they entered the bedroom, then collapsed out of breath. It was far too early for that, Rosina thought, setting down her bag. A hysterical mother did neither herself nor her baby any good. If she didn't calm down she would have no strength left for pushing.

She took Carmela's hands. "What happy news, cousin! Your baby will be born soon. We'll do this together, you and I. Will you want the birthing stool, do you think?"

"No, I don't want that horrible thing." Carmela crescendoed into another contraction.

"That's fine," Rosina said, unpacking her bag. "Daniele, could you please leave us?"

"I'm staying. Carmela and I have discussed it, and we think I should be here."

He sounded resolute, though his pale face betrayed his fear. Hopefully he would manage to convince himself he meant what he said. "Very well. Then would you please hold her hand?"

She didn't like having him there, but what could she do? There was a reason most men got drunk while their wives gave birth—they couldn't stomach the pain and suffering. She prayed Daniele wasn't one of those men who fainted at the sight of blood. He was panicky, which worried her because he might make Carmela panic too, which would make her less able to cope with the pain. For a midwife, a husband in the room was a complication, one more thing to think about and tend to, especially if things went wrong.

But tonight nothing could go wrong. Nothing *would* go wrong. Rosina pushed her shoulders back and straightened her spine. She was in charge here. She knew what to do. She would do it.

Angelo followed Rico out of the kitchen back to his buddy, then over to the scuffle near the cockfighting area, which had erupted into a team effort of two on two, bets welcome. He spotted Nico. "Have you seen Carlo?"

"Not in a while," Nico said, his eyes on the fight.

"Let me know if you do."

"Why, what's up?"

"Nothing yet."

Best to keep an eye on Carlo too, if he could find him. Angelo circled the yard, then went back to shadowing Rico and his pal, who had planted themselves near the fence to watch the fight, but as soon as it ended and money was changing hands, they were on the move. Angelo followed. They were stirring up trouble as far as he could tell. He couldn't hear everything they said, but "Vittorio" and "Gabriele" jumped out of Rico's mouth more than once, and not in a kindly way. If Carlo heard Rico criticizing his brothers, he'd go after him like a rabid dog. And then there'd be trouble, big trouble.

Angelo stopped abruptly, hope sinking. Up ahead, smack in the path of Rico and company, was more trouble—Paolo, who liked nothing better than fighting, especially when he'd had a few drinks. And from the looks of him, he'd already indulged in both. Dirt stained his trousers and he was breathing hard between gulps of something that wasn't beer. Angelo ran toward him, intent on getting him away, but Carlo came out of nowhere and beat him there. It took no time at all for the two of them to put their heads together like they were plotting something. *Cazzo*! Now Nico was headed their way.

Angelo intercepted him. "Listen, I need your help. See those two over there? They're talking shit about your father and his brothers and I think Carlo heard them. I'm afraid there's going to be trouble. Can you get him and Paolo out of here?"

Nico swore under his breath. "Rico? Yeah, I know him and so does Papà. A real *figlio di puttana*, I can tell you that. You're right, Papà will beat the crap out of him and make short work of it too. To tell you the truth, I wouldn't mind watching."

"I don't think that's a good idea," Angelo said. The words were barely out of his mouth when Carlo lunged at Rico.

Rosina set out her supplies in a hurry. Carmela's frantic screams could split eardrums, which meant, given the short time she'd been laboring, either she had a very low pain tolerance or she was further along than Rosina thought.

"Carmela, I need to check on the baby's progress."

"Noooooo," Carmela groaned. "I need to push."

"No! You mustn't, not until it's time. Pushing too early can cause swelling and make it harder for the baby to get out, do you understand?" Rosina folded the sheet back. "Now open your legs, that's good. A little more, try to relax. Now let's see. Good news, you're halfway there!" Halfway in only a few hours? Please, Saint Nonnatus, make it a quick delivery but not a precipitous one. "Now let's take a listen."

With her Pinard horn pressed into the low rise of Carmela's belly, Rosina told her to breathe slowly. "Hmm, let's try again." She moved the horn higher—still nothing—then higher. "There it is!" She spoke lightly, reassuringly. "A strong heartbeat. Hold still now, let me count. Perfect, a hundred and forty beats per minute." What wasn't perfect was finding the heartbeat there, above Carmela's navel. The baby was a breech.

"Can I listen?" asked Daniele as Marietta bustled in with a stack of towels and swaddling blankets. Rosina held the horn in place for him. "I hear it!" He looked up, radiant. "It sounds like the ocean!"

"You're a good husband, staying here with her," Marietta said. "Your father would never have set foot in the room with me, and good thing too. I don't believe he would have survived. Young people today are so modern minded." She kissed Daniele's head. "Rosina dear, I've put water on to heat. Is there anything else you need?"

Yes, a prayer for a quick delivery and a healthy baby. Rosina touched the chain at her neck. "Yes, in fact. One minute." She palpated the baby's skull, its rounded back. She couldn't tell if the feet were tucked against Carmela's spine, meaning the baby would likely come out bottom first, or if the feet were lower in the pelvis, meaning they would come first. Neither was good.

"Carmela, we need to do something."

"What's wrong?" Daniele asked.

"It seems your baby has decided to come out right side up instead of upside down."

"What does that mean?" Carmela said, panicked.

"He's not coming headfirst, and it would be better if he did. I'd like to try to convince him to move. Is that all right? It won't be comfortable for you."

"I'm afraid," Carmela said.

"What if it doesn't work?" asked Daniele.

"Then the feet or the bottom will come out first. It happens sometimes."

"All right." Carmela grabbed Daniele's hand.

Rosina oiled Carmela's belly, then she and Marietta positioned their hands at the baby's head and bottom. "Between contractions," she said to Marietta, "you push and I'll pull. Ready, Carmela? Relax after your next contraction. Remember, don't push!" Carmela nodded, her eyes huge with fright.

The contraction came and went. "Now, Zia." They pushed and pulled, Carmela moaning all the while, until her abdomen tightened for the next contraction.

"Stop. We'll try again in a minute." Three more contractions, three more attempts. The baby's heart rate didn't budge, fortunately, but neither did the baby. "You've got a stubborn one in there. Bottom first it is," Rosina said lightly. No point in mentioning that the doctor should have detected the breech and tried to turn the baby weeks ago.

"Oh, I wish he would turn around," Carmela said.

"Don't worry, dear ones, I'm sure everything will be fine," Marietta said brightly.

Rosina began to sing softly, to calm herself as much as Carmela and Daniele. "*Dormi, mio vanto, colomba bianca, la mamma è stanca, lavora tanto. La mamma è stanca perché lavora tanto, ma con te accanto non sente pene, tanto ti vuole bene.*" As the contractions came, she talked Carmela through them, Daniele echoing her: "Breathe, don't push! You can do it!" Between the contractions she sang, softly, soothingly, the same song urging the white dove to sleep because her mother is tired, but she loves her so much, until finally her preoccupied mind found another. "*Ninna nanna, ninna oh, questo bimbo a chi lo do*?" She checked the baby's progress every ten minutes, warranted under the circumstances. And she prayed to the Madonna and Saint Raymond Nonnatus that this baby would come out screaming with lung power to spare, with ten fingers and ten toes and a good, strong suck. She would do her part as best she could. As for the rest of it—chance and fate and God's will—all she could do was hope.

Angelo swore he didn't see Carlo move, it happened so fast. Carlo took Rico by surprise with a tap on the shoulder and a right hook to the jaw. Rico staggered and Carlo struck again, knocking him breathless with a blow to the chest. Rico hit the ground and the cocks charged, pecking at his throat until Carlo landed on him and the squawking birds scattered. Rico flipped Carlo and both men rolled to their feet.

"You talk shit about me and my brothers behind my back? Eh? You think Vittorio doesn't give a damn about Gabriele and me? You think I wanted to end the strike because my brother died? You've got a lot of opinions, you *figlio di puttana*!" Carlo wiped his eyes with his sleeve. "You don't know the first thing about me and my brothers! *Nulla*!"

"I know men died because of you," Rico sneered.

A few men noticed the fray and rushed over, ready for blood. "He's nothing, Carlo!" someone yelled. "Crush him!" More and more men came to watch and soon a throng ringed the fighters.

"Is this how you operate?" Carlo shouted. "You keep your mouth shut at meetings, then talk shit about me to your idiot friends?"

They were circling each other now, Rico's mouth open in a distorted grin like he was having the time of his life. Nico was watching them nervously, his eyes flicking from Carlo to Rico and back.

"See what I mean?" Angelo said. "This could go bad real quick."

"Papà, let's get out of here!" Nico shouted. "That piece of shit's not worth the effort."

Paolo shoved him, muscling in as close to Carlo as he could. "Fight with us or shut up and get out of our way!"

"You boys stay out of this," Carlo said. "Go on, get out!"

Now money was changing hands, the men taking sides. Angelo couldn't believe it—fistfights, cockfights, it was all the same to them. He searched the crowd, hoping none of Rico's friends had enough balls to want in on the action.

"You got something to say about me, you say it to my goddamn face!" Carlo bellowed. "And fucking leave my brothers out of it!"

Then the whole game changed. Rico's face opened in a wide, lewd grin. "You, nah. But that pretty girl of yours, yeah, I got something to say about her. I bet she's a fine piece of—"

Carlo roared and charged, a rabid dog, but Rico was ready. He sidestepped him, tackled and straddled him, punched his face. Blood spurted and a roar went up. Paolo was dancing on the sidelines, Nico holding him back. "Get up, get up!" Paolo screamed. Carlo got Rico in a headlock but he broke free and the men staggered to their feet, circling with fists primed, eyes bright in faces dark with dirt and blood.

"You touch her, I'll kill you." Carlo's whole body heaved.

"Rico!" Angelo shouted, hoping to distract him. The man glanced up and Carlo charged again and they hit the ground in a rolling tangle. Rico twisted Carlo's arm and slithered free, a slippery eel. On his feet, he searched the crowd while Carlo struggled to stand. Then Rico's friend dashed into the circle. A flash of steel, then Rico crouched, moving in.

"Carlo! A knife!" Angelo shouted. "He's got a knife!"

Rico lunged and Carlo blocked him and the blade flew skyward. Carlo kneed Rico in the groin and both men hit the ground like granite, Rico screaming and retching, Carlo pounding the shit out of him. Paolo threw Nico off and ran toward the men and Nico took him down in a flying tackle. The roaring crowd parted, then closed ranks again.

Angelo went low, frantic to find the knife before someone else did, before they handed it off to Rico and Carlo ended up dead. Then he stopped, realizing his mistake. There were other knives, sure there were. And a gambler with a knife would give it to the man he favored to win. What to do, what to do? Something to stop the fighting, a distraction. But what?

Two hours passed, then three, then four. Carmela dozed as the urge to push eased. The birth canal opened little by little, slowly enough that Rosina no longer feared a precipitous birth, and the baby stayed put, head up, bottom down. Daniele paced, went into the hall and paced and smoked. Marietta followed him, offering reassurances he ignored. He came back into the room, asked incessant questions about how much longer and whether the baby seemed healthy, whether, because Rosina kept saying "*lui*" instead of "*lei*," she thought it was a boy. Hiding her irritation, she smiled and told him she couldn't say but they would find out soon enough. These men and their obsession with having a son! Whenever new fathers heard the word *boy* they crowed like roosters. Didn't it occur to them that those sons would want to marry someday, and where would all the girls be then? Who would give these overly proud fathers of boys the grandchildren they wanted?

She checked Carmela's progress again. Fully dilated and effaced, time for her to push at last. Except . . . instead of the baby's soft bottom, Rosina's fingers touched a foot, then something ropy and hard. *Madonna santissima*, the cord was prolapsed, an emergency she'd never encountered. She opened her fingers, forcing the vaginal walls apart. Carmela screamed.

"Zia, Daniele, come quickly. Turn her onto her left side. Quickly!"

"Is that normal?" Daniele asked. Marietta put a hand to her throat, fear in her eyes.

"Please, now! Zia!"

Marietta startled, then launched into action. "Over you go, dear," she said with forced cheerfulness, and Daniele leaped to help her.

Rosina moved with them, her hand a cage around the cord. "Good, now get her left arm out from underneath her so her chest is down, and put a folded blanket under her hips. No, fold it more or get a pillow, I want her hips higher."

"I need to push," Carmela groaned.

"Don't push! Stay calm, shallow breaths, please. Don't push."

"I can't. I need to—oh, oh!" Carmela shrieked as the next contraction hit.

"Don't push, quick puffs! Breathe!"

Rosina forced her hand higher, her fingers spanning the birth canal, making space for the cord, checking for pressure. She could hear Donata's voice: *Be careful with a footling breech. If the cord slips out first, it's very dangerous.*

Carmela screamed and thrashed. "You're hurting her!" Daniele shouted. "Jesus Christ, stop!"

"Tend to your wife," Marietta said sharply.

"Hold her hip in place so she doesn't roll back," Rosina said. "Do it, Daniele! Forward, toward the bed. Good." Keeping pressure off the cord, she felt for the other foot. Descending, not tucked up inside. Thank God the baby was small and Carmela's pelvis of normal size.

"Only a minute more, I promise. Now push with the next contraction, as hard as you can, and don't stop until I tell you to." There was no time to explain and it was better if she didn't. "Deep breath, Carmela. Now!"

Carmela heaved and pushed, her breath a long, shuddering groan. Still shielding the cord, Rosina delivered the left foot, then the right. "Good, easy now, hold still, hold still." Two feet out, two spindly legs, the skin dusky. She eased the baby's bottom out and the cord fell free. "All right, on the next contraction you're going to push hard. Like last time. Don't stop until I tell you." Rosina wiped her forehead on her sleeve. "You can do it. One long push, as hard as you can, and you're done."

Carmela took a great breath and bore down. Rosina felt for the baby's chin. Nicely tucked. Good. "Keep pushing, don't stop!" The head was free. She eased the baby onto the bed. He lay still, breathless and blue, limbs splayed like a puppet's.

"Oh my God," Daniele said.

Angelo took an elbow to the back and hit the ground, nearly knocking the feet out from under a man holding a lantern. It swung wildly, kerosene sloshing and flames spiking against the glass. Could have started a fire, he thought as he got up. Pushing forward, he saw Carlo and Rico circling again. Rico hadn't used the knife yet, but Angelo knew in his gut this was going bad. As he moved closer, the men went into silhouette against a blazing lantern opposite. Then it came to him—a fire, a small one, nothing dangerous, a few flames that a bucket or two would drown. Enough to distract the fighters so Nico could get Carlo out of there.

Angelo unhooked a lantern and dropped it where there was more dirt than grass, praying no one saw him. The flames searched for fuel, faltered. Good. He turned toward the crowd and shouted, "*Fuoco*! Fire! Someone get water!"

A cry went up, a few voices echoing his at first, then more and more, calling for haste. "*Fuoco*! *Acqua*! *Sbrigati, sbrigati*! Move it, get water!"

They were panicked. Too panicked. Confused, Angelo turned, stared in disbelief at the flames devouring the underbrush and spreading fast. The grass must have been drier than he'd thought, the breeze stronger. But how—

"*Attenti, attenti*!" someone shouted as a fireball the size of a horse erupted, leaping for the trees. Angelo stumbled backward.

Dio santo, what had he done?

All hell broke loose, panicked men scattering like roaches. "Go to the firehouse for Christ's sake!" "*Vai, vai*! "Run!" "Get water!" "*Acqua, acqua*!" "Where's a fucking bucket?" Rebuzzi dragged out a hose and men swarmed the kitchen, handing out buckets, dishpans, empty wine bottles, whatever they could find. "Make a chain," Rebuzzi yelled, aiming at the flames. "Move your asses!"

The blaze jumped to the trees, zipped up branches and obliterated leaves, licked at a rooftop too close for comfort. Angelo grabbed a bucket from the chain of men and heaved it. A tall birch exploded and he fell backward under raining embers and smothering heat. Men shouted and ducked and took to the ground, covering their heads. Feet planted wide, Rebuzzi arched backward, painting the flames with plumes of water.

Angelo scrambled to his feet. "Nico! Carlo! Paolo!" He ran into the throng, desperate to find them, praying he wouldn't find them dead.

Faint in the distance, the fire bell clanged.

"He's not dead," Rosina said, praying the words were true, praying for the Madonna's blessing. *Santa Maria, benedica questo bambino, La prego.* Carmela was sobbing, Daniele circling, his voice a questioning drone that Rosina barely heard. She worked quickly, clearing the baby's nose and mouth. Her fingers at the baby's throat. A pulse. *Grazie, Madonna santissima, grazie infinite.* Her mouth over his nose and mouth. Breathe for him, make him breathe. No breath. Flick his chest. Nothing. Another breath. Nothing. Breathe for him again, again, again, again. Then the limp body tensed and stirred and the baby coughed and cried, a shrill, beautiful sound. Rosina shook with relief. *Grazie, San Raimondo Nonnatus.* Swaddling the baby loosely, she watched his skin warm to pink, his eyes flicker open.

"He's alive!" she said as if his mewling cries weren't proof of that. She tied off the cord and cut it, wrapped him snugly and held him to her chest for warmth.

"Give him to me," Carmela said through tears. "Wait, I have to push again."

"Already? It will be the afterbirth. Let me see." Rosina gave the baby to Daniele.

It wasn't the afterbirth, it was a tiny head. Another thing the doctor had missed.

"Carmela, keep pushing. You're having another baby."

"What?" Carmela paled.

"Zia, please help me. Daniele, please sit down," Rosina said. God forbid he fainted and dropped the baby.

The child came easily, another boy, a rag doll two-thirds the size of its twin, underdeveloped and blue. Breathing, but poorly. This one wouldn't live. Rosina caught Marietta's eye. Her grim face said she knew it too.

"Carmela, it's another boy, but I must tell you he's very small and weak. He hasn't grown properly." Rosina paused to let them grasp her meaning. "I'm very sorry, but I don't think he will live."

Silence, the family in shock. Rosina worked quickly to clean and wrap the baby, praying that by some miracle the taint of blue would warm to pink.

Carmela's face stretched with grief. "He won't live? How do you know? No, you don't know that, you can't!"

"He's breathing, but not well. You'll have a day or two, I think, probably no more. I'm very sorry, I know it's hard to accept. Do you want to hold him?"

"Yes," Carmela sobbed. "My sweet little son," she murmured as Rosina placed the baby in her arms. "My beautiful baby boy."

Daniele sat next to his wife, crying. When the baby stirred in his arms, he stroked the small head. "Shhh, *piccolino*. Our dear little Teodoro Vittorio." He looked at the sickly twin and his face sagged. "We don't have a name for him."

"Give me one," Rosina said. "He must be baptized."

"Leonardo, for my father," Carmela said, her voice breaking. "Leonardo Daniele." Daniele nodded.

Rosina took a small vial of holy water from her bag and crossed herself, the others following suit. Touching drops of water to the baby's forehead, once for each mention of the Trinity, she said, "Leonardo Daniele Bottinelli, *io ti battezzo nel Nome del Padre, del Figlio, e dello Spirito Santo.*"

Carmela sobbed, her face pressed into Daniele's shoulder. Rosina gave them a few minutes, then took Teodoro from Daniele and tucked him into Carmela's free arm. "Let's see if he'll eat." He latched on well, his suck sufficient. His eyes were open, a dark slate blue, fixed on his mother's face. Leonardo lay with his eyes closed, mouth at the teat, too weak to suck.

When Marietta left to find Vittorio and Cosimo, Daniele took Rosina aside, speaking softly. "There was a problem with Teodoro, wasn't there? Besides not coming out headfirst. When you said not to push, something was wrong."

She held his gaze. She couldn't lie even if it would make him feel better, not after he'd seen his child lying limp and blue. She explained about the prolapsed cord, the risk of pressure cutting off the oxygenated blood coming from the mother. "This is more common when the baby comes feet first," she explained. "There's enough space around the legs that the cord can slip down there."

"But he wasn't breathing."

"There might have been some pressure on the cord, hopefully not much. He revived quickly, which is a good sign."

"And you knew what to do. You didn't stop for a second."

"There was no time."

"And Leonardo." Daniele struggled to control his voice. "Was there anything we could have done?"

Despite the *we*, Rosina knew he meant *you*. Before she could reply, the door swung open. Vittorio and Cosimo hurried in, kissed Carmela, congratulated the new parents, admired the babies. Then Vittorio ushered Rosina and Daniele into the hallway.

"What happened? Marietta says the second twin isn't well." Vittorio reached a trembling hand toward Rosina, then let it fall. "Is there no hope for him?"

"He is very weak," Rosina said. "It happens sometimes, one twin grows normally and the other doesn't, but we don't know why. I'm sorry."

"But shouldn't the doctor have known there were two?" Daniele's voice shook. "Couldn't he have warned us?"

Rosina hesitated. She wanted to blast the doctor's incompetence with all the contempt he deserved, but that wasn't what the family needed to hear. Their anger would come without any provocation from her. Still, she wouldn't lie to them.

"He should have known about the twins, although he might not have known Leonardo was weak and small. It would depend on how the babies were positioned in the womb. However, with twins there are always more risks, for the mother as well. He could have prepared you for that possibility."

Daniele clenched his fists. "I will have words with him. Carmela deserved better. Our sons deserved better!"

"And the problems with Teodoro?" asked Vittorio.

"The breech position is common enough. However, babies don't usually change position shortly before birth, so it's likely that he was in that position for a while. It would have been easier to turn him before Carmela went into labor. As I told Daniele, when a baby comes feet first, there can be problems with the cord."

"I regret the day we met that incompetent fool," Daniele said.

"As do I," said Vittorio, "and for my part in convincing you to trust him. Niece, I must ask you—" He hesitated. "How do we know Leonardo wasn't hurt during the birth?"

"Truthfully, we don't know, but I don't believe it would matter. He is small and weak because he didn't grow properly, not because of the birth. I believe his lungs don't work as they should. Most likely his heart doesn't either."

Daniele wept softly. Vittorio was quiet, his face grave. Rosina wondered what would come next—anger, accusations of blame for Leonardo's poor chances of survival?

Instead, Vittorio embraced her. "Thank you, niece. You saved Teodoro's life and we are more grateful than I can say. I know Donata will be proud of you. As for Leonardo . . ." His tears wet her cheeks until he found his breath. "It seems our dear Leonardo was meant to be with God."

Rosina cried with him, her sadness lightened by joy. This was the uncle she remembered, kind and loving. A family man who loved her like a daughter.

The house quieted. Marietta went to see about a meal, insisting Vittorio leave too and give the new parents their privacy. Cosimo had already disappeared. Carmela dozed with both babies in her arms, Daniele beside her, while Rosina kept watch from a rocking chair. Through her exhaustion, a familiar sense of quiet exhilaration was growing. How she had missed this, all of it—the uncertainty, the excitement, the joy, the sadness, even the fear. The thrill of life heightened beyond the ordinary. And she had done well, as Zia Donata used to say. Though Leonardo would die, she had done what was needed, and done it well. His fate would be tragic, but it was beyond her power. Zia Donata could have done no better. What had she said that terrible day when Mrs. Riva died? Midwives weren't miracle workers. How true.

Rosina rocked gently. She was a midwife again, and there would be more babies, more joys and more reasons to grieve. A future with hopes and expectations, without knowledge of what might come.

She rose quietly, took from her bag a pencil and the notebook Donata had given her. Before Leonardo died, she would draw him alone, a portrait to memorialize his birth and his death, but now she would sketch all of them together, mother and father and sons.

Her hand moved quickly, instinctively. Line, highlight, shadow, form. The image took shape—a moment suspended, a life too short, the visible traces of grief on Carmela's face. Here was a young mother sleeping, her face ravaged by emotions both fleeting and forever, her arms a nest for her children. Rosina drew, absorbed in her work, mindless of the hour.

When the portrait was done, she closed her eyes. She was a midwife. Yes. An artist too. She had a voice and she would use it. She would preserve these precious moments of childbirth and family as she saw them. She would tell the stories she witnessed as only she could, like Angelo told his about Barre, and they would be as visible as anything carved in stone. Zio Gabriele would have been proud.

TWENTY-SIX

AT DAWN, MARIETTA INSISTED THAT ROSINA GO HOME and sleep. "Cosimo will drive you. I'll send for you if needed." Rosina left her sketch on the bedside table where Carmela would see it when she woke.

At home, voices drew her to the kitchen. She stopped in the doorway, shocked to see her father's bandaged face and hands. "Papà! What happened?"

"There was a fight," Carlo said.

"Which you started," Clementina pointed out.

"A man disparages me, that's one thing. He brings my family into it, that's another. That's all I'm going to say, Clementina. I don't want to hear another word about it."

"Where's Paolo?"

"Out buying a newspaper," Nico said.

"I have news too." Rosina poured a cup of tea and joined the others at the table. "I delivered Carmela's babies. Twins, Teodoro and Leonardo. Leonardo is too small. I'm afraid he won't live."

"Oh no," Clementina said softly. "To lose a child . . . but Teodoro is well?"

"Yes. There were problems, but everyone was grateful and kind. Zio Vittorio cried and hugged me."

"Will miracles never cease," Carlo muttered.

"I thought you weren't a midwife anymore," said Nico.

"I thought that too."

"*Grazie a Dio* the one child will live," Clementina said. "The loss of the other will be unbearable. Carlo, you must—"

"I know," he said, his eyes full of pain. "You don't have to tell me. I'll go see him today."

"I think tomorrow would be better," Rosina said.

Carlo shook his head. "Today. I won't do what my brother did to me."

Footsteps pounded up the stairs, and seconds later Paolo burst into the kitchen. "Look at this!" he said, holding up the *Daily Times*. The front-page headline shouted, "FIRE ON SOUTH MAIN!" followed by "Barn Destroyed, One Man Presumed Dead."

"Someone died?" Rosina said. "How terrible. Where was the fire?"

"At Rebuzzi's, we were there," Nico said. He grabbed the paper and began reading in a dramatic voice. "A fire erupted last night on South Main Street at Orazio Rebuzzi's house, claiming the life of at least one man, it is believed, a vagrant by the name of Sam 'Stumper' Mahoney."

"You were born for the stage, Nic," Paolo said.

Nico swatted him and went on. "Barre's fine volunteer fire brigade reported to the scene at approximately eleven thirty last night after seeing flames."

Marcello would have been there, Rosina thought, then the notion disappeared as quickly as it had come.

"Witnesses say a party at Rebuzzi's, known for cockfights that draw an unsavory crowd—"

"Hey, we're unsavory!" Paolo laughed.

"—turned ugly when a brawl broke out over differences of opinion about the recent, devastating stonecutters' strike. During the melee a fallen kerosene lantern ignited the brush behind the house and the flames raged out of control, consuming an abandoned barn. Mr. Mahoney, who locals say had taken up residence there, appears to have been killed, though the fire brigade has yet to discover his body."

"It's a miracle more people weren't hurt," Rosina said.

"The blaze took several hours to contain," Nico continued, "burning itself out at river's edge in the early-morning hours. Police questioned the few remaining men at the site, who were uncooperative. No one admits to knowing who started the brawl or the fire. Other than a backyard fence that burned, no damage to Mr. Rebuzzi's property was incurred. Investigations of both the fire and Mr. Mahoney's probable death are pending."

"There you have it, the partial truth as always," said Carlo.

"Rosina, tell me what it said. I didn't understand half of it," said Clementina.

"We'll read it together, Mamma. It'll be good practice for you." Rosina stood. "Toast and coffee, anyone? I'm starving."

"I'll make it, you sit." Clementina put the kettle on. "I'm proud of you, *cara*."

"We all are," said Nico. He nudged his brother. "You'd better hurry up and get married and give our sister some business."

"You first."

"You're older."

"By three minutes!"

Nico tossed the paper aside. "Hey, did anyone see Angelo afterward? I lost him during the fire."

"If he was smart, he got the hell out of there before we did," Paolo said.

"He's probably home sleeping, which is what I'm going to do now." Carlo stood with difficulty and hobbled out of the room.

What a strange night, Rosina thought. For everyone. Two births and a fire, one death a certainty, another a possibility. She prayed that the missing vagrant would be found safe and sound. Angelo too. Surely he was at home like her father said, safe and sound asleep.

Angelo had walked all night, or what was left of it. What an idiot he'd been, starting a fire. His legs felt like rubbery logs, but he couldn't sit still, couldn't shake his shame, so he kept charging forward without direction, avoiding the few people he came across. Past dawn he realized he was streaked with soot and dirt. Anyone who knew about the fire might think he looked suspicious and call the police, and then they'd question him and he'd end up in jail. He was an arsonist. A criminal. What would Rosina think of him now?

After washing his face and arms in a fountain as best he could, he bought a *Daily Times*. It didn't take long to find out he might be a murderer as well as an arsonist, a thought that sent him running to the edge of town where the road to Montpelier bent through forest and he'd be alone. What else could he do? If he went home, he'd see his father passed out on the floor like a dead man, like Stumper Mahoney, the man Angelo had killed as surely as if he'd put a knife in his throat.

When he couldn't walk another step, he fell onto the ground under a maple tree and sobbed, pulling his hair until his scalp ached. How could he live with himself, knowing what he'd done? How could he ever face Rosina again?

Then the answer, terrible and inevitable, came to him—he wouldn't. He would keep away from her. Or he wouldn't have to because the police would find him and arrest him. If they didn't, he should turn himself in.

He curled up on his side, despairing at the thought of never seeing Rosina again, never making art, never being a stonecutter. His life was over. He'd killed a man. He should turn himself in.

He dozed a little, dreamed fiery nightmares that made him cry out in fear, woke to the worse nightmare of knowing the fire was real and Stumper Mahoney was probably dead.

He should turn himself in. He got up and walked back toward town.

Wait—didn't the paper say no body had been found? But it could have burned up, couldn't it, every last bit of bone? He'd thrown the paper out, had no more coins in his pocket. But he had to read the story again, to confirm his guilt.

On the northern fringes of Main Street he peered into a coffee shop, hoping for an abandoned newspaper, then kept walking, his mouth like flypaper. His eyes ached and his teeth felt sticky and a blister stabbed with every step. At the Depot Square newsstand he nicked a paper, strolled off like the innocent he wasn't. So he'd added theft to his list of crimes, so what? Nothing new. He'd grabbed clothes from wash lines, eggs from a stranger's sitting hens, so what was the difference? Except this time the theft seemed like a bigger crime.

He found a quiet street, sat in a corner patch of half-dead grass, snapped open the paper. A different headline now: "BLAZE RAISES QUESTIONS," followed by "Investigation Continues." Amid speculation that the fire was accidental was the hope that Mahoney still lived. No remains had been found, not a bone, not a scrap of cloth. Angelo lay back, eyes closed. It was like his blood had drained out of him in ten seconds, he was that weak with hope. Please, please, please.

But still, he should turn himself in.

He walked east again, toward City Hall and the police station, then kept going down South Main past the firehouse to Rebuzzi's. In the backyard were skeletons of trees, charred earth, a pile of blackened boards that had once been a barn. His doing.

Voices. Two policemen approached from past the barn. "We're going to have to ask you to leave," one of them said in an Irish lilt. "This is a crime scene."

"Yeah, I heard about it." Could they hear his voice shake? He cleared his throat. "Say, have you found that fellow who slept in the barn? I hope he's all right."

"Can't say," the same cop said. "You can read about it in tomorrow's paper. Now get out of here."

"Yessir." Angelo headed back to town. They had a lead. He would wait for the next headline before he decided what to do. If he was going to confess, he needed to know what he'd done.

At six the next morning he was at the Depot Square newsstand, waiting for the early edition. He was a wreck, what with all this waiting and not sleeping, not being able to eat despite the gnawing in his belly. If he didn't show up for work at seven, he could lose his job. It wouldn't matter, though, not if he turned himself in. Go to jail or go to work? Right now neither one seemed possible.

Thirty minutes later a wagon rattled up and the driver hoisted bundled newspapers onto the sidewalk. Angelo slapped a nickel he'd found onto the counter—he wasn't a thief this time, at least—and yanked a paper from the stack. When he saw the headline—"STUMPER LIVES!"—he let out a breath that came all the way from his toes.

He took off into the maze of train tracks, sat in the shadow of a single boxcar going nowhere. The story said Mahoney had given up the barn some time ago for a burrow under Widow Antonioli's porch, and he'd been slumbering there, no doubt aided by cheap booze, throughout the manhunt. Late yesterday afternoon he'd stumbled out and found that he'd been reported dead, to which he responded thusly: He was as tough as a fifty-year-old whore and planned to die when he was good and ready. As for the investigation, it was closed due to a lack of witnesses and evidence. By all accounts the fire had been an accident—in an editorial aside, the suggestion was made that drunken brawls and kerosene lanterns were best enjoyed separately—however, if any witnesses came forward or evidence was found, the case would be reopened and pursued with all the rigor it deserved.

He leaned his head back, waiting for his blood to slow its course. Then he heard voices, familiar ones, of men headed toward Burnham Meadow. It had to be close to seven. He scrambled up. Go to jail or go to work? He wasn't a murderer. No one had been hurt, and that abandoned barn was no loss. As for the fence, he could help Rebuzzi build a new one.

If he was quick, he could beat the starting whistle. Tossing the paper aside, he ran.

TWENTY-SEVEN

THE INVITATION HAD COME FROM VITTORIO, for a family dinner on a Sunday afternoon in mid-October, fifteen days after the twins' birth and thirteen days after Leonardo's death. Rosina had stayed with Carmela nearly around-the-clock for the two days of Leonardo's life. Together with Marietta, she cleaned and wrapped his tiny body for burial. Daniele and Vittorio asked Carlo to design and carve the headstone, and he said he'd be honored.

As the days passed, Teodoro kept Carmela busy, a tonic for her grief. He was more vigorous every day, ravenous all the time and gaining weight quickly. His nose was Carmela's, his fingers Daniele's, while his sturdy body predicted his grandfather's build. He had soft, black swirls of hair that Rosina couldn't resist touching, and a sweet little rosebud mouth. Whenever she held him, he gazed at her with serious eyes, trying to charm her into forgiving him for nearly dying.

Vittorio had proposed the dinner to celebrate the births of the twins, the first Bottinellis to be born American, and to honor Leonardo's passing. They had buried him quietly and privately, and though they would continue to mourn, now it was time to think of the living. Of family. Everyone had to come; there could be no excuses. It would be the first time in more than three years that the whole family would be together.

Carlo was hesitant, despite Vittorio's gratitude to Rosina and his delight that Carlo had defended his honor at Rebuzzi's. One day, a nice gesture and brothers reunited, the next, their political differences reborn, perhaps a stab in the back. You never knew.

"It's a peace offering," Clementina said. "He's trying to mend fences. Let him."

Marietta had told Clementina not to bring anything, instructions she knew would be ignored. They lived by the same rule: Don't show up with your hands in your mouth. Clementina decided on a pot of basil grown from seed, six eggs laid that morning, and a crostata in case Marietta's dessert wasn't to Carlo's liking. She told Rosina that making sure Carlo was in a good mood all evening was worth possibly offending Marietta, to which Rosina replied that as far as she knew offending her aunt wasn't possible, and anyway her father would be happy enough with some good wine or whiskey.

Clementina smiled. "*Brava, cara.* You speak like a woman who understands men."

"I wouldn't say that."

"No? You knew enough to refuse Marcello." Clementina placed the crostata in a basket, topped it with the eggs and basil, and covered the whole thing with a dish towel. "I see he's taken up with Isabella again. That's quite a ring she's wearing. He certainly didn't waste any time."

"I'm sure they'll be very happy together," Rosina said, though she thought no such thing.

"Speaking of young men," said Clementina as she untied her apron, "where is Angelo these days? Nico says he keeps his distance, even at work."

"How would I know, Mamma?" Rosina hadn't seen him since the night of the fire except once, at a distance, and he'd disappeared like a flash. If he was avoiding Nico, she supposed he had his reasons. But why her? It made no sense, not after he'd shown her that portrait, then sat at the dinner table making her insides quiver like gelatin.

She did *not* understand men.

"Your father likes him, you know. He's a good boy." Clementina bustled around the kitchen wiping counters and clearing clutter.

"Mamma, leave it," Rosina said. "Let's go before Papà changes his mind."

Marietta had festooned the house with bunches of flowers, bright yellows and rich reds reminiscent of autumn foliage. After drinks in the parlor and a visit to the nursery, during which Teodoro slept through all the compliments he received, the family sat down to a feast of salumi and cheeses, risotto with mushrooms and saffron, and a massive venison roast served with potatoes, cooked greens, and plenty of red wine. Carmela ate with one hand, an arm wrapped around still-sleeping Teodoro in her lap.

Vittorio raised his glass. "To Teodoro, my beautiful grandson, and to dear Leonardo, never to be forgotten. And to Carmela and Daniele for making me a grandfather. And to my niece Rosina, one of the two finest midwives in Barre. The other being my dear sister, of course."

"As if it could possibly be anyone else!" Rosina laughed and gave Donata a wineglass salute.

"And to this," Marietta said, "the first Bottinelli family dinner in far too long. Here's to all of us."

All of us. They were a family again, raising their glasses together, drinking, laughing, talking with their mouths full. A loud, opinionated, maddening, kindhearted bunch, and Rosina would love them forever. Yet she felt sad, and not because of Leonardo. She felt alone, in a way she never had. Why?

She glanced around the table. Everyone fit into pairs or trios, she realized—her parents, the twins, her father and Vittorio, Vittorio and her aunts, her cousins, Daniele and Carmela. Everyone except herself. Was that it? No, because it wasn't true, she was Nico and Paolo's third. What, then?

Daniele leaned over, whispered to Carmela, and she listened, smiling, then looked into his eyes. The two of them in their own little world. An intimate moment, shared with no one else.

Ah, that was it.

Her brothers would find new pairings someday, maybe Cosimo would too. Would she? Would a man who wasn't a Bottinelli occupy the chair next to her someday? Not that long ago she would have said no, or she didn't care. Lately, though, she found herself imagining the lives of strangers, specifically their love stories. That middle-aged man hurrying across the Common last Friday, flowers in hand and his tie askew—surely he was on his way to a tryst. And that gray-haired woman sitting on her front stoop on Berlin Street with an old man in shirtsleeves, their manner suggesting a familiarity decades long—did she call him lovingly to bed each night? Only yesterday Rosina had been riding the trolley when a young man stopped at a corner to let it pass. He'd seen her in the open car, clinging to a pole with a hand anchoring her hat, and smiled as if overjoyed. Her first thought had been that she must have reminded him of his sweetheart; her second was that his hair, coppery in the sunlight, looked like Angelo's.

Angelo. She thought about him too often lately, a fool's pastime.

After coffee served with Marietta's almond cake and Clementina's crostata, everyone dispersed—Vittorio and Carlo to the study, the younger men outside to admire the Oldsmobile, the women to the kitchen. Carmela excused herself to put Teodoro to bed.

"Let me," Rosina said. "Please, I'd like to."

In the nursery she sat in the rocker and gave Teodoro her finger, which he clung to with surprising strength. He felt good in her arms, solid and warm. He must miss his brother, she thought. How hard it must be to snug up next to someone for nine months, then find yourself alone. Someday she would take him to Hope. They would visit Leonardo's grave and she would tell Teo about his own birth and his brother's death and how much he was wanted and loved. She kissed his silky head. His warmth, his weight, those trusting eyes—she could almost imagine wanting a child someday.

Teodoro slept. Rosina gazed at her drawing of Carmela and Daniele with the twins, framed and hung opposite the door alongside the babies' portraits. Now she sketched every mother and baby she tended and gave the drawings to the families when she left. Word had spread quickly, and when women called to request her services they asked for "the artist midwife," which tickled her no end. Even Mrs. Basso had wanted a sketch of herself with her daughter Luisa, the baby Rosina had delivered months before, and Mr. Basso liked it so much that he decided to organize a showing of Rosina's sketches at St. Monica's community events room—when she'd done enough of them, of course, and assuming the families would part with them temporarily. Rosina said she would be honored. Her first show!

She laid Teo in his bassinet and placed her hand on his solid little back, feeling the rise and fall of his breath. A new life, and all the promise that came with it. "*Sogni d'oro, mio piccolo tesoro*," she whispered.

In the kitchen the women were flushed with drink, giddy with laughter. "Are Papà and Zio still talking?" Rosina asked.

"Yes," Clementina said. "Have some sherry."

At midnight, Rosina and her mother and the twins left, arriving home breathless after being shuttled in the Oldsmobile, in pairs and at great speed, by Cosimo, every turn promising disaster. Carlo and Vittorio were still in the study. Whatever it was they were talking about, Rosina took it as a good sign. At least they were talking. She fell asleep wishing she were eavesdropping outside the study window. Her sleepy mind sketched in Angelo beside her, the two of them side by side, arms touching.

When the clock struck midnight, Carlo was listening to Vittorio say things he never would have dreamed possible. Yet the soft leather of the easy chair he sat in, the cool glass in his hand, and the warm liquor on his tongue proved he wasn't imagining it.

Vittorio hadn't wasted any time getting to the point. "I'm selling the Milano," he said. He waited for Carlo's shocked expression, smiled with satisfaction when it arrived. "And I'm buying a shed. A big one. *Mal d'america* has got the Fontana boys running scared and they want out. You'll be foreman. Oh, don't worry, you can still carve stone, but you'll be managing the men too, hiring, setting policies, and so on. I'll be too busy to do that."

"Selling the Milano? I don't believe it, you worked so hard for it." Carlo clutched his glass as if he might drop it.

"Aren't you going to ask me why I'll be too busy?"

"You'll tell me anyway."

"Because I'll be running for office. Mayor Barclay had better watch his back because I plan to boot him out. If a Scottish stonecutter can become mayor, then so can an Italian one."

"I don't know what to say."

"Say you'll vote for me."

"You honestly want to leave the Milano for the granite business?"

"I'm halfway there, aren't I? I won't lie, selling the Milano will leave a hole right here." Vittorio thumped his chest. "However, I'm a practical man and my sons are too, and they're on board. I don't need to tell you that the granite industry is a sure bet for years to come. That's not true for liquor licenses in Barre. You know how many businesses have one? Four, including mine. The hotel survives because of the bar, and you know how fickle temperance laws can be. I can offer the best food at the best prices, but without booze to wash it down the business would stagnate. A liquor license isn't something I can count on from year to year, and I'm not interested in stagnating."

"No offense, but you've alienated a lot of the men. Who's going to work for you?"

"If you work for me they'll line up at the door, I have no doubt of that. I wish I were half as persuasive as you are."

"Learn to be more bullheaded."

"Point taken. Now, here's the best part." Vittorio paused to top off their drinks. "I'm looking for someone to buy me out of Lombardi's shed, and when I find him, that money will go toward an air filtration system for my shed. The men who come to me won't have to worry about dying of *mal d'america*. Including my nephews, I hope."

"You astonish me."

"Regrets keep me awake at night. *Basta*." Vittorio waved a dismissive hand. "Lombardi is an ass and always will be. I've realized it would be a mistake to tie my future to his. This is a way out for both of us. Think about it, talk to Clementina and the boys."

"I don't have to think about it, the answer is yes. With one condition."

"Name it."

"I can only do so much with the union—don't get me wrong, I won't step down as president—but what if, you've got me thinking now, what if I ran for alderman? Of Ward Five, the North End. If I had a voice in city policy, I could help the stonecutters where they live as well as where they work." Carlo jumped up, energized. "*Cristo santo*, I can't believe I'm saying this. So yes, I'll be your foreman if you'll tolerate me campaigning when the time comes. And with the understanding that if I get elected I'll have to leave the shed."

"Understood." Vittorio raised his glass. "*Al nostro futuro*. Think of it, Carlo. Think of what our future will be if we dream big enough."

"If we dream big enough and we do it together. For Gabriele."

Vittorio echoed him, and they drank.

Carlo swirled his whiskey, thinking, questioning, daring himself to reconsider. The road ahead would be rocky if not dangerous. He and Vittorio would always have their differences. At the least, it would be risky to take a paycheck from his brother. He refused to be a subservient flunky, and over time, with this warmhearted night only a distant memory, Vittorio might think of him as one. And if someday he were an alderman and Vittorio the mayor? *Dio mio*, what damage they could do to each other.

"One thing, brother. If you think we won't go head-to-head in city politics, you're dumb as an ox."

"I look forward to it." Vittorio beamed.

"I won't make it easy for you in the shed either. I'll expect as much from you as I will from the men. In your case, that means spending money."

Vittorio stubbed out his cigar. "Be prepared to do battle there too."

"We could end up hating each other again. We probably will."

"I'll take the risk. Will you?"

"I will."

They shook hands. Where would they be in five or ten years? Vittorio wondered. Here, he hoped, having Sunday dinner together, both of them grandfathers several times over. In the meantime, knowing Carlo, there would be plenty of shouting matches. And that was fine, to be expected even, as long as they remembered they were brothers.

Vittorio raised his glass again. "To us, Bottinellis in America." It was what he'd dreamed of. That there were no longer three of them was a fact still raw and tender. But two brothers dreaming together wasn't bad. Two brothers who would do their damnedest to make their mark on Barre.

TWENTY-EIGHT

ON THE SECOND OF NOVEMBER, FESTA DEI MORTI, Rosina and her mother rose before dawn. This year, the traditions to honor the dead were more important than ever because of Gabriele and little Leonardo. Their first task was to bake batch after batch of *ossa dei morti,* their numbers steadily depleted by the thieving twins until Clementina banished them from the kitchen. By midmorning the lanterns had been cleaned and their wicks trimmed, fresh chrysanthemums lay on the counter wrapped in butcher paper, and four extra places, for the family's departed spirits, filled out the dinner table.

"We're ready to go, I think," said Rosina. After wiping an invisible spot off one of the dinner plates, Clementina agreed.

The day was crisp, with a blustery wind turning dried leaves into confetti. At the cemetery, fresh flowers adorned the hundreds of graves and brightened the snow-scattered grounds. Vittorio and his family were already there, except for Carmela, who had decided the day was too cold for tiny Teo.

Everyone got to work, and an hour later a lantern burned beside each grave, the Bottinelli headstones were free of dirt and lichen, and a blue-striped blanket Carmela had knitted warmed the mounded earth where Leonardo lay. Marietta and Donata placed white chrysanthemums on the graves and Rosina added colorful ones, pink for Agnese, burgundy for Gabriele and Carletto, and yellow for Leonardo.

Everyone stood quietly for a few moments, heads bowed. Then the men drifted off to talk. Now that the finishing touches were being put on the Lombardi-Bottinelli shed, Carlo and Vittorio talked of little except Vittorio's planned escape.

"I think we're in for a bad winter," Rosina said, rubbing her gloved hands and bouncing her heels to keep warm. "I don't remember it being this cold on All Souls' Day last year."

"As you get older, you feel the winters more," Donata said. "Old bones mind the cold."

"Please, I'm not old yet!"

"Old enough to think about a husband," Clementina said. "*Allora*, dinner won't cook itself. Carlo, boys, are you coming?"

"Not yet. We'll see you at home," Carlo called.

"Husband dear, don't forget to come for us," Marietta said. Then, to Clementina, "I'm taking no chances. His head has nothing in it except the shed and the Milano sale these days. Carmela and I have no intention of walking across town with the baby."

"I should think not!"

"Mamma, you go on," Rosina said. "I'll catch up to you, there's something I need to do first. Zia Marietta and Zia Donata, please don't bring anything. Mamma seems to think we're feeding the whole town today. Honestly, I doubt there will be room on the table for plates and silverware."

Of course her words would go unheeded. The table would overflow with food and the kitchen would be overcrowded, everyone seated shoulder to shoulder. As it should be.

"Aren't you mysterious," Clementina said. "Don't be long."

After the three women left, Rosina hurried off in the opposite direction, to Antonella Lucci's grave. Angelo wasn't there, to her dismay. Something was wrong, it had to be. Why else would he have become invisible?

She turned back, cursing the cold. A voice in her head said to leave it alone, let Angelo come to her if he wanted to. But he was acting strange and she had to know why. Was it because he no longer had feelings for her, if he ever had? Or because he did, but he thought she was sweet on Marcello? Suppose, instead, he showed up one day and declared his love? She needed to prepare herself for that possibility, steel herself to walk away. And the only way to do that was to see him again and find out exactly what was going on.

The voice in her head was probably right, which was annoying. And, frankly, unacceptable. Since when had she ever left alone something that bothered her? And today Angelo was bothering her, very much.

Twenty minutes later she was standing in Foss Street, her mind whirling and her body a trembling mess of anxiety and doubt and hope. In front of her was a dismal building with peeling ochre paint and some broken ground-floor windows that she'd identified as Angelo's boardinghouse by finding his name and address in the *Barre City Directory*: "Lucci Angelo, tool boy, bds 19 Foss."

What, exactly, was she hoping for? That he was safe and well, that was all. Oh, and that they would be friends again. Yes, that was all.

"Get on with it," she said under her breath. Crossing herself, she prayed for courage and guidance, then rang the bell. A buzzer echoed faintly.

"*Chi cerchi*?" asked a quavering voice from above. Rosina looked up at an elderly man leaning out of a second-floor window.

"Angelo Lucci."

"They're out for the day, I heard them say. Him and his father. Come up and knock if you like. Second floor, third door on the right."

Out for the day? Where? He had no relatives to visit as far as she knew. But of course he could have gone anywhere. Telling herself knocking was pointless, she climbed the stairs anyway, noting the cracked walls and threadbare carpets. Angelo deserved more than this depressing place.

Her tentative knock was greeted with silence; a vigorous one yielded the same result. The old man emerged from a door down the corridor. "See? Like I said."

"Yes, it seems so." This time the disappointment was crushing. Angelo's absence was a message, Fate telling her, like the voice in her head, that she should leave him be.

"Good day to you," she said to the old man.

She ambled home, feeling bereft all over again, which was silly. So what if they'd kissed? So what if he'd romanticized her in his drawing? Neither meant anything. "Forget him," she muttered. "You've got more important things to think about."

She had barely opened the apartment door when Clementina bustled into the parlor, wiping her hands on her apron. "*Eccoti*! Where have you been? No, no, keep your coat on! Angelo came here looking for you. He was on his way to the cemetery, he'll wait there an hour at least. He said he has something important to tell you if you want to hear it. I told him you do, of course." She brushed imaginary lint from Rosina's sleeve, then kissed her. "He's a good boy, Rosi. Don't be a fool. *Sbrigati*!"

"I'm hurrying!"

She arrived at Hope breathless, her wool collar itchy with sweat. Angelo was sitting beside his mother's grave, arms wrapped around his knees.

He stood as she approached. She looked fine in her dark green coat and matching hat. More than fine—perfect. Perfect for him. Which was a goddamn shame because now he had to ruin any chance he'd ever had with her by telling her what he'd done. Who he was. She deserved to know the truth. Tell her, then forget about her.

As if he could forget.

"You came." He'd known she would, yet had doubted it too.

"Of course. Mamma said you wanted to tell me something. I haven't seen you in forever, so I figured it must be important." Could he see how nervous she was? She gestured toward a spray of red and pink chrysanthemums lying on the gravestone. "Those are beautiful."

"Her favorite colors."

"She must have been a lively person, then. Those are vital colors, like blood."

"I suppose. It's hard to remember." His tone changed, bitter now. "She was proud of me when I was a kid. Always said I'd amount to something."

"She'd be proud of you now. Papà told me you're going to cut stone in his shed. That's something, isn't it? It's what you wanted."

"Yeah." He shrugged. Then, in a harsh voice that didn't sound like his, "I started that fire."

"What?"

"The fire at Rebuzzi's. I started it."

"I, I don't understand. The papers said it was an accident."

"It wasn't. Your father and Rico were fighting and there was a knife, Rico's friend had it, and I wanted to get it away from him, but then I remembered that lots of fellows had knives, so what good would that do? Someone was going to get killed if I didn't do something and there wasn't a chance in hell I was going to let it be your father."

"You started the fire to save him?" Rosina covered her mouth, her eyes filling.

"It was supposed to be a small one," he said miserably. "A distraction, that's all. To stop the fighting."

"It *was* an accident, then! A mistake. Please don't blame yourself."

She stepped closer and put a hand on his arm. He could feel her warmth burning through her glove, through the wool of his coat. He wanted to tell her to let go, but he couldn't do it.

"I thought about turning myself in that night. The next day too, when I thought I'd killed Stumper. I'm an arsonist, that's all there is to it. I wanted you to know. I won't blame you if you never want to see me again."

"That's why you've . . . Angelo, listen to me." His muscles tightened under her hand. "You're not an arsonist, you were trying to save my father's life. And you most likely did! I'm glad you didn't turn yourself in."

"I still can. I might," he mumbled, moving away.

"Please don't." Say it. Take a chance. "Honestly, visiting you in jail wouldn't be any fun at all."

He turned then, to see her eyes, see if she meant it. "You'd visit me?"

"Every day."

They hovered in place, debating what would come next. Then a gust of wind spun the dried leaves at their feet into a wild airborne spatter of yellow and brown and Rosina bent to brush leaf fragments from her coat. "This wind!" she said, laughing. "It's like the dead are telling us they know we're here." When she straightened, his kiss took her by surprise. That familiar feeling, her stomach cartwheeling, blood thinning.

He released her slowly, tucking a windblown curl into her collar. Then he pulled her close again and they stood without moving, without talking. He felt the rise and fall of her breath, matched his own to hers.

"I gave up midwifery, did you know?" Rosina said, her cheek pressed into his coat.

"I didn't."

"I've gone back to it now. And I delivered my cousin's babies. Twins. One died, bless his soul." She pulled away, watching his face. "It's what I want to do. It's what I am."

"Then you should do it."

"Marcello didn't think so."

"He's a fool."

"He is. And a pig," she said, laughing. "A sweet one, sort of, but still a pig." He moved to kiss her again and she stopped him. "I won't give up midwifery for any man. Or for marriage."

"Why should you?"

"Or my suffrage work."

"Good." He kissed her nose, then her mouth.

"Why is it good? Do you believe in women's rights?"

"Never thought about it. But I guess you do, and I don't mind if you convince me."

"I don't know if I want to have children."

"Time will tell."

The sun was behind him, copper-tipping his hair. She thought of the sheer chance of their meeting, how they'd crossed an ocean from different towns and ended up in the same place. He'd proved he cared for her when he took her to the Hall to eavesdrop even though he could go to the meetings. He'd chosen to listen to Debs outside, with her, when he could have met the man in person. He'd stood with her father and brothers and uncle during the strike, suffered alongside them when he didn't have to. Taken a foolhardy risk to save her father. Shown her over and over again, and as clear as day in the portrait he made of her, that he loved her.

She took his hand, rough and warm. "What do we do now?"

"This." He kissed her again, until an old woman crutched on a young man's arm crept past them, scowling. "We're causing a scandal," he whispered in mock alarm. "There must be a rule against kissing in cemeteries."

"Let's break it again."

At last Rosina stepped away, her skin flushed in the chill air. She shoved her hands in her pockets and they stood, eyes locked. "What now?"

"Do you float?" Angelo said.

"What?"

"My mother used to say we floated, me and her. She meant we were dreamers."

"I am too. I guess that means I float." She hesitated. Their futures shifted here. "I can't promise anything."

"I can. Let's try, all right?" He held out his hand, and she took it.

"Have dinner with us. You know Mamma is hoping you will."

"I can't disappoint her, then, can I?"

They walked, unhurried, past the sea of graves dotted with flowers, the headstones carved by stonecutters waiting to die or by the ones who hadn't waited. Like Aldo Nappi. "Wait. This way," Rosina said, tugging Angelo's hand. They crossed to the cemetery's southern boundary, past family after family celebrating this day for the dead, sharing memories while their children played, mindless of the past and unafraid of the future. In a few years' time, she thought, some of the children they would see here would have taken their first breaths in her hands, like Teodoro. The portraits she made of them might stand on mantels or hang on bedroom walls.

Aldo's grave was a smooth granite block engraved with a weeping willow. On it was an explosion of white chrysanthemums bound with a red ribbon. Rosina kissed her fingers and touched the stone. "He was such a kind man."

"He was." Angelo took her hand again. At the cemetery's entrance, where the road curved and fell, he stopped and pointed toward town. "Look how clear it is now." The wind had brushed away the veil of stone dust and they could see for miles, past Burnham Meadow to the blue rim of mountains, to hidden quarries and train tracks with no end. "You know where the air is always clear?"

"Where?"

"Out west. Montana, Nevada, California, Oregon. We could go there someday. Anywhere."

"We could." Trains went west every day, to Detroit, Chicago, Denver, Salt Lake City, San Francisco, Los Angeles, places Rosina had thought she'd never see. The West, where the fight for women's suffrage had met defeat after defeat yet went on, unstoppable, its leaders strong and vocal and determined. They could go there together, she and Angelo. Not now, when there was plenty to do here. But someday. She could join those strong women, work with them, deliver their babies.

A wild, whipping wind erased the clouds over Barre, freeing shafts of pale sunlight. "*Dare alla luce*," she whispered. To give to the light, to give birth. She thought of Emma Goldman, her talk of enlightenment, of Zia Donata's belief in the future. *We women*. She lifted her face to the sun, inhaled. The air tasted sweet, rich with possibility.

ACKNOWLEDGMENTS

My heartfelt thanks to the Cynren Press team, particularly publisher Holly Thesieres Monteith, who apparently has unlimited patience, not to mention a sharp yet sensitive editorial eye, and Roderick Brydon, for his evocative cover design. I'm grateful to both for making my words into tangible art that I can hold in my hands and share with readers.

Endless gratitude to my trusted critique partners Judith Turner-Yamamoto and Daniela Petrova, fellow authors who always say yes to reading another draft and often tell me (thank god) what I don't want to hear.

Karen Bjorneby shepherded this book through its genesis and was kind enough to critique a much later version. ZZ Packer told me, at the Napa Valley Writers Conference way back in 2009, to "go home and finish this book," and I'm grateful for her encouragement. Steven Damron, Emily Dreyfuss, Carol Jauch, Alka Joshi, David Lenoe, Michael David Lukas, Hillary Read, Robin Silverman, and Jim Wood provided early feedback and encouragement. Later drafts benefited from the sharp eyes and excellent ideas of readers Deanna Moyers Chavez, Graham Hofmann, Patrick Kane, Yukari Kane, Julie Ann McLaughlin, Lisa Wallgren Okuhn, Mark Swinney, Mignon Sardi Swinney, and Mary Ann Thompson. Nancy Gile provided enthusiasm when I needed it most. A big thank-you to all of them.

In Barre, Karen Lane, former director of Aldrich Public Library, offered research assistance and her magical librarian powers. Paul Heller, a Barre and granite industry historian and writer, offered wise counsel and his own books to expand my knowledge. My cousin Stephen Restelli, a fellow genealogy freak, opened the door onto a hidden part of my family's past that influenced this book. I'm grateful to have such smart, kind people in my corner.

In Viggiù, Giuseppe (Beppe) Gallo, the town's devoted local historian, told me stories about the town and its stonecutters, gave me a book he wrote about the *viggiutesi* who emigrated to Barre, and convinced me to follow him into abandoned quarries, an unsafe but fascinating adventure. His generosity is endless. *Un ringraziamento di cuore*, Beppe.

In Perugia, my generous friend Carlo Chiecchi helped me with idiomatic Italian expressions and in general saved me from language errors. *Grazie mille*, Carlo.

Warm thanks go to the kind folks at Bordighera Press, who published an excerpt of an earlier version of the book in *VIA: Voices in Italian Americana* 35, no. 2 (2024).

Years ago, Nina Schuyler opened my eyes to style and made me an eternal devotee of the spectacular sentence. I'm grateful for her ongoing support and advice.

Many resources have enriched my storytelling, and I'm grateful to their authors, researchers, and creators for paving the road for me. For more information, please see the Historical Note and Sources.

GLOSSARY

ACQUA water
ACQUA IN BOCCA keep a secret (*literally*: water in mouth)
ALLA NUOVA LEVATRICE to the new midwife
ALLORA well, then
ANZIANO/A elderly person
ARRIVEDERCI goodbye, we'll see each other later
ASCOLTAMI BENE listen well
ASSOLUTAMENTE absolutely
BASTA enough
BELLISSIMO very handsome/beautiful
BELLO handsome, beautiful
BENE good, well
BENVENUTO welcome
BUONGIORNO hello, good day
CALMA calm down
CALMATI calm yourself (*familiar*)
CAPITO understood
CARA/MIA CARA dear/my dear
CARISSIMO very dear (person)
CAVOLO darn it (*literally*: cabbage)
CAZZO fuck, prick, damn
CHE BELLO how beautiful
CHE C'È? what is it?
CHE SCHIFO how disgusting
CHI CERCHI? who are you looking for? (*informal*)

CIN CIN   cheers
COGLIONE   idiot, fool
COM'È ANDATA OGGI?   how did it go today?
COSA?   what?
CRETINO   idiot, cretin
CRISTO SANTO   Jesus Christ
DA QUANTO TEMPO?   for how long?
D'ACCORDO   agreed
DAI!   come on!
DARE ALLA LUCE   to give birth (*literally*: to give to the light)
DIO   God
DIO MIO/MIO DIO   my God
DIO SANTO   holy God, my God, good Lord
DISTRUGGERLO!   destroy him/it! (*imperative*)
DOVE VAI OGGI?   where are you going today? (*familiar*)
DUE GOCCE D'ACQUA   two drops of water (*meaning* two people who are alike)
ECCOCI!   here we are!
ECCO COM'È ANDATA   here's how it went
ECCOMI!   here I am!
EHI   hey
È IN CUCINA   he/she is in the kitchen
È PERFETTA   she is perfect
È TARDI   it's late
FESTA DEI MORTI   All Souls' Day
FIGLIO DI PUTTANA   son of a whore/bitch
FIGLIOLA   my daughter (*affectionate*)
FUOCO   fire
FUTURO   future
GIOVANOTTO   young man
GRAZIE   thank you
GRAZIE A LEI   thank you (*formal*)
GRAZIE ALLA VERGINE   thanks to the Virgin Mary
GRAZIE INFINITE   infinite thanks
HAI FATTO BENE   you did well
IL BUE CHE DÀ DEL CORNUTO DALL'ASINO   the ox that gives horns to the donkey (*meaning* "the pot calling the kettle black")
IL BUON GIORNO SI VEDE DAL MATTINO   a good beginning bodes well (*literally*: you see a good day in the morning)
INFEDELE   unfaithful

LA GATTA FRETTOLOSA FA I GATTINI CIECHI the cat in a hurry has blind kittens
L'ALTRA SIGNORA È ARRIVATA the other lady is here
MA CERTO CHE SÌ of course I am/you are/we are
MA COSA STAI DICENDO? but what are you saying?
MADONNA SANTISSIMA blessed Lady (Virgin Mary)
MAI never
MALEDETTO COGLIONE damn fool/moron
MALOCCHIO evil eye
MANNAGGIA darn it/damn it
MARIA SANTISSIMA blessed Virgin Mary
MERAVIGLIA a marvel, a wonder
MERDA shit
MIO CARO FRATELLO my dear brother
(MI) SCUSI excuse me (*formal*)
NOI DONNE INSIEME we women (together)
NON C'È NIENT'ALTRO DA FARE there's nothing else to do
NON CI CREDO I don't believe it
NULLA nothing
ODDIO oh God
OSSA DEI MORTI almond paste cookies, often bone shaped (*literally*: bones of the dead)
PADRONE master
PERFETTO/A perfect
PETTEGOLA a gossip
PEZZO DI MERDA piece of shit
PICCOLO TESORO little darling
PORCA MISERIA damn it (*polite*; *literally*: pig misery)
PUTTANA whore
RESPIRA! breathe! (*imperative*)
SANTA MARIA, MADRE DI DIO Holy Mary, Mother of God
SANTO CIELO good heaven!
SBRIGATI hurry up
SCALPELLINI stonecutters
SCUSAMI excuse me (*informal*)
SEI A CASA? are you home? (*familiar*)
SENZA CUORE heartless
SIGNOR Mr.
SIGNORA Mrs., ma'am

SIGNORINA Miss (*title*)
SOGNI D'ORO sweet dreams (*literally*: dreams of gold)
STA MALE he/she is sick
STA PER CROLLARE it's about to topple
STRONZO/I asshole/s
TESORO treasure, darling (*affectionate*)
TESTA DI CAZZO dickhead
TRADITO/TRADITA betrayed
TRAGEDIA tragedy
TUTTI all, everyone
TUTTO BENE all good
UFFA ugh
VA' A CAGARE fuck off
VA BENE all right, very well, okay
VAFFANCULO go fuck yourself
VAI (you) go (*informal command*)
VATTENE get out of here
VERGOGNATI shame on you
VERO/A true
VIENI come (*familiar*)
VI PREGO I beg/pray you
ZITTO! quiet!

HISTORICAL NOTE AND SOURCES

Many hours of research over many years went into this book, and if it contains any factual errors, they are mine alone. I did my best to represent Barre, its inhabitants and the circumstances of their lives, its granite industry, and its volatile politics as they were in the early 1900s. However, as is inevitable in a work of fiction, I made some changes to fit the narrative.

Both Emma Goldman and Eugene V. Debs did speak in Barre, but not when I say they did. Debs appeared at the Labor Hall in 1904 and again in 1910, on a presidential campaign tour. His speech in chapter 13 is adapted from his address "Industrial Unionism," delivered at Grand Union Palace, New York, December 10, 1905. Goldman visited Barre in 1899 and gave two speeches at Tomasi Hall, a public venue on North Main Street; a third speech was canceled after a mob barred her entry to the building and armed anarchists rose up in protest. She spoke in Barre twice more, in 1907 and 1911. Her speech in chapter 23 is adapted from "What I Believe," printed in the *New York World* in 1908, and from a 1933 speech, "An Anarchist Looks at Life." These well-known radical figures in labor history spoke eloquently and powerfully, thus the words I attribute to them are their own. If you'd like to read their speeches in full, please see the list of sources that follows.

Luigi Galleani, editor of the anarchist newspaper *Cronaca Sovversiva* from 1903 until 1918, did appear at the Barre Opera House with Emma Goldman. However, that happened in 1907, and their purpose was to encourage people to vote.

The 1903 strike in the book is completely invented, though a small one did take place that year. The five-month 1892 strike that Clementina mentions is real, though, and Italian strikers did burn down the shop of a Scottish man who wouldn't issue them credit. The fictitious shooting at the Labor Hall on Primo Maggio is a tip of the hat to a real event, the murder of stonecutter Elia Corti in an anarchist uprising there in 1903.

Speaking of bad guys, someone had to play the heavy in a story involving union struggles, and for my purposes, those "someones" had to be the shed owners. Certainly not all of them were as despicable as Ugo Lombardi, or as soulless as I've depicted them in general. (Apologies to my relatives Andrea Restelli and Joseph D. Ossola, themselves shed owners in the early 1900s, and to their other descendants. I mean no offense.)

The Labor Hall (now the Old Labor Hall, a National Historic Monument since 1998) and its history and uses are as I've described them, with the exception of the store where Rosina works. The actual store in the Labor Hall's basement was a cooperative, not privately owned. The Hall was the site of annual performances of *Il Primo Maggio*, written by anarchist playwright Pietro Gori, but as far as I know, the play has no character named Gianluca. Other businesses named in the book, such as Halliday's Pharmacy and Dodge's Creamery, are fictitious.

These exceptions aside, I stuck to the facts. Barre's past is well documented, and old maps, books, newspapers, and online sources helped me to see it as it was. The streets and buildings named in the book existed in 1903, including the Hotel Milano (which might not have been as elegant as the one in the book). However, at least one appellation has changed: the small park near the Opera House and City Hall that Rosina calls the Common is now named City Hall Park. It still has a bandstand.

Speaking of City Hall, Barre did have a Scottish mayor, as Vittorio mentions. His name was William Barclay, and he served three terms in the early 1900s.

Hope Cemetery was and always will be an art gallery, filled with evocative monuments made exclusively of Barre Gray granite and carved by Barre's stonecutters (who often carved their own). Many of my family members are buried there. Since the 1930s, two lovely statues of the Virgin Mary have flanked the entrance, designed by master sculptor Carlo Abate. The model was Louisa Liberty Ambrosini Fuller, a stonecutter's daughter.

Barre's North End was, as depicted, home to Italian immigrants, who lived in apartment buildings, commonly called tenements, and boardinghouses. (In 1903 Barre, the term *tenement* was not synonymous with squalor and overcrowding, though certainly such conditions existed.) Many widows—who constituted, between 1880 and 1918, 45–51 percent of the town's workingwomen—supported their families by taking in boarders, primarily stonecutters.[1] Barre's grander

1. Susan L. Richards, "Making Home Pay: Italian and Scottish Boardinghouse Keepers in Barre, 1880–1918," *Vermont History* 74 (Winter/Spring 2006): 48–66.

homes could be found on North Main Street and in neighborhoods to the east and southeast. Vittorio and Marietta's home on Washington Street is modeled on a turreted mansion built in 1887 by Scottish shed owner George C. Mackie.

Barre's long history of *mal d'america* and its devastating effects on the stonecutting community are a shameful blot on America's past. For decades the granite industry unions fought a valiant but futile battle against *mal d'america*. (Barre was an early adopter of unions; by 1899, 90 percent of its workers were members of various locals, compared to 7 percent, the national average of union representation.[2]) With the introduction in the early 1890s of pneumatic chisels and a surfacer called the "bumper," the incidence of "stonecutters silicosis," as *mal d'america* was also known, rose dramatically.[3] However, the unions' efforts in the early years were thwarted by the erroneous belief that the disease was a form of tuberculosis; thus the immigrant families and their supposedly dirty habits were blamed, freeing the shed owners from any responsibility. Later, a cause-and-effect connection between silicosis and tuberculosis was established: Silicosis, an occupational disease, made the men more susceptible to tuberculosis, an infectious disease.

By 1903, a few pitiful regulations were in force to limit the amount of stone dust, such as sweeping and watering down the stone, but they did little to solve the problem. A study of mortality among granite workers from 1926 to 1936 showed that they died approximately eleven years younger than other Vermont men (other sources say sixteen years younger). It wasn't until 1936 that manufacturing sheds were required to install suction equipment. The agreement came with a price: a reduction of the men's wages to defray the cost of the new equipment.[4]

For a concise yet accurate picture of early twentieth-century Barre, I recommend Robert Weir's article "Solid Men in the Granite City: Municipal Socialism in Barre, Vermont, 1916–1931." In it he writes, "In 1900, the average American died at 50; in Barre they passed at 42. Stone workers suffered mortality rates 33 percent higher than the general populace into the 1940s, and air quality did not substantially improve until the passage of the Occupational Safety and Health Act of 1970."[5]

A quote Weir attributes to granite cutter Roaldus Richmond lays out, concisely and grimly, the reality of working with Barre Gray granite: "I cut stone all my life and I drank all my life. Both will kill a man in his 40s."

---

2. Robert E. Weir, "Solid Men in the Granite City: Municipal Socialism in Barre, Vermont, 1916–1931," *Vermont History* 83, no. 1 (2015): 43–81.

3. David R. Seager, "Barre, Vermont Granite Workers and the Struggle Against Silicosis, 1890–1960," *Labor History* 42, no. 1 (2001): 61–79, https://doi.org/10.1080/713684518.

4. Wendy Richardson, "'The Curse of Our Trade': Occupational Disease in a Vermont Granite Town," *Vermont History* 60, no. 1 (1992): 5–28.

5. Weir, "Solid Men in the Granite City."

Many of Barre's stonecutters came from Viggiù, a small town near the Swiss border in Lombardy. There, a museum is devoted to the town's stonecutters: Museo dei Picasass (*picasass* is dialect for *scalpellini*, or "stonecutters"), and in that museum is a block of Barre Gray engraved as follows: "City of Barre, VT, USA—Comune di Viggiù (Va), Italy—October 6, 2009." It was given to the town by Barre's mayor to recognize the link between two communities shaped by stone and the men who carved it.

And what of the women? They are certainly less well documented. The midwives in Barre didn't find their names in the newspapers; they worked quietly in the shadows. The Vermont Woman Suffrage Association that Donata and Rosina joined was formed in the early 1880s and became, in 1907, the Vermont Equal Suffrage Association. Roughly forty years later, when the Nineteenth Amendment became law in 1920, Vermont women finally had the right to vote.[6]

Among suffragettes in the United States, Italian surnames weren't common. Boston can claim Rosa Marie Finocchietti Levis, born in 1878 and thought to be the first Italian American suffragette in Massachusetts; however, evidence of other Italian Americans or Italian-born women who fought for the vote is scarce. This means that whether Rosina stayed in Barre or headed west with Angelo, she would have been an outlier. Exceptional, in a sense. No doubt that would have made her happy.

6. Gene Sessions, "Women Get the Vote, 1920," Vermont History, https://vermonthistory.org/women-get-vote-1920.

Sources

Articles

Barre Daily Times. "Debs Predicts Panic Coming and That Wave of Socialism Will Embrace Country." September 9, 1910.

Bielenberg, Kristina L., and Karen Lane, eds. *Barre, Vermont: An Ethnic Bouillabaisse*. Barre Ethnic Heritage Studies Project, Vermont Department of Education, 1978.

Bushnell, Mark. "Then Again: A Controversial Voice for Change." *VTDigger*, April 9, 2017.

Colodny, Roby. "Vermont's Untold History: Labor in Barre: 1900–1941." *Public Occurrence*, October 4, 1976.

Frey, Kate. "United States: Barre's Hidden History of Italian American Radicalism." *Links International Journal of Socialist Renewal*, February 23, 2018.

Martini, Alessia. "Scolpita nella pietra: Testimonianze scultoree della comunità italiana di Barre, Vermont." *Italian Canadiana* 36, no. 1 (2022): 201–27. https://doi.org/10.33137/ic.v36i1.39391.

McDonald, Marian. "The Granite Years: Barre, Vermont, 1880–1900." Unpublished manuscript.

Mueller, Robert, and Greg Guma. "Vermont's Untold History: Labor and Capital in the Green Mountains." *Public Occurrence*, October 4, 1976.

Mulvaney, Joelen. "46 Granite Street: A History of Barre Granite Workers." *Vermont Sunday Magazine*, August 9, 1992.

Richardson, Wendy. "'The Curse of Our Trade': Occupational Disease in a Vermont Granite Town." *Vermont History* 60, no. 1 (1992): 5–28.

Schneiderman, Jo. "Vermont's Untold History: Beyond Midwifery and Motherhood." *Public Occurrence*, October 4, 1976.

Scott, W. F. "The Granite Industry." *Inter-State Journal*, 1902.

Seager, David R. "Barre, Vermont Granite Workers and the Struggle Against Silicosis, 1890–1960." *Labor History* 42, no. 1 (2001): 61–79, https://doi.org/10.1080/713684518.

Sessions, Gene. "The Anarchist Movement in Barre, 1920." Vermont History. https://vermonthistory.org/anarchist-movement-in-barre-1920.

Sessions, Gene. "Women Get the Vote, 1920." Vermont History. https://vermonthistory.org/women-get-vote-1920.

Tomasi, Mari. "The Italian Story in Vermont." *Barre Daily Times*, August 7, 1958.
Vecoli, Rudolph. "Make My May Day." *Vermont Guardian*, April 27, 2007.
Vecoli, Rudolph J. "Mass Amnesia Makes Americans Forget the Story Behind May Day." *Times Argus*, April 26, 2007.
Vecoli, Rudolph. "Primo Maggio in the United States: An Invented Tradition of the Italian Anarchists." In *May Day Celebration*. Quaderni della Fondazione G. Brodolini. Marsilio Editori, 1988.
Vecoli, Rudolph J. "Primo Maggio: May Day Observances Among Italian Immigrant Workers, 1809–1920." *Labor's Heritage* 7, no. 4 (1996): 28–41.
Vermont Historical Society. "Barre Italian Life 1890–1920: Home/School Life." Digital Vermont. https://www.digitalvermont.org/exhibits/show/barre-italian-life-1890-1920/home-school-life.
Vermont Historical Society. "Barre Italian Life 1890–1920: Politics of Barre." Digital Vermont. https://www.digitalvermont.org/exhibits/show/barre-italian-life-1890-1920/politics-of-barre.
Vermont Historical Society. "Barre Italian Life 1890–1920: Work in the Granite Industry." Digital Vermont. https://www.digitalvermont.org/exhibits/show/barre-italian-life-1890-1920/work-in-the-granite-industry.
Walsh, Kevin M. "Honoring Their Own: The Stonecutters of Barre." *Italian America*, Winter 2019.
Weir, Robert E. "Solid Men in the Granite City: Municipal Socialism in Barre, Vermont, 1916–1931." *Vermont History* 83, no. 1 (2015): 43–81.
Wood, Paul. "The Architecture of the Granite Shed." *Times Argus*, November 5, 2007.

Books

Allen, Donald G. *Barre Granite Heritage with Guide to the Cemeteries*. Friends of the Aldrich Public Library, 1997.
Bacon, Elisabeth Ramon. *Santander to Barre: Life in a Spanish Family in Vermont*. Greenhills Books, 1988.
Belding, Patricia, Ellen E. Griggs, and Elizabeth Ralph, eds. *Barre in Retrospect II: 1776–1995*. Friends of the Aldrich Public Library, 1995.
Belding, Russell J. *From Hitching Posts to Gas Pumps: A History of North Main Street, Barre, Vermont, 1875–1915*. Potash Brook, 2003.
Blow, Richard. *Barre Vermont Remembered*. Yankee Books Galore, 2002.
Brayley, Arthur Wellington. *History of the Granite Industry of New England*. 1923. Legare Street Press, 2022.

Chambers, Doreen, and Brooke Lorentzen. *Images of America: Barre*. Arcadia, 2014.

Clarke, Rod. *Carved in Stone: A History of the Barre Granite Industry*. Rock of Ages, 1989.

Fenwick, Carol, ed. *Barre in Retrospect: 1776–1976*. Friends of the Aldrich Public Library, 1975.

Heller, Paul. *From Barre to Montpelier: Writings on Central Vermont History*. Paul Heller, 2018.

Knoblock, Glenn A. *Images of America: Hope Cemetery*. Arcadia, 2018.

Litoff, Judy Barrett. *American Midwives: 1860 to the Present*. Bloomsbury Academic, 1978.

Loomis, Erik. *A History of America in 10 Strikes*. New Press, 2018.

Mitchinson, Wendy. *Giving Birth in Canada, 1900–1950*. University of Toronto Press, 2002.

Mitford, Jessica. *The American Way of Birth*. Dutton, 1992.

Quinn, Bridget. *She Votes: How US Women Won Suffrage, and What Happened Next*. Chronicle Books, 2020.

Ulrich, Laurel Lee. *The Midwife's Tale: The Life of Martha Ballard, Based on Her Diary, 1785–1812*. Vintage, 1991.

Wertz, Richard, and Dorothy C. Wertz. *Lying-In: A History of Childbirth in America*. Yale University Press, 1989.

Films

Barre Memories: Quarrying the Past. Peregrine Productions, undated.

The Blood of Barre: A Portrait of the Granite Industry. Carolina Sculpture Studio, 2022. https://www.youtube.com/watch?v=Z3pmyZJztyw.

If Stone Could Speak. Dir. Randy Croce. Labor Education Service, University of Minnesota, 2007.

Mal d'America: L'emigrazione degli scalpellini lombardi e ticinesi nel Vermont. https://lanostrastoria.ch/documents/01k818848rssnerfkdnkagyoaz.

Interviews

All interviews are from the American Life Histories collection of the Federal Writers' Project, 1936–40, available from the US Library of Congress.

Richmond, Roaldus. "Dust on His Clothes: Men Against Granite." July 31, 1940.

Richmond, Roaldus, and Mari Tomasi. "Both Will Kill a Man." September 14, 1940.
Tomasi, Mari. "A Barre Family: Men Against Granite." August 23, 1940.
Tomasi, Mari. "A Stonecutter's Holiday." August 1940.
Tomasi, Mar[i]. "The Boccinis Are Good Marriers: Men Against Granite." July [3, 1940?].
Tomasi, Mar[i]. "Granite Worker, Vermont 1938–9." Undated.

Speeches (Excerpts)

Debs, Eugene V. "Industrial Unionism." Republished as "Industrial Unionism," *Industrial Union Bulletin* [Chicago] 1, no. 36 (1907): 5. Reprinted under the same title in *International Socialist Review* 10, no. 6 (1908): 505–8.
Goldman, Emma. "An Anarchist Looks at Life." Speech given at Foyle's Twenty-Ninth Literary Luncheon, London. March 1, 1933.
Goldman, Emma. "What I Believe." *New York World*, July 19, 1908.

DISCUSSION GUIDE

A. Rosina came to America thinking the door to her future would be wide open; instead, she finds that women's options are as limited by social constraints as they were in Italy.

1. Which actions does Rosina take that you admire, or in what ways do you think she's too idealistic or even misguided?
2. Is she cruel to initiate a courtship with Marcello knowing she's not interested in marriage, or is she right to put her needs first?
3. Which of the book's open-minded women (Rosina, Donata, and Marietta) do you most identify with, and why?
4. If you were a young woman circa 1900, would you be brave enough to partner outside of marriage and/or have a child? Why or why not?
5. Rosina sees Angelo as a threat in part because of her physical attraction to him and in part because he, like her brother Nico, treats her like a person with a brain. Why can't she see that her own biases about men prevent her from considering Angelo as a romantic option?

B. In the United States today, doctors are the norm for obstetrical care, yet according to the Commonwealth Fund,[1] the country has the highest rate of maternal death of all high-income nations—double and sometimes triple the rates of Norway, Switzerland, Sweden, the Netherlands, Japan, Austria, Germany, the United Kingdom, France, Canada, Korea, New Zealand, and Chile. In many of these countries, midwives greatly outnumber OB-gyns.

---

1. Commonwealth Fund, "Insights into the US Maternal Mortality Crisis: An International Comparison," issue brief, June 4, 2024, https://www.commonwealthfund.org/publications/issue-briefs/2024/jun/insights-us-maternal-mortality-crisis-international-comparison.

1. Do you think midwives should play a bigger role in the US health care system?
2. Have you used or would you ever choose to use a midwife? Why or why not?

C. The Bottinelli family's rift is rooted in pride as well as in political beliefs and values.

1. Are the Bottinelli brothers justified in allowing their rift to go on for years and affect their families?
2. Does Vittorio have a moral obligation to help Carlo achieve his goal of obtaining the equipment that would help to save the stonecutters' lives, given that his brothers and nephews are at risk?
3. Does Rosina's alliance with her aunt Donata contribute to the return of family unity?

D. The book opens with the death by suicide of a Barre stonecutter who had *mal d'america*.

1. Do you think suicide is ever justified, even if it spares those who are terminally ill and their families from long-term suffering?
2. A stigma of shame increases the surviving family's suffering. Why do some people consider suicide to be shameful?

E. The qualities that make Barre Gray granite desirable also make it deadly to the men who work with it.

1. Does society have a responsibility to reject what causes physical harm or to provide safety measures to prevent it?
2. What role should society play in balancing the right of an individual to profit and the right of an individual not to suffer harm?

F. Carlo, as president of the Barre Local of the Granite Cutters Association, is a driving force in the 1903 strike.

1. Is Carlo right to feel responsible for the events and outcome of the strike?
2. How much does Gabriele's death affect Carlo's decision to call a vote to end the strike?
3. Is striving for progress that would benefit the greater good always a worthwhile effort, even when it puts workers at risk?

G. The Italians who emigrated to the United States during the Great Migration of 1880 to 1920, particularly those from southern Italy, faced discrimination and racial slurs like *wop*, *guinea*, and *dago*. Italians were considered as dirty and low status as Blacks were at the time. In today's America, however, Italians are considered white.

1. Why do you think society's perception of Italians has changed?
2. Which factors drive a society's movement toward or away from racial discrimination of a particular ethnic or national body?

A full, downloadable Reader's Guide is available from the publisher at http://www.cynren.com/bookclubs

CHERYL A. OSSOLA is a second-generation Italian American and a descendant of the stonecutters who shaped Barre, Vermont's, granite industry. Her fiction and poetry explore Italian heritage, art, labor history, and the immigrant experience. She is the author of the novel *The Wild Impossibility* (2019), and her work has appeared in *Fourteen Hills*, *Writer's Digest*, *Switchback*, *VIA: Voices in Italian Americana*, and *Eastern Iowa Review: Best Prose Poetry 2025*. A former editor and freelance writer with an MFA from the University of San Francisco, she writes *Italicus: a writer's life in Italy* from a hilltop town in Umbria.